ABOUT THE AUTHOR

Sally Bothroyd grew up in Victoria but now lives in Darwin, although she doesn't much like the heat. She was the inaugural winner of the ASA/HQ Commercial Fiction Prize in 2020. *Brunswick Street Blues* is her first novel. Her other claims to fame include once writing headlines for the *NT News* and being the carry-over champion on *Sale of the Century* for two nights. Readers can visit her website (www.sallybothroyd.com) to learn more.

BRUNSWICK STREET Blues

SALLY BOTHROYD

FICTION
HQ

First Published 2022
First Australian Paperback Edition 2022
ISBN 9781867216018

BRUNSWICK STREET BLUES
© 2022 by Sally Bothroyd
Australian Copyright 2022
New Zealand Copyright 2022

This is a work of fiction. Names, characters, businesses, places, events and incidents are either the products of the author's imagination or used in a fictitious manner. Any resemblance to actual persons, living or dead, or actual events is purely coincidental.

Published by
HQ Fiction
An imprint of Harlequin Enterprises (Australia) Pty Limited (ABN 47 001 180 918), a subsidiary of HarperCollins Publishers Australia Pty Limited (ABN 36 009 913 517)
Level 13, 201 Elizabeth St
SYDNEY NSW 2000
AUSTRALIA

° and TM (apart from those relating to FSC°) are trademarks of Harlequin Enterprises (Australia) Pty Limited or its corporate affiliates. Trademarks indicated with ° are registered in Australia, New Zealand and in other countries.

A catalogue record for this book is available from the National Library of Australia
www.librariesaustralia.nla.gov.au

Printed and bound in Australia by McPherson's Printing Group

MIX
Paper from
responsible sources
FSC
www.fsc.org   FSC° C001695

For the people of Melbourne, who set a world record for pandemic lockdowns in October 2021. If you read this novel I hope it makes you smile, and that you'll forgive me for taking a degree of creative licence in writing about your town.

CHAPTER ONE

October 2007

This wasn't the first time I'd encountered a dead body. Having grown up in inner Melbourne in the 1990s when heroin was at its peak, I'd passed the occasional overdosed junkie on the way to school. I couldn't immediately see the man's face, but this didn't look like an overdosed stranger. The bright white hair made him unmistakable—it was Mayor Dickie Ruffhead. His leering portrait hung in the foyer of the council's chambers, and when I took a few more steps towards the body, I could see that even in death he had the same smile on his smarmy, perma-tanned face, although his dentures were now on the floor among a scattering of bulldog clips and I couldn't help noticing that his pinstriped trousers were down around his ankles.

It was true that the mayor had been missing for several days, but no one seemed too concerned. Council gossip suggested his wife had sent him to rehab again for sex addiction—or gambling, drinking or possibly cocaine; the mayor was a man of varied interests. I took a closer look at his mottled face. Stroke or heart attack was my guess. On the plus side, the discovery explained the weird smell on the second floor of the council building, which had been a hot topic of discussion for several days. (It had been mooted that a disgruntled rate payer had hidden prawn heads in an air-con duct again.) Of course, no one had checked the archives storage. No one had checked anywhere. Council staff were sticklers for job descriptions and frowned on anyone who strayed outside of their strict parameters. Even cleaning out the office fridge was unthinkable.

I'd lived in Melbourne all my life. In 170 years the city had grown from a scrawny settlement founded by the syphilitic son of a convict on the banks of the Yarra River to an unwieldy metropolis. I've heard it said that John Batman was the only person in Australia's colonial history to attempt a treaty with the Kulin people whose land he wanted. It was an unfair contract, of course, but that's bureaucracy for you.

Recently, the city had become my employer and as far I could see, Batman's act set the tone for Melbourne and the ongoing management of its boroughs. I had a PR job and I hated it, but the money was good and it was nine to five, which meant I could keep working nights for my Uncle Baz. He owned a pub in Fitzroy, an inner suburb just north of

Melbourne city known for its live music, coffee culture and a football team that had moved to Brisbane in the 1990s due to money troubles.

When I saw an advertisement for a job in the Yarra City Council's PR department, I figured it could help me find out who was behind a slew of complaints being levelled at Baz's pub; it seemed to me that someone at council— or someone with influence over council affairs—was very much hoping that Baz would sell up and move on. One of our regular bar patrons helped me fudge a CV and application letter—he'd worked in bureaucracy for decades and knew all the right buzzwords—and before I knew it, I had my foot in the door.

But, as it turned out, information was proving hard to come by. Three months into the job, I was still struggling to get my head around the basics of PR, and I was no closer to uncovering any inside scoop regarding the complaints against Baz. So when I happened to learn that there was a store of council documents in an archive on the third floor of the council building, I thought it wouldn't hurt to take a look. I waited until ten past five, when the building was mostly deserted (council workers not being fond of overtime), then I got past the lock with the help of a lock-pick kit I'd acquired from an old boyfriend—one I suspected of breaking into my apartment and stealing my stereo after we broke up.

The archive room had high ceilings and the light coming from the windows revealed faded paint and unloved plasterwork. Utilitarian shelves crowded the space, stacked to overflowing with cardboard box files, and one shelf at the far wall seemed to have collapsed completely. I'd closed the door behind me and had taken a few steps into the large room when I realised something was very wrong. There was a strange smell, and it was intensifying as I approached the area of the collapsed shelf. That's when I realised I wasn't alone—but I was the only one breathing.

Maybe I should have rung the cops straight away, but among the many things I've learned from Uncle Baz over the years, one of the more important ones is that it's best not to get involved with the authorities if you can help it. I didn't want to explain how I'd found the corpse of a public official after gaining unauthorised access to the archives department. I closed the door and crept silently away.

* * *

I left the council building and grabbed my bicycle. The benefit of cycling, apart from avoiding Melbourne's trams, was that it gave me a chance to clear my head of what I'd just seen—and clear my sinuses of the lingering smell. I headed directly to Uncle Baz's joint in Fitzroy.

When Baz first arrived in Melbourne in the 1960s, the inner northern suburbs were inhabited by factory workers and newly arrived immigrants—authorities had already razed the slums that were there in the forties and fifties. Since the 1990s, however, Melbourne's real estate prices had started heading for the stratosphere, and I didn't really see that they could go any higher. If I ever managed to qualify for a mortgage, I'd only be able to afford the outer, outer,

outer suburbs and, considering the commute time, I'd prefer to live in outer space. Better views.

Baz's pub was called the Phoenix and it was in the couple of blocks at the end of Brunswick Street that had managed to stay slightly seedy. According to Baz, he bought the Phoenix in the 1970s after a stint working as a session musician in the US. It was a long story that varied depending on how many whiskies he'd consumed, but the gist was that Baz went to Chicago to look for his father, a Black American GI who'd been stationed in Brisbane during the Second World War. His parents had met at a social club established for the 'coloured' members of the US military well known as a jazz hotspot. Baz's father played saxophone in his civilian life while Baz's mother was a singer. Since segregation was still a thing in the US at the time, it was mainly Aboriginal women who were employed to work at the club. The story explained Baz's almost preternatural musical ability, but it didn't quite explain how a session guitarist—even a very good one—had earned enough money to buy a pub.

I locked my bike to a lamppost outside the Phoenix, which stood on the corner of Brunswick Street and one of Fitzroy's many bluestone-cobbled lanes. The outer brick walls of the Phoenix came within two metres of the gutter and its facade had dirty cream-coloured paint visible between a peeling layer of posters while all the windows had bars, giving it the air of an old-time police lockup. Inside, what the Phoenix lacked in hygiene it made up for with ambience—which was a polite way of saying it had sticky carpet and hadn't been seriously refurbished since the 1960s.

On entering, I was enveloped in a comforting miasma of second-hand smoke, stale sweat and yesterday's beer. Flora was behind the bar. I imagine Flora had been quite a looker in her youth, but she hadn't been refurbished since the sixties either. She greeted me with her usual: 'Hello, hen.' Flora was from Glasgow and thirty years in Australia had barely dinted her accent. Flora had tried to retire a few times, but it never seemed to stick. She was currently working pro bono like me because she also had a soft spot for Baz.

Two of my favourite regulars were sitting at the bar with one of my least favourite. They were doing a crossword while arguing about saxophone players.

'It's John Coltrane or Stan Getz,' said Tony, a diamond dealer who'd seen many jazz greats in his world travels, but tended to favour the more mainstream artists.

Graham played bass, and was pretty good, but kept his day job as a public servant stooge, rather than go 'full muso'. He was the one who'd helped me with my CV. 'What about Archie Shepp?' he asked, always one to stir the pot.

'Get out of here with that experimental shit! That's not jazz, in my book.' Tony slapped the counter with one tastefully jewelled hand.

'There was an Archie Wilson who played for Carlton once,' piped up Phil. Phil could turn any conversation to football. His emotional investment in Carlton winning another premiership was the only thing keeping him from drinking himself to death, as far as I could tell.

Flora just winked at me and sighed. 'In Glasgow it's talking about football that'll get yer a glass in yer face—here, it's sax players. And it's not football, by the way, it's Aussie Rules.'

'You're in Fitzroy now, not Glasgow,' said Tony. 'But you can keep your hair on. No one's going to glass anyone.'

The Phoenix regulars were a disparate bunch, loosely tied by a love of music, or a cancelled driver's licence that kept them close to home, Phil being a case in point. The line-up changed slowly over the years. Occasionally someone died or moved interstate. But many had been coming to the Phoenix for years and I had learned more from them than I ever learned at school, including practical skills like how to pour the perfect beer or how to hustle in pool. Other skills were more niche: how to appraise a diamond or crack a safe. I'd spent so many hours at the Phoenix that, if Baz was forced to close it for good, it would leave a huge hole in my life. More than a hole.

Baz was sitting at one of the tables reading the sports pages of a newspaper. He was wearing his usual black shirt and trousers with green braces. A big man with bad knees thanks to a youth playing football, Baz was only mildly padded around the middle; it was his salt-and-pepper hair and whiskers that gave away his age. When he saw me, he hastily stubbed out a cigarette in a beer glass, and then tried to hide the evidence under the table.

'How's the council job treating you, Brick?' asked Graham, no doubt trying to draw my attention from Baz's attempted subterfuge. 'You know anything about this talk of an East-West tunnel? I just heard something on the news.'

Greater Melbourne was notoriously traffic-clogged and tunnels have long been proposed as the cure-all, especially one to burrow under Melbourne's notorious traffic snarls between the east and the west.

'I haven't heard anything,' I said. 'But I'd hardly be the first to know. Everyone at the council is so secretive I feel like I'm working for ASIO.'

'They'll never be able to build a tunnel,' interjected Tony. 'The government would have to buy up too much real estate and then tear it down. This is a historical area. Bulldozing a few square blocks would not be a popular move with voters.'

'I dunno,' said Phil. 'The premier we've got now might just be the bastard to get it done. I remember when he played for the Demons. He was a real hard case.'

'What do you reckon, Baz?' asked Graham. 'Anyone come by here offering you heaps of money to clear out and make way for a tunnel?'

Baz looked away. 'I've just got to go and make a phone call, fellas.' He headed for the stairs to his office.

'You okay, love?' Flora asked me. 'You're looking a wee bit peaky.'

'Just tired.' I went behind the bar and helped myself to a double vodka.

'Go on home then. I can manage. Working two jobs must be wearing you to a frazzle.'

'Thanks, Flora.' I squeezed her shoulder. 'I'll just go up and see Baz first.'

'Take this post up to him, would you, hen? I found it wedged in a box of napkins.'

I entered Baz's office without knocking and caught him in the process of searching through his desk drawers. No doubt hoping he'd hidden some cigarettes in there.

'Baz, it looks like there's another complaint letter from council here.' I handed him the envelope and continued leafing through the others.

'Thanks, bub. Just what I need.'

'And God knows what this is, the handwriting's atrocious.' The spidery writing on the envelope was written in all capitals.

Baz opened the letter and glanced in it briefly before hastily shoving it in his desk drawer. 'I'll read that later,' he said.

I sat down on the chair opposite Baz's desk. 'What are we going to do about the council complaints?'

'I dunno, bub. I'm thinking that maybe we should shut down for a few weeks. That'll stop the noise complaints at least. Although it doesn't bring us any closer to getting the electrics up to speed.'

I hated to see Uncle Baz look so tired and dispirited. I called him uncle, but for all intents and purposes, he was my father. If he hadn't adopted me, I don't know where I'd have ended up. My early years were a blur of foster carers. Nobody kept me for long, maybe it was because a lazy eye and a childhood stutter made me seem slow, or maybe people figured my parents were junkies. I was a foundling— to use an old-fashioned term—found outside a betting shop in Melbourne's CBD, wrapped in a dirty blanket and stuffed inside a sports bag. I generally avoided dwelling on my origins. My dark hair had a distinct red tinge, which hinted at some Irish heritage—but then my skin tanned well in summer, and my hazel eyes could look green or brown, depending on my outfit.

'There's got to be something more we can do,' I said, as Baz shuffled through some papers on his desk. 'What about that old mobster who used to come in here? I know you used to give him money in a paper bag.'

'That was years ago, love. I didn't think you even knew about it.'

'I know more than you think,' I said, but I wasn't being completely honest. There were some things I didn't know about the history of both the Phoenix and Baz.

'It wasn't much money, bub—less than council rates. Old Nino liked jazz. He wanted the club to stay open and the payment let him save face. But he's real old now. He'd be ninety at least.' Baz smiled and gave me a hug. He smelled of cigarettes and Old Spice. 'God knows we've had hard times before. We'll get through this.'

I was less sure. Melbourne was going through a period of massive change. It was not the same town as when Baz had first arrived in the 1960s, and some people were being left behind.

* * *

I farewelled Baz and the Phoenix crew and got back on my bike. It was only a short ride to my place, but first I took a detour past the payphones near the housing commission towers on Gertrude Street. A phone call from there was unlikely to be traced, since the local drug dealers vandalised any street surveillance cameras quicker than they could be fixed. Seeing the regulars in the Phoenix—Phil in particular—had made me feel guilty. The mayor wasn't lovable, but there had to be some friend or relative who cared about him, and they might even want him to have an open-coffin funeral.

I'd planned to give the police an anonymous tip-off but chickened out at the last moment. Instead I left an anonymous message on my boss's voicemail. I knew my boss wouldn't answer her phone. Despite being the head of the council's PR department, Gail Fawcett never ever answered her mobile phone. Like with a drug dealer, you left a message and she rang you back ... or not. Come to think of it, drug dealers in Melbourne were way more efficient. They'd have to be or they'd go out of business.

'I have some information for you, Ms Fawcett,' I whispered in an attempt to disguise my voice. 'The reason the second floor smells so bad is that the mayor has died and his body is in archive storage.

'This is not a prank call,' I added as an afterthought.

CHAPTER TWO

As I parked my bicycle outside the council building the next morning, I scanned for any sign of unusual activity, like a crowd gathering to watch a body being wheeled out on a gurney, but the only person I could see was a homeless man named Morrie. He was sitting on an iron bench surrounded by plastic bags filled with bits and pieces.

Morrie was a local character. He looked at least a hundred, but he was probably somewhere between fifty and seventy—a pretty good innings for a homeless Aboriginal man. 'Whenever I think the old bugger's finally gone and carked it,' Baz often said of Morrie, 'he turns up the next day. It's bloody spooky.' Still, Baz called Morrie uncle as a sign of respect and often slipped him a couple of bucks. 'The way he's survived so long living on the streets. That's not easy, I'll tell ya. Not easy at all.'

On this day, Morrie was drinking what I assumed was a can of beer wrapped in a paper bag while writing in a hardcover notebook. 'Baz's girl!' he said as I approached.

'Hey, Uncle. This isn't one of your usual spots.' Morrie didn't often stray much past Brunswick Street.

'Nah, with a mate. He's gotta pay a fine to get his dog back. I told him to ask about my dog too. Bastards.'

Morrie was obsessed with the idea that someone had stolen his dog when in truth it had either died or run away a long, long time ago. A car went past and Morrie squinted at it, before adding something to his notebook.

'What are you writing there?'

'I'm keeping track of all the cars coming and going. Been here all night. This way I can prove which bastard took my dog.'

'Did an ambulance come by? Or a police car maybe?' I tried to keep my tone casual.

'Nah.' He closed his notebook. 'Say, you got a spare dollar? I'm nearly out of grog and it's been a bugger of a decade.'

'Uncle, I'm on the bare bones of my arse.' I scrabbled in my bag and reluctantly handed over my emergency $10. Maybe karma would keep me and Baz off the streets as well.

'Bless you, darlin'. Baz grew you up right.'

I left Morrie to his notetaking and went to chain my bicycle to a No Standing sign. The council offices were in an imposing building with a grand facade of columns and sweeping stairs, a legacy of the Gold Rush years, when Melbourne was Australia's most cashed-up city. Inside, the entrance hall was similarly lush and opulent, but beyond the ground floor either the gold ran out or a 1970s renovation had stripped away the charm. From the second floor up, it was mostly grey partitions, fluorescent lights and the odd depressed-looking plant.

As I reached the second floor, I still hoped I might see some crime-scene tape or maybe a hot detective carrying a lukewarm coffee. Instead I was met by Gail, my boss—the human equivalent of an ice bath. She was looking as brittle as her bleached hair.

'Brick, I'm glad you could make it,' she said in her usual passive-aggressive manner. 'Something terrible has happened.'

For a moment I relaxed, thinking my anonymous phone call had done the trick and the mayor's body had been found without me having to raise the alarm. My relief was short-lived: as I followed her to her office, the stench hit me like a wall of despair. The mayor was definitely still in the building.

Gail shut the door to her office behind me, which muted the reek a notch. Or maybe it was being smothered by the incense. A handful of joss sticks were burning on her desk. 'That dickhead new councillor Hugo, the fat fuck, has been talking to Channel Nine again. As if I didn't already have my hands full with Meddling Mavis.'

Gail lived to impress the elected council members, but she didn't like any of them. Mavis DuBois was a particular thorn in her side. Mavis claimed to be a PR consultant and whenever she was in the council building, which was often, she popped in to see us so we could benefit from her words of wisdom. This was usually a bid for us to put out a press release with her name at the bottom and if it led to 'a photo opportunity at a playground or dog park, all the better!' Now it seemed that another councillor, namely 'fat fuck' Hugo Clark, was making moves on the PR bandwagon.

'I have a hair appointment,' said Gail. 'I need you to get on the phone and tell him that he has to talk to me before he talks to any of those pricks again. Okay?'

'Sure.' I used my most businesslike tone. 'And do you want me to call someone in to deal with the weird smell? Maybe a possum's died in a wall cavity.' It was becoming clear to me that Gail had not listened to the voicemail message about the mayor decomposing on the floor above.

'What smell? I can't smell anything,' said Gail, although her eyes were watering. 'Your job is public relations. Stick to it. I don't want you messing around with things that are not in your job description.'

I went to my desk and coaxed my computer into life. I had 114 new emails waiting, but none of them appeared useful. I added to the traffic by emailing Councillor Hugo Clark rather than pick up the phone.

'Dear Mr Clark,' I typed. 'Ms Fawcett would like to remind you that it's council policy to refer any media inquiries to the PR department.'

I pressed send with a flourish and congratulated myself on my growing bureaucratic acumen. That would sort him out. I'd come a long way since I began with the department three months earlier, but it was still a work in progress. Like a jigsaw puzzle of a forest at night, there was very little to go off. I'd had to slowly piece together my boss's expectations via snippets of information let slip by other members of the PR team during unguarded moments. Gail's nineteen-year-old PA, Brucie, was an especially fruitful vein due to his love of office gossip. As I was slowly coming to understand it, my role was to field media enquiries on a variety of issues—car parking being one that tended to get the public very excited—and fetch coffee for my boss whenever she felt like a long macchiato, extra hot. I didn't mind fetching coffee. During my high school years, I did an early morning barista shift for some easy pocket money. I understood coffee better than I understood office politics.

Besides myself, my boss Gail Fawcett and her luckless PA Brucie, there were six other people in the PR and communications team. Two were on stress leave, one was on maternity leave, and one—in charge of our web pages—was doing such an outstanding job of avoiding me that I wasn't even sure of his name. I'd narrowed it down to Gavin or Grant, and I absolutely couldn't blame him for wanting to steer clear of the rest of the PR team: they were bad at PR, terrible at communicating and pretty crap at teamwork. The only thing everyone agreed on was we weren't allowed to divulge too much information to anyone, but especially not to members of the media.

The smell from the body on the third floor, which had first been noticeable only in the second-floor lunchroom directly below the archives storage, was starting to spread across the entire second floor.

'Where's the maintenance department?' I asked Brucie, who was slumped at his desk outside Gail's door. He wasn't a morning person. 'I'm going to ask if they can find out what's causing the smell.'

Brucie gave me a desultory look. 'That's not in your job description, Brick. I wouldn't do it.'

By now I knew the 'job description' argument got council workers out of most things, except meetings, but it had taken me a while to get my head around the concept: when working at the Phoenix my duties ranged from bartender to cleaner to back-up singer, depending on the night. Not to mention accountant and door bitch. I'd even turned my hand to plumbing on occasion.

'I won't tell if you don't. It's probably just a dead rat in the ceiling. They'll get it out in a jiffy.'

'I honestly can't smell anything,' said Brucie. 'Although I do have a bit of a cold.' Brucie sniffed again, to demonstrate, but it would have been more believable if his pupils weren't pinpoints.

In the end I had to tell the maintenance department I feared some kind of gas leak: a funny smell wasn't enough to get them moving. A guy called Dave was reluctantly despatched.

'Yeah, there is a bit of a pong.' He opened a few cupboards in a half-hearted manner. 'It's probably some off food.'

'Do you think it could be coming from the floor above? Through the heating vent?'

He looked confused so I pointed directly at the vent.

He shook his head as if I'd told him a joke. 'Yeah, nah, I wouldn't think so. Have you tried an air freshener?'

By now the smell seemed to be intensifying by the minute and I was beginning to feel queasy. I retreated to the fourth-floor toilets, the only ones with windows that opened. They were popular with smokers—at least, they were popular with the ones who could still make it up the stairs, since the lift didn't go all the way to the fourth floor.

I'd give Gail one more day to listen to my voicemail message about the dead body and if there'd still been no action, I'd call the police.

CHAPTER THREE

The next day I arrived at work at seven in the morning, mentally prepared to call the authorities so they could rid the building of the mayor's body. Morrie was still stationed near the No Standing sign, but was thankfully asleep, because I was totally out of cash.

The second floor was quiet, apart from the buzz from the fluorescent lights that seemed to burn day and night. I took a cautious sniff and found that the air was breathable. It was a good sign, but not definitive. I fired up my computer and was waiting for my inbox to load when the phone rang. I jumped. The phones in the PR department rarely rang since emails were the preferred manner of communication. I answered with trepidation.

'Hello, this is Selena McManus from *Today Today*.'

My heart froze. It was something I'd been dreading, but it still caught me by surprise. Selena had made my life hell from ages ten to twelve when she was the meanest girl at our primary school. I knew she had become a television reporter, albeit with a new surname and a weird new accent. She'd started out doing traffic reports while hovering over the Monash Freeway but had since climbed the tree to a current affairs show on TV. It was the kind of show that loved doing stories on evil parking inspectors, dodgy dog inspectors and anything generally involving angry rate-payers. I had been resigned to the fact that one day my new job would lead to our paths crossing in a way that required civil communication rather than our usual tactic of ignoring each other if we happened to be in the local Greek deli at the same time.

'How can I help you?' I tried to keep my voice as normal as possible. Selena was like a dog that could smell fear.

She got straight to the point. 'I've heard that the mayor's dead. Can you confirm this?'

My mind raced. Gail's tactic with journalists was 'deny, deny, deny', but I didn't think that was going to cut it. If you can't deny, lie.

'Sorry, I've just walked into the office. I'll get someone to call you back in a second. Everyone's in a meeting.'

Selena wasn't happy, but she hung up. I felt sick. Before I could even start to formulate a plan of action, the phone rang again. I gave serious thought to not answering it at all but relented through force of habit. Lucky, because it was Gail.

'It's council policy to answer within three rings, Brick, you might want to remember that.' Needless to say, I'd never heard of this policy. 'I need to you to write a press release. Have you read the memo Hugo Clark sent out to all the council staff? About the mayor being dead? It was totally against my advice, but what can you do when you're dealing with amateurs.'

My inbox chose this moment to reveal its latest cache. Top of the list was one tagged as urgent and titled *Sad News*. It was an official memo from the elected council members saying that the mayor had passed away at home after having a heart attack.

'Do you want me to send out a press release about his death?'

'No, for God's sake, no.' Gail's disgust at my lack of professionalism was evident. 'Start with an illness. We'll tell them he's dead tomorrow.'

'But what if someone tells a reporter about this memo? They might ring and ask—'

'Well, you shouldn't be answering the phone, should you?' She slammed the phone down with a thud so deafening, I suspected she'd thrown her receiver against a wall. I hazarded a guess that we weren't going to see her in the office that day. Being absent was Gail's way of managing staff in general and today it would also allow her to blame us for any media stuff-ups.

I'd formulated a theory about Gail's office phobia. It involved her being so overwhelmed by the sheer volume of her email inbox that she could only face it while being three sheets to the wind—not always advisable during office hours. The other theory (formulated by a more low-minded colleague, aka Brucie) was that she was having an affair with someone inappropriate, but that seemed highly unlikely. I suppose that technically Gail could be considered attractive—she was tall and broad shouldered with long legs. But her tendency to wear a lot of black made her resemble one of those spiders that devours their partner after mating. If indeed she was having an affair, I was sure to unwittingly uncover it sooner or later. I've always had a talent for accidentally finding things. I'd found the mayor, after all, and I currently had three stray cats living with me.

The phone rang again. This time I ignored it in case it was Gail testing me and started on a press release; common sense told me it was going to be needed. But what to say about Dickie Ruffhead? He'd stopped by the PR department a few times and had struck me as the sleazy conman type, much akin to various music promoters I'd met over the years. I was instantly wise to his efforts to have me crawl under the desk to retrieve a dropped pen. To fill in the blanks, I did a quick internet surf.

Ruffhead was a one-time bookie. Some friends in high places, more friends in low places. Three wives. No kids. He'd been mayor for a long time despite not being all that good at it. Could I put that in the release?

'Oh. My. God!' Gail's PA Brucie had arrived without my noticing, or perhaps he'd slept under the desk again. Sometimes he didn't have the taxi fare to get back to the suburbs after a night in clubland. 'Have you read this email? The

Gruesome Groper has groped his last arse! Did I tell you about last year's Christmas party where he even took a stab at me?'

Only about a million times.

Brucie's face was lit up like a full-moon rave. 'I wonder if he went on the job?'

I'd wondered that myself.

'I bet it was in a titty bar or something,' continued Brucie before another thought harshed his gossip high and he went pale. 'Does Gail know yet?' he whispered.

'Yes, so we'd better think of a plan of action.'

He started to panic. 'Oh shit, oh shit. This is going to be worse than when that Selena chick from Channel Nine did the cat registry exposé. Gail is going to be livid. We'll have to hide all the staplers in case she throws something.'

* * *

The next few days went by in a blur as the PR team was actually forced to do some work. Phones rang nonstop and the ping of emails arriving sounded like rain on the roof. The culmination was a memorial service for the mayor held in the council chambers. All staff were mandated to attend. On the plus side, it was catered.

While alive, Dickie Ruffhead was often said to be the shonkiest bastard who'd ever darkened the doors of the council chambers. Not to his face, obviously. For his memorial, the word 'larrikin' was proving handy. Even creepy Hugo Clark said a few words. 'We all know he wasn't perfect,' he rasped, and there were nods, in particular from staff members who well knew this was an understatement. 'He had a soft spot for the ladies—and one or two of you, I know, will be missing him especially.' Confused looks were cast about, lingering on anyone under forty, including— much to my horror—myself.

But the general atmosphere was one of relief, as if an ancient pet dog with a skin complaint and incontinence had finally been run over. Gail was absent, claiming to have a long-standing appointment with a specialist, so the PR team was more relaxed than it had been in days.

Brucie suggested I take some photos for the social pages of the staff newsletter and it gave me a good opportunity to observe reactions through the camera's viewfinder. I was curious as to whether the person who'd moved the body was present. But the only person who seemed the least bit upset was Mavis DuBois. This was odd since I'd only ever seen her treat the mayor with barely veiled contempt. As a PowerPoint of photos played showing the mayor cutting ribbons and/or drinking, Mavis seemed to be shedding some genuine tears, but then, death can affect people strangely; maybe she'd lost a loved one recently. Or a pet hamster.

I gave up taking photos and grabbed as many sausage rolls as I could comfortably hold on a napkin. Gossip was rife as worker drones hovered around the buffet, but it mostly centred on who was going to be the next mayor, and although there was a subcurrent of speculation about which of Dickie's various addictions had caused his heart attack, I didn't hear any theories that he'd popped his clogs while actually in the council building, nor that he was behind the phantom stink that came slowly and left suddenly, so whoever had removed the mayor's body had kept it very, very, *very* quiet.

Once again it occurred to me that while 170 years had passed since the days of John Batman, madness and corruption remained at the heart of Melbourne's governance.

* * *

We got an early mark after the memorial service, so I went to the Phoenix. Working two jobs had left me unsure of what to do with any spare time. I needed to find a new hobby. My previous hobby had been good-looking men with no money, and working at council was definitely helping me go cold turkey. It seemed that they had a mandate to only employ men who were terminally unattractive, completely devoid of charm or charisma or gay.

I arrived at the Phoenix to find an impromptu jam session in progress. Graham was playing bass and a guy in drag was singing a bluesy version of 'California Dreaming' while dressed as Mama Cass. He was actually pretty good.

'Is Baz here?' I asked Flora, who was behind the bar as usual.

'He's left town for a few days, hen. He asked me to use up the kegs tonight and then keep the Phoenix closed for the rest of the week. Does he owe money to a supplier or something? He said he left you a message on your machine.' Baz knew I rarely listened to messages on my mobile phone because my plan charged me to pick up voicemail.

Sure enough, when I got home there was a message on my answering machine. 'I'm worried about this complaints thing and I know you're busy with your council gig, so it'll give you a break from working two jobs. We can open up again when I get back.'

I immediately dialled his mobile, but there was no answer and I didn't bother leaving a message. Baz didn't pay to pick up voicemail either.

The message made me feel uneasy. Baz had mentioned the idea of closing the Phoenix for a few days, but I thought he'd consult with me before he actually took such a drastic move. Our regulars didn't bring in heaps of cash, but it was a steady trickle and we didn't need them finding another watering hole. I hoped Baz knew what he was doing.

CHAPTER FOUR

Back in my second week of working for council, my boss Gail had informed us that someone from the PR team needed to attend the council meetings on her behalf because she was 'too busy'. It was more likely that she just couldn't be bothered, but she was offering overtime so I was happy to step into the role. At the first few meetings I attended, I dutifully took notes, thinking Gail might ask me to report back, but she never did. So I gave up taking real notes and instead spent the time daydreaming and doodling in a notebook, although I did make myself responsible for setting up the tea, coffee and biscuits. This was better suited to my skill set and made me feel (and look) useful.

The council meetings were held in a large room on the ground floor that had the Federation glamour of glossy wood panelling and moulded ceiling flourishes. From the walls, the portraits of former mayors glared down like vengeful ghosts.

On this evening, the death of Dickie Ruffhead seemed to have invigorated the council members, and I could tell it was going to be a long session of debate and counter debate, interspersed with some petty quibbling.

The only friendly face sat behind the councillors in the seats assigned to the public: Sue Day was the reporter for a free weekly newspaper that generally included one page on council affairs and fifty-eight pages of real estate listings. She caught my eye and silently mimicked shooting herself in the head with her biro. I was about to respond with my own death by self-strangulation, but a movement drew my attention away. A man was waving through the double glass doors of the council meeting room in an impatient manner. He was obviously a first-timer to the building or he would have known to ignore the signs and push not pull.

I left my seat and opened the door just wide enough to converse.

'Yes?' I whispered, noticing with an uneasy frisson that this new interloper was under forty and not wearing brown. He was carrying a battered leather satchel that didn't close properly. A notebook and a laptop were in danger of falling out.

'I'm Mitch Mitchell.' He produced a business card from his pocket and held it between his index and middle finger, as if he were about to do a magic trick.

I'd been afraid that one day a reporter other than Sue might come to the meeting and tonight was the night.

Gail was not going to be pleased. She feared reporters like vampires feared sunlight, as I'd learned on my second day with the PR department. I'd been sitting there hoping someone would give me some work to do when the phone started ringing. Gavin (or Grant) was acting like he couldn't hear so I'd thought I'd better answer it. The woman on the other end had asked, very politely, to speak to Gail Fawcett. I was feeling quietly proud that I'd managed to transfer the call, since I'd only had five seconds of instructions from Brucie (who'd been speeding like Keith Moon on tour at the time), when Gail's office door flew open with a noise like a gunshot as its handle hit the wall. Then she was in front of me, bright red and almost incoherent with rage. 'Don't. You. Ever. Do. That. Again,' she'd shouted, each word punctuated with a jab from a talon-like finger. 'I. Do. Not. Take. Calls. From. Anyone. Hear me? Anyone!'

'The meeting's nearly over, I'm afraid,' I lied, knowing that there was at least three hours to go. I hoped he'd turn tail and leave, but he didn't budge. Instead he stuck his foot in the door.

'Can I come in? I believe this meeting's open to the public.'

Great. A looker with a shitty attitude—all he needed was a gambling habit and he'd be the man of my dreams.

I gave up trying to close the door. 'You can sit over there.' I gestured in Sue's direction and was shocked to notice her run a surreptitious tongue over her teeth before flashing the man a smile.

I felt uneasy as I returned to my seat. Nothing on the agenda had struck me as particularly newsworthy. A cold prickle ran across my skin. Maybe this interloper knew something about the circumstances of the mayor's demise. There was still a chance I could be dragged into the whole sordid saga, forcing me to resign immediately.

'Now we move to Item 12,' announced the deputy mayor. The new arrival's ears pricked up like a dog that had just heard a tin opener. I stopped pretending to take notes and paid attention.

'I'm sorry to have to announce that councillor Mavis DuBois has decided to step down as chair of the Development Consent Committee. Her mother's very ill and she needs to spend more time with her.'

I'd heard about the Development Consent Committee because Mavis DuBois invariably mentioned it every time she stopped by our department: it was a powerful committee that could veto building applications, demand extra car spaces be added to multi-apartment developments and generally make life difficult for developers. Its meeting agenda papers were as long as the phone book, so Mavis preferred a staff member to print it out for her, rather than do it herself.

My eyes went to Mavis. She was looking even worse for wear than she had at the mayor's memorial. Usually she was the epitome of corporate chic: cream-toned power suits with elegant jewellery and subtle make-up. Today she had a layer of ill-matched foundation that had left a mark on the neck of her jacket, was blinking erratically, and her mascara was smudged.

'I've only received one nomination so far, from Councillor Hugo Clark, but considering the late notice I'm willing to take more.' The deputy mayor scanned the assembly.

Like Mavis, Hugo Clark was much younger than the other councillors—I pegged them both as only a few years older than me, so in their early to mid-thirties—but Hugo didn't look like a born politician. He looked more like a real-estate agent who'd eaten too many pies. He favoured shiny suits and had an ill-advised Ned Kelly–style beard. He was also very creepy. I was pulling beers before I was old enough to legally drink, so I was used to creeps. Hugo Clark took creepy to a whole other level, however. His eyes were dead and his voice was sticky and unpleasant.

I looked around at the other councillors. There were no other nominations. I suspected they all had their eyes on the prize of being the next mayor. They'd waited many long years for their chance at the top job.

'Well then, Councillor Clark,' said the deputy mayor. 'It seems as though your nomination has been successful. Congratulations.'

I saw Sue making a few notes while glancing covertly to her left to see what the unexpected visitor was doing. He hadn't even taken out his notebook and was sitting with his arms crossed, staring intently at Hugo Clark in the manner of an old Western film, the kind where a gunslinger arrives in town with nothing to rely on but his wits and his luck.

* * *

When the meeting finally wrapped up, Sue and I decided we needed a drink after wasting four hours of our still young lives. Sue's mother was visiting from South Australia and she was keen to make the most of the free babysitting.

As we walked to Sue's station wagon, I shrugged off my long-sleeved work jacket (a beautiful green fitted number that I'd found in an op shop) and let my hair loose from its tight bun.

'I wish I could shake out my hair and look like a million bucks,' said Sue, using her rearview mirror to put on some lipstick. 'These days I'd need Spakfilla to cover the bags under my eyes.'

We drove the short distance to Carlton. Sue wanted to check out a pub that apparently had a beautiful pressed tin ceiling, but when we got there we found it had been replaced by a giant hole in the ground surrounded by scaffolding. 'Well, that sucks,' she said. 'Where will we go instead?'

We settled on the nearby TAB since it had half-price pots on offer. It was a squat 1970s-style building with all the charm of a supermarket. We took our beers as far as possible from the poker machines.

'So who was that guy at the meeting?' I asked as Sue ripped opened a packet of salt and vinegar chips.

'What do you mean?' Her expression combined both shock and outrage. 'Didn't you recognise him?'

'Is he a reporter?' I didn't want to tell her that I rarely read the newspaper and almost never watched the TV news.

'He's Mitch Mitchell.' She paused for me to express some sign of recognition.

'Jimi Hendrix's drummer?' It was the best I could come up with.

'No. He's only Australia's most influential war correspondent since Wilfred Burchett.'

I nodded as if I'd suddenly remembered, but I still had no idea who she was talking about. Obscure Blues artists of the 1930s are more my specialist topic, thanks to Baz.

'He covered Somalia, Afghanistan, Iraq. He was recently kidnapped by the Taliban and held hostage for three months before escaping. You must have heard about that. He's a real journalist—not some half-arsed real estate reviewer. Plus, tell me he's not the sexiest thing you've ever seen in council chambers?'

'Well, the bar's not very high there,' I pointed out. 'But what the hell was he doing at council if he's a war correspondent?'

'He must have a lead on a story. Either that or he's having trouble sleeping.'

Whatever Mitch Mitchell's motives, my boss wasn't going to like a real journalist showing an interest in council affairs. Gail was still recovering from a TV report about council buying a bad batch of ticket paper for the parking meters: the tickets went black when exposed to sunlight, completely obliterating anything printed on them. Parking-meter-paper-gate, I'd joked at the time, but Gail's wrath hadn't been funny at all.

'It was definitely something to do with Hugo Clark getting that committee chairman gig,' said Sue. 'What do you know about that?'

'Not much,' I said. 'I usually only see Hugo Clark at council meetings and he only talks to me if the biscuits run out. He especially likes the Monte Carlos. But my boss did have her tits in a twist the other day because he gave an interview to Channel Nine about something.'

'Yeah, I saw him on the TV news. The idea of another cross-town tunnel has reared its head again. Ever since Errol Grimes became premier, he's turned into the biggest bastard on Earth. Good looking though, the camera loves him. Grimes—not Hugo. Hugo looked like a sack of shit and didn't say anything much … but I *was* surprised to see his head on television. I phone all the councillors at least once a week hoping for something resembling a news story and Hugo never returns my calls. The only time I've ever managed to interview him was when he was running for council. He had a bit of a weird vibe about him.'

'It's not just because he looks like a sleazy real estate agent?'

'Sleazy real estate agents I can handle. I talk to them every day. No, I mean he's really creepy. Zombie-style creepy? You know?'

I knew what Sue meant. Since I'd begun working for the council I'd met more than one person I suspected of being a zombie. But I'm sure it didn't make them bad people. Or did it?

After downing her beer and getting a second one, Sue returned to the topic of the council's visit by journalistic superstardom. 'If you really want to know what Mitch Mitchell's up to, you could go along to one of the development consent meetings,' she said. 'I think there's one later this week.'

More meetings were the last thing I wanted.

'I'm surprised Mavis DuBois gave up the gig, though,' continued Sue. 'She loved being on that committee. It's

almost as powerful as being the mayor. Maybe Mitch
Mitchell's investigating her. If anyone's in bed with developers, it's Mavis. Apart from the late mayor, of course. I'm
sure he was taking kickbacks hand over fist, but no one's
ever found any concrete evidence. Too late now he's dead, I
guess. If the council's chief executive's got a lick of sense he
will have gone in and shredded every scrap of paper in the
mayoral office.'

I sipped my beer quietly. Letting Sue drink and think
aloud was turning out to be a good strategy for gathering
information without looking too stupid.

'It's unbelievable the amount of development that's going
on,' she said. 'Melbourne's going to lose everything that
makes it Melbourne if things keep going this way. They may
as well just dig up the Gold Coast and plonk it down on top
of us. You look away for a second and they've built a thirty-
storey apartment block—all with two tiny bedrooms and
six bathrooms. For God's sake, who needs six bathrooms?
And if it's not some ugly high-rise it's vast seas of McMansions with no eaves and five aircon units sucking us straight
down to hell.'

Sue drank some more beer. 'And there are McMansions
in Brunswick these days. Not your good old Greek palaces, but honest-to-God McMansions. In Brunswick!' Sue's
dream was to buy and renovate (tastefully, of course) an old
Brunswick bungalow—instead she and her husband had a
massive mortgage on a pre-fab in Caroline Springs, one of
the more recent outer suburbs that had been built next to a
twelve-lane freeway.

'So you think this shit-hot journalist guy's chasing up something to do with a development proposal that's going to the committee?'

'It's got be. There's a million killer stories there. If I didn't have to write thirty real estate reviews a week before driving an hour home to three screaming children, I'd consider doing some digging myself. That said, I'd probably be sacked since developers make up eighty per cent of *The Weekly*'s advertising revenue.' She paused. 'I'm kind of surprised he's back in Australia, though. Maybe he's got burnout after being kidnapped by militants.'

'That'll do it.' The kidnapping could explain the slightly manic gleam I'd noticed in Mitch Mitchell's eyes.

'Mitch Mitchell was certainly interested in knowing who was going to be the new chairman. Maybe I'll go along to their next meeting. After all, I'm going to have to change jobs one of these days. There's only so much selling out you can do before your soul dies completely.'

I thought I'd better lighten the mood. 'Are you sure you don't just want to have another perve? What would your husband say?'

'I doubt he'd care. Too tired, like me. Sleep deprivation is a recognised form of torture, you know.' Sue sighed, then downed her second drink with the efficiency of a true journalist. 'Speaking of, I'd better go and rescue Mum from the kids. The DVD player's on the fritz, so God knows what they'll all be up to.'

The pub ambience had left me feeling homesick and I decided to pop by the Phoenix on my way home. I hadn't heard from Baz since his strange phone message at the start of the week.

I'd always enjoyed walking at night. I liked looking in windows lit up like TV screens. A famous bass player once told me that the French have a word for it: 'flaneur' (or 'flaneuse' for a woman). I'm not sure how that differs from 'voyeur' (or 'voyeuse'), but I'm glad the French make a distinction.

Melbourne's weather has the changeable nature of a meth addict, but this October evening, it was particularly fine. The denim-clad bottom of the man walking ahead of me was also particularly fine, making my walk more enjoyable. I'd sworn off men but there was no harm in looking. This man was tall and well built with a loose-limbed swagger and thick, wavy hair well past his collar. He slowed to take a call on his mobile phone, so I paused and pretended to check out some overpriced boots in a shop window while trying to catch a glimpse of his face in the reflection. He finished his call and slung his bag back over his shoulder. It was battered leather and I was just wondering where I'd seen it before when I got a look at the man's face. It was the man who'd barged into the council meeting earlier that night, the journalist Mitch Mitchell: the *famous, award-winning* journalist, as I'd learned from Sue. I quickly turned back to the window in case he noticed me staring, but I needn't have worried. He shoved his phone in his pocket and continued walking without a backward glance.

He and I were headed in the same direction, so I followed him a little longer. He crossed the road and went into a small bar that had cropped up in a shopfront that had previously housed the last independent video store to go out of business; a fresh coat of paint had obliterated the LIGHTS OUT VIDEO sign. I wondered if he was meeting someone special.

A breeze sent a skitter of leaves along the footpath. It looked like we were in for a storm. Curiosity got the better of me so I crossed the road and was about to peek casually in the window of the bar when Mitchell emerged again suddenly. His hand whipped out like a snake and grabbed me by the wrist.

'If you're following me, you're not very good at staying unnoticed. Have I met you before?' He looked me up and down, lingering momentarily on my chest as if it would help jog his memory.

I opted not to remind him of our brief interaction at the council meeting. 'I work at the Phoenix, down the road,' I said. 'I wasn't following you, I just thought I recognised you, is all. Are you Mitch Mitchell?'

He dropped my wrist and gave a thin smile. Up close I could see that his eyes were brown. 'That arsehole? No, I'm not him, I just have an arsehole kind of face.' With that he loped off down the street.

* * *

As I neared the Phoenix, I could see it was closed, but I decided to pop in anyway and see if Baz was back from his mysterious jaunt. I unlocked the door, then locked it behind me. The bar was dark and the air was stale, indicating no one had been in for a few days. I went up the stairs to Baz's office and it likewise had a stale smell.

The office was a converted storeroom with a desk and a couch in the corner. The desk was its usual mess of paperwork. I uncovered the phone and tried Baz's mobile again. It buzzed from under a stack of paperwork to my left and when I uncovered it, it showed twenty-five missed calls.

Out of habit, I stacked up the papers I'd dislodged. I'd spent a lot of time sitting at Baz's desk: doing homework, making up the pay packets back when we could afford to pay staff and, most recently, doing a financial plan and a list of renovation jobs, in order of urgency. I felt physically ill at the possibility of Baz losing the Phoenix. It had been his life for more than forty years, and mine for nearly twenty.

I exited his office via a second door which led to a small concrete balcony. Another door off this balcony led to Baz's apartment while a set of concrete steps went down to a tiny walled courtyard, graced by three doors and a bunch of wheelie bins: one door led back into the Phoenix, one led to a poky toilet, and the third opened onto the street.

I knocked on the door to Baz's apartment, waited about fifteen seconds and then opened it using a key he kept stashed behind a loose brick. The apartment was 'bijou', to use yet another French term that's supposed to make crap stuff sound more glamorous. It took all of thirty seconds to establish that Baz wasn't inside and another thirty to check he wasn't downstairs in the dismal courtyard dunny. I'd begged him to get a toilet inside the flat, but excess cash is hard to come by when you run a live venue.

I returned to the lounge room and sat on the faded two-seater. The only other items in the room were Baz's piece-of-crap TV—used mostly for watching football—his state-of-the-art Garrard 401 turntable and Tannoy Arden speakers, and his shrine to Lionel Rose, which was made up of a framed photo of Rose, victorious after his fight at Festival Hall in 1969, beside another frame holding Baz's ticket to the fight. Festival Hall was Baz's sacred place. His flat was definitely not; more and more it was just becoming a place to store his record collection and endless boxes of photos. You could be forgiven for thinking Uncle Baz was in the process of moving house.

Baz had taken up photography as a hobby in the 1960s. 'It's important to have something outside of your work,' he'd tell me whenever I complained about the chemical smell in the bathroom, which doubled as a dark room. In the last year I'd been going through some of his photos, hoping to find proof regarding his claim of spending a night on the town with the Beatles during their visit to Australia in 1964. 'Those cats were pretty wild,' Baz had said.

I was thinking more of the money that could come from selling a rare John Lennon photo, but I also liked looking at the pictures—especially when I found shots of Baz himself. I'd framed one photo I'd found of him in his footy gear and presented it to him as a Christmas gift.

'Look how young I am there!' he'd said.

'What year was this, do you reckon?' I'd asked.

Baz ran his fingers down his face as if to aid his think-ing process. His fingers were long and gnarled, bringing to mind tree branches. 'Must be about sixty-two. When I started playing for Fitzroy Reserves. It was my first winter in Melbourne and I nearly froze me bloody balls off. I'd never seen frost before—I thought that someone had spilled flour all over the oval. No word of a lie!'

Baz was born in Brisbane but had moved around and lived in all kinds of places—especially after his mother's death. I'm yet to get to the bottom of how, why or when he ended up in Melbourne, but the photos were suggesting it was around 1960.

'You're looking pretty smooth here, Baz,' I said, laughing at the Brylcreem that had turned his wiry hair into a slick-looking helmet.

'Harry Belafonte, they used to call me on a good day. Other days they'd call me a Black cunt to me face. Pardon my French. Melbourne was a different town back then. Blackfellas were expected to stay in Fitzroy. There were some suburbs that were definitely off limits. A lot of things were off limits.'

A yellowed box of photos was open on the coffee table. I pulled out some prints that showed a small skiffle outfit on stage at the Phoenix. Two guitarists—one with a nice-looking Gibson and the other some piece-of-shit six string—a drummer and a dark-haired woman singing. The Phoenix hadn't changed much but the people were unmistakably from another era. For a start, everyone was smoking and the men were all wearing suits, their hair cropped to a short back and sides. The women were wearing dresses and high heels, sitting with their legs crossed at the ankle. I flipped over the photo to read Baz's careful lettering: *Betty Jones and the Jive Kings.*

I continued pulling out photos. Another showed a thickset woman behind the bar. Something about her eyes reminded me of Baz's Aunty Dot, but she was way too large. Dot had always been the tiny, birdlike type. I wondered if it was one of Dot's sisters, but when I turned the photo over, there was nothing written on the back.

The storm arrived with a clap of thunder and the kind of winds that sent tree branches crashing and debris flying. I decided to stay put. The tiny room that had once been my bedroom had been totally consumed by boxes, but with the help of some bourbon I found in the kitchen, I managed to fall asleep on the threadbare couch.

I woke suddenly to the sound of a door slamming. Although it was too dark to see much, I was perplexed to find that I was now lying on my stomach underneath the couch. The dusty carpet was pressed into my cheek, making me want to sneeze. I tried to move but was paralysed; a sure sign that I was dreaming.

As I looked out from under the couch, I saw a pair of high-heeled shoes. A woman was standing mere inches from my face. A feeling of dread had begun in the pit of my stomach and was steadily growing. I was about to dig my fingernails into my own flesh—a tactic I'd found effective against the night terrors I'd suffered since childhood—but a voice stopped me. It was Baz. He was calling out from a distance. 'Nora! Nora! Christ! Nora!' My heart was hammering in my chest. The high-heeled shoes had disappeared now, but I could hear footsteps and banging, as if someone was tearing the house apart. 'Little girl, where are you?' Baz's voice was even more hoarse and frantic than before. 'Where are you? Are you here? Jesus Christ!'

I awoke with a jerk, sending the empty bourbon glass spinning onto the floor. I was on the couch, my neck stiff, my mouth gluey and dry. Dim light was coming in from a crack in the curtains and my watch told me it was five o'clock in the morning.

I stumbled into Baz's room to see if he'd returned, but the blanket and sheets hadn't been disturbed. I sat down heavily and looked around. Baz's bedroom also had a share of stacked boxes. His suitcase—the same one he brought back from the US all those years ago—was in its usual place on top of the narrow wardrobe. His bedside table featured a photo of me and Aunty Dot wearing Christmas cracker crowns next to a glass of water for his dentures and an old-fashioned alarm clock.

Then I noticed Baz's guitar stand in the corner. It was empty. The relief was akin to making it to the outdoor dunny on a cold night after holding on for way too long. I did another check of the house, but Baz's guitar and its case were definitely missing. It was a very good sign. Baz might leave behind his luggage, he might leave behind his mobile phone, he might even leave behind his front teeth, but he would never leave behind his guitar. I now felt reasonably assured that Baz had gone somewhere with some degree of planning. Half-arsed planning, seeing as he'd forgotten his suitcase, but planning nonetheless.

It wasn't unusual for Baz to be out of touch for a week or so: for a fishing trip, a cheeky fling or a weekend spent scouring regional record stores for rare 45s. Everyone has their methods of stress relief.

I filled a mug with water from the tap and washed down a couple of painkillers that looked almost as old as Baz's kitchen cabinets. Then I stuck a note on the fridge asking him to call me as soon as he got in.

Outside the storm was over and it was abnormally still, like the atmosphere had worn itself out in a childish tantrum and was now fast asleep. Houses were dark, streetlights were dimming and the rush-hour traffic was yet to start. The air carried the newly washed smell of leaf litter and wet concrete.

Before my new life as a council drone, it had been a good five years since I'd started my day before ten o'clock. Usually I hadn't left the house until midday unless it was for a triple espresso and a bacon sandwich. When you work until two or three am that's just what you do.

It had been a surprise to rediscover early mornings. The streets looked different. After midnight, inner Melbourne's streets were littered with young men smelling of cheap booze and cheaper aftershave. Their mission was to get pissed, punch someone and then get a souvlaki before heading back to an outer suburb called something adjectival like Upper Plenty or Federal. Suburbs I had happily never visited in my whole life.

In the early morning the hooligans, creeps and bogans were safely tucked away in their burrows (or the emergency room, depending on the evening) and it was like Melbourne's inner city lowered its mask and returned to a more innocent, old-fashioned time. The morning people emerged: joggers, power walkers, mothers of babies—people who were less likely to attack you just for looking at them. They might even smile and say hello. They almost never yelled obscenities from passing cars.

Some mornings you could look up and see hot air balloons hanging silently in the sky like huge, overripe fruit. They always gave me a tingle of excitement, like the balloons were a link to another time and place. I wasn't sure I'd ever be that keen to go up in one, though. What if it burst, sending me plummeting back down to Earth?

* * *

Once—when particularly bored—I'd mapped every house I remembered living in and found I'd never moved more than two kilometres from the Phoenix; eleven houses within the same area of about four square kilometres. You'd think I'd been raised in a village during the Middle Ages instead of a cosmopolitan city of more than three million people.

At the moment, I was house-sitting for an old friend who was overseas. Bunny and I had met in our late teens while dating members of a garage band who were squatting in a disused bank in Fitzroy. They'd had their glory days in the grunge era and were reluctant to move on.

I was involved with the bass guitarist, Derek. His main attractions were some high-quality tattoos and a deceptively healthy complexion for an early adopter of meth. Bunny was with the lead singer, Warren, who had skanky, greasy hair he was constantly flicking back off his acned face, as well as a sinus problem that meant he sniffed loudly all the time (also meth related, in hindsight).

Bunny was quicker than me to learn that musicians were a waste of time. She moved out of the mould-infested bank vault, finished a medical degree and was now working for an overseas aid agency. The worst part of the whole story was that her greasy ex changed his name and ended up being one of Australia's most bankable movie stars. We try not to ever mention it.

Bunny and I had reconnected a couple of years back over a house-sitter notice she'd posted at the Black Cat Cafe. My duties were to water the plants, feed Bunny's pet snake once a month and keep the place safe from break-ins. Over time it evolved into a house-share arrangement since Bunny travelled for work a lot. More recently her baby brother had moved into a clapped-out caravan in the tiny back yard. I wasn't expected to feed her brother, but Bunny hoped I'd keep an eye on him. She said he was 'socially challenged' and needed some degree of adult supervision.

Bunny's house had been renovated sometime in the 1980s, judging by the decor in the bathroom. There were two bedrooms at the front with a corridor down the middle. At the back was a tiny spare room-cum-junk room, a kitchen and lounge. The laundry was in a lean-to in the backyard. Bunny had inherited some money from a grandmother and was smart to invest it in buying the house when North Fitzroy still featured a slew of unrenovated rat traps rented by arts students who didn't mind using the gas ovens for heating during winter. Gentrification was edging out the students now.

The phone was ringing as I unlocked the door. Not many people knew the landline number and I almost tripped in my haste to answer, hoping it would be Baz.

'Brick, my wee hen.' It was Flora. 'Sorry to ring your house so early, but I couldn't get through on your mobile. I'm wondering if you've heard from Baz. I thought he'd be back by now and of course he's not answering his mobile.'

I sat down on the floor in the corridor and removed my boots. 'No, I haven't heard from him. I know he said he was leaving town, but I thought it was just for a day or two. I've been to his flat and he's not there—and neither is his guitar. It makes me wonder what he's up to.'

Flora's sigh made the phone's receiver hiss. 'Ah well, I guess he'll turn up when he's ready. But if you speak to him, tell him to call me.'

I put down the phone, wondering what to do next. There was a chance Baz had gone to visit family interstate. If anyone knew, it would be his Aunty Dot, the matriarch of Baz's vast family—members of which were spread right across Australia. Dot and her builder husband had moved to Darwin in the 1980s during the post-cyclone reconstruction, and although Dot had since been widowed, she'd stayed on there. She said the heat soothed her arthritis.

'Brick, love, you're calling early. What's up?' Dot's voice was so vibrant, it was hard to believe she was nearly eighty.

'Actually, I'm ringing because Baz has done one of his disappearing acts. I was hoping he might be there.'

'Not unless he crept into town without telling me, and he knows I'd be wild with him if he tried that.'

'Could he be visiting someone? Are any of the cousins in strife? Or a grand final?'

'I don't think so. He's not chasing some young bird, is he? He needs to marry Flora before she loses patience with him.'

'I'm wondering if it's something to do with the Phoenix,' I said. 'I don't know if Baz has told you, but we've been having some money troubles.'

'Well, you know Baz—more of an artist than a business-man. It's a good thing he's got you and Flora to help him take care of the financials.'

'Aunty Dot.' I paused, wondering how to phrase it. 'Do you remember the exact year Baz bought the Phoenix?'

'It wasn't long after he came back from the US; 1974 or 1975, I reckon.'

'Did you think it was a good idea for him to buy it?'

'Oh yes, he needed to settle down, have some little ones I could bounce on my knee, though I'm glad I didn't hold my breath on that front. Thank goodness you came along to calm him down a bit.'

Her words caused an echo of my dream from the previous night. Baz had been calling out for me in panic. Was it an omen? Or was it just my subconscious working overtime? All my life, especially during times of high stress, I'd had a recurring nightmare of being chased by a faceless bogeyman.

'Did you think it was a good idea for Baz to adopt me?'

There was a pause and I could hear Dot's breathing down the line. 'I remember the first time I set eyes on you. I came down to give Baz a hand—help settle you in. You had hair like a bird's nest and Baz had no idea how to get the tangles out. You reminded me so much of my own little girl. Bless her soul.' Aunty Dot's only child had died of scarlet fever.

Again the echoes of my dream were in my mind, and I continued before I could lose my nerve. 'I had a dream last night about a woman called Nora. I think it might have actually been a memory. Do you know about anyone called Nora, Aunty?'

I thought the line had dropped out, but then Dot cleared her throat. 'I didn't ever meet her, bub. But I believe she was your foster mother for a while. Baz said she loved you like you were her own daughter, and she would have kept you with her … but …'

Something made me unwilling to hear what Dot was going to say next. 'Sorry, Aunty, I've just realised the time. I've got to go and get ready for work. I'll ring you later.'

I mulled over Aunty Dot's words while I took a hot shower. Memories of my life before Baz were hazy, and I'd been happy to keep a curtain drawn between my life before Baz and my life after Baz. The finer details of my adoption were not discussed, and I'd only needed to ask questions recently when I'd inquired about getting a bank loan with a view to helping Baz pay for an electrical overhaul. I'd discovered that my birth certificate extract listed me as Beloved Brown rather than Brick Brown and Baz was not keen for me to show it to the bank—just as he'd been reluctant to produce various documents relating to his purchase of the Phoenix. It was unusual for us to have a disagreement, but Baz and I had clashed over my plan to beg money from the bank.

'I don't want you going into debt for the Phoenix,' he said.

'Why not? Isn't it the Australian way? To go into debt for real estate?'

'It's my problem, bub, I'll handle it.'

Baz's words stung. Sure, I always referred to the Phoenix as Baz's joint, but deep down I felt ownership as well. I'd lived above it for ten years and had worked in it for twenty. The whole reason I'd taken the job at council was for the benefit of the Phoenix, so it felt like he was shutting me out. It also felt like there was something more he was hiding from me, and I'd hoped to find some answers in the council's archives, but after seeing the mess the files were in (not to mention finding the mayor's body), I'd given up on that idea, although I still wondered what the mayor had been doing in the archives department—and why someone had secretly moved his body.

CHAPTER FIVE

Amazingly, after my uncomfortable night on Baz's couch, I was only ten minutes late to work. Unfortunately it was Tuesday, and a 'Monday' meeting was in progress.

'Brick, nice of you to join us.' My boss looked pointedly at her shiny gold watch. 'We've been waiting for your action-ing update.'

Although Gail liked to avoid the office, when she did visit it was to hold a long meeting to discuss something called 'performance outcomes'. These meetings were supposed to be held on Mondays but were usually held on other days because too many people were chucking sickies on Mondays in order to avoid the meeting. I quickly grabbed a folder which I kept on my desk for these occasions. A folder can make anyone look more professional.

I'd just settled into an empty seat at the meeting table when Gail fixed me with a beady stare.

'Let's start with the council meeting last night,' she said. 'How was it?'

I was instantly on guard. Gail had never expressed an interest in a council meeting before, so I opted to keep my answer general. 'I think the councillors made a lot of good ground—it was a pretty big agenda.' I gave her my best knowledgeable expression.

Gail arched her eyebrows—or at least the skin where her eyebrows would be if they hadn't been plucked to oblivion. 'Were there any media inquiries?'

It was clear someone had told her about Mitch Mitchell's appearance at the meeting. My mind raced. Should I play the innocent idiot or pretend I was managing the potential threat in an efficient and businesslike fashion? I went for the second option. 'Yes—the award-winning journalist Mitch Mitchell stopped by. Quite an honour.'

There were signs of recognition from my colleagues, who obviously followed current events more closely than me.

'He hadn't given me notice beforehand,' I continued. 'But I'm having a meeting with him this week to find out if I can assist him in any way. He just wanted a general overview of council governance procedure for an in-depth piece he's doing on … kerbside recycling in Melbourne. I think it's a great opportunity for us to highlight our strategy regarding hard-waste rubbish collection.' It was weak, but all I could come up with under pressure.

I could see from Gail's expression that she didn't believe a former war correspondent like Mitch Mitchell was the slightest bit interested in hard rubbish, but there was a good chance she thought *I* was dumb enough to believe it. That would buy me time to find out what was really going on. She surveyed me like a snake eyeing a small furry animal while trying to assess how wide it can stretch its jaws. Then she turned her attention to the next victim, Phil, who was still being punished for suggesting that someone needed to clean out the office fridge. He was drunk at the time. He kept a bottle of homemade hooch in his bottom drawer and I really couldn't blame him.

'Any more reports of phantom smells in the office kitchen, Phil?' she asked. 'You may need to get yourself checked out by a doctor. I've heard that brain tumours can cause people to imagine strange smells.'

Phil looked like he wished he had a brain tumour—or else he was wishing he hadn't given up drinking.

After two hours, I could see Gail was desperate for caffeine so I grasped the opportunity to escape. I offered to do a coffee run and was inundated with a dozen orders, all of them slightly bespoke: it required a photographic memory and the bicep strength of a cocktail waitress. Luckily I had both.

I went to the nearest cafe, gave the order to the barista, then picked up a newspaper and sat down to wait. The front page had an eye-catching photo of a tall, blond and expensively dressed man who'd been pelted by something that looked like excrement. 'Suits you, sir!' read the headline.

On reading the article, I learned that someone with a good throwing arm (and gloves, you'd hope) had lobbed a large turd at the Victorian premier, Errol Grimes, in protest against plans for a six-lane freeway to be expanded to ten lanes. There was speculation as to the origin of the turd— dog or human? The thrower was believed to belong to a particularly feral group who called themselves the Anti-Freeway Protest Alliance. I turned the page. People were always protesting against freeways in Melbourne, but it didn't stop more and more of them getting built. You couldn't have a sprawling monster of a city like Melbourne without some seriously big roads.

'Talk about a PR fiasco.' A woman had sat down next to me. She also had a copy of the newspaper. 'Not to mention a waste of a good suit. Of course, it made for a great news story. Did you see me on television last night?'

I froze. It was Selena McManus and she was pretending we were old school friends instead of nemeses: the last time we'd spoken she'd called me an 'ugly dog, who deserved to go to the local high school with the other losers'. The irony of this was that teachers had mixed us up all the time due to an apparent likeness. Not to mention that she'd have given up a lifetime supply of hairspray to go to the local high school. She went to the orthodox convent, where even Chapstick would get you beaten half to death by the hundred-year-old nuns who ran the place.

'No, I missed the news last night,' I said trying to keep my voice casual.

'Don't worry. There'll be more riots for sure. The premier's not going to budge an inch; he's one hard bastard. Great-looking for a politician, though, usually they're hideous. But you'd expect an ex-footballer to keep in shape. My boy-friend plays for Richmond and he's got a six-pack you could eat lunch off.'

That explained why the man in the dog poo suit looked familiar—he was a former AFL footballer. Thanks to Uncle Baz I'd spent many a freezing winter's day watching a bunch of men run around a muddy paddock, although as I grew older I developed an appreciation for the finer points of Aussie Rules (mostly the footballers' legs).

'My boyfriend won the Brownlow Medal last year,' Selena continued. 'You probably saw me in the paper.'

'Gee, I'm sorry, but I missed that too,' I said as insincerely as possible.

'Actually, I'm glad I ran into you, Brick. I hear you're working for the council now.'

The penny dropped. She'd been staking out the cafe in hopes that a council worker would come in so she could pump them for information.

'A friend of mine dropped by the council meeting last night,' she continued. 'Maybe you've heard of him? Mitch Mitchell?'

First Gail asking questions and now Selena: Mitch Mitchell was obviously a man to watch. I tried to think of a topic so unsexy that it would scare Selena off her fishing expedition. 'He's writing an in-depth piece about plastic recycling by councils around Australia. Recycling is becoming such a major issue these days. The planet's in real danger. Koalas at risk. Not to mention quolls.'

At that moment the barista arrived with my coffee order and a free side of flirtation. 'Ah, bella signorina, you're meeting your just-as-beautiful sister today.' He treated Selena to his most winning smile.

Selena looked at him as though he'd just put a tray of full-fat lattes in front of her.

'We're not sisters,' I said quickly. 'Just old school—' The right word escaped me: 'friends' was the wrong term; even 'mates' was a stretch. 'We went to school together.'

Selena exited after the barista's unintentional insult and I hoped she'd stay away. She'd always had the kind of cunning that could ferret out secrets. At primary school her favourite move was to steal things out of people's bags by bumping into them. Brucie had told me about some of the fanciful TV stories she'd done in the past and I didn't want her writing any more stories about council affairs, lest Gail's brain explode with fury.

I returned to council to find the meeting was entering its third hour. The coffees were received like Elvis in the Vegas years. I promptly spilled mine down the front of my shirt as theatrically as possible and rushed out again, indicating I'd just pop to the loo to rinse the stain. With everyone else still stuck in the meeting I'd be able to make some personal calls from my office phone without anyone listening in. Not only was our section of the office open plan, but it had bizarre acoustics that meant you could hear every sniff, chew or fart of your colleagues. I needed to ring Mitch Mitchell and find out what he was up to before anyone else started asking questions.

I attempted an internet search first, but the hamsters that powered our system must have been sleeping, so I retrieved the card he'd given me at the meeting. It was plain black on white, regular font with just the basics: name, mobile phone number, email. I dialled the number and he answered right away.

'Mitch Mitchell.'

It didn't surprise me that he was too arrogant to bother saying hello. I decided to play the clueless PR girl, seeing as the clueless part wouldn't be a stretch. 'Hi. This is Brick Brown. I didn't get a chance to introduce myself properly last night at the council meeting. I'm with the PR department, I helped you when you had trouble opening the door.'

'Brick Brown.' His voice was low and as rock'n'roll as his scruffy hairstyle, and I could tell by his tone that a smart-arse comment about my name was coming. I decided to keep talking and hopefully head off any witticisms.

'We were so honoured to have a journalist of your calibre at one of our little meetings.' I used the most gushing tone I could muster. 'Can I ask what brought you there?'

'You can ask,' he said, 'and maybe I'll tell you.'

I gritted my teeth. 'Well ... is there any way I can assist?'

'No thanks, Brick Brown. I don't feel you'd be able to provide me with anything useful.'

'I'm such a fan of your work,' I gushed a bit more. 'Please tell me if there's anything I can do—'

'I've already had a call from someone at your council—a rather unpleasant woman called Gail Fawcett.'

I nearly snorted with shock and tried to disguise it with a cough. I had never known Gail to communicate directly with a journalist. Was he telling the truth or was this a sneaky journalist ploy aimed at tricking me into giving something away?

'She told me I could expect legal action if I attempted to enter council chambers again without notice.'

It certainly sounded like something Gail would say. Maybe she'd been testing me earlier by not mentioning it. 'Oh, that's great!' I was babbling by now. 'But still, if there's anything I can do, just give me a buzz or flick me an email.'

'Sure thing, Brick Brown. Is that really your name?'

'That's what it says on my driver's licence.' There was no need to mention to him that my driver's licence was fake. It was a good fake though, and cheaper than forking out for a real one since I rarely drove. 'Does yours really say Mitch Mitchell?'

I put down the phone before he could answer, which gave me a smidgen of satisfaction, but I doubt he even noticed.

My computer chose that moment to load a page. It was about Mitchell's kidnapping in Iraq. The photo released by his captors was disturbing: he still had the rockstar look, but it was more like a rockstar who'd just been arrested for crashing a car while high on drugs. There was something about his gaze, as if he was looking at his own death and saying, 'Bring it on.'

I was about to return to the meeting when my mobile phone rang. It was Mick O'Toole, one of Baz's oldest partners in crime from his football-playing days. 'Hello, sweetheart,' Mick wheezed. 'Listen, I'm trying to get hold of Baz, but the Phoenix is closed up and he's not answering his bloody mobile phone. He was supposed to come and watch the footy training with me last night. One of my nephews has got the call-up to the Reserves.'

I frowned. Baz could be absentminded about appointments—particularly if I made him a doctor's appointment—but it was rare for him to miss a date that involved football. Baz sometimes mentored young players, specifically ones who'd moved from regional areas to play in Melbourne. 'It's similar to mentoring musicians,' he'd say. 'Gotta try and keep them off the grog, gambling and girls. It's a bit like pissing in the wind.'

I licked a tissue and attempted to lift the coffee stain on my shirt. 'I think he's gone out of town, but I don't know where or why.'

'I don't want to worry you, love,' said Mick. 'You know what Baz is like. He'll turn up. Tell him to call me.'

As soon as Mick hung up, I tried ringing the Phoenix, Baz's favourite betting shop and even his mobile—although I was pretty sure it was still on his office desk. There was no answer on any of them. Reluctantly I returned to the meeting.

* * *

When the meeting wrapped up an hour later, I don't think I was the only person who could have used a hit from Phil's stash. I returned to my desk and pretended to read my inbox while really wondering what excuse I could concoct to borrow a car from the council fleet. It would be quicker to drive over to the Phoenix and see if there was any sign of Baz rather than ride my bicycle.

'Does anything need to be picked up?' I asked Brucie. 'I'm happy to go on an errand. Even if it's not in my job description.'

Brucie ignored my attempt to poke fun but was happy to have me go and pick up a month's worth of newspapers. 'We're supposed to keep a copy of all the newspapers on file,' he said. 'In case the council's being shit-canned in one of them. Not that anyone reads them these days. Unless they're a total dinosaur.' He rolled his eyes.

Brucie gave me the spare key he had hidden in his desk drawer, which saved me filling in a mountain of paperwork. The council fleet was kept in a basement carpark and once I'd managed to extract the car from its tight spot with only a minimal amount of paint scraped off, I drove to Brunswick Street and parked in the Phoenix's loading zone. I entered via the side door and took the concrete stairs straight up to Baz's flat. It was just as I'd left it the previous night, as was his office.

I wasn't sure where to look next. Baz's 1985 Datsun had blown a gasket on the South Eastern Freeway a while back, and he'd decided it wasn't worth fixing, much to everyone's relief. If he'd gone off somewhere further than walking distance, he'd either borrowed a car or taken the train.

I sat down at his desk. Baz couldn't use the computer, so I dug out his phone message pad and had a flip through it.

It was often my best way of finding out what he was up to. A page was torn out, so I did the old lead pencil shading trick on the next blank page. A ghost impression of the most recent note appeared. It was a list of names:

Daphne

Delilah

Margaret

Perhaps Baz was cheating on Flora after all.

I scanned the desk for any further clues and tried the desk drawer. It was locked, which was unusual. I took out my lock-pick kit and the drawer soon sprang open.

Inside I recognised the letter with the spidery writing which had arrived the last time I'd spoken to Baz. I looked inside and was shocked to see a stack of hundred dollars bills: several thousand dollars' worth. I hastily returned it and re-locked the drawer. Who was sending Baz money? Why hadn't he told me about it? And why had he left it in his drawer?

Something brushed against my leg and I nearly hit the ceiling, but it was just a semi-stray cat that seemed to be able to infiltrate the Phoenix via mysterious feline means. The cat had started hanging around a few years back after getting stuck in the space where an old dumbwaiter had joined the cellar with the bar above.

Suddenly it occurred to me I should check the cellar. What if Baz had had some kind of accident down there? I went down to the bar and flicked on the cellar light switch concealed under the counter. Then I took a deep breath and heaved open the cellar door in the floor behind the bar.

A waft of cool air rose up to greet me, carrying the slight smell of salami. Before the Italian lady next door had sold up and moved to Frankston, Baz used to let her cure all kinds of smallgoods in the cellar. Now the only things kept there were the kegs and a haunting smell of ham. It's probably why the cat was in the cellar in the first place.

I looked around for the cat, thinking it would be better than no company at all, but it must have buggered off when it sensed it was needed. I went down the metal stairs as fast as possible before I could change my mind.

The next thing I knew I was flat on my face on the cold stone floor—I'd tripped over a knee-high object right at the bottom of the stairs. On the plus side, the pain took my mind off my panic.

I rolled over, wiping my smarting palms on my skirt. The object looked kind of like a vacuum cleaner, but without the bag attachment. I checked out a model number stamped into the metal, then staggered to my feet.

The solid brick walls and the cool, dry atmosphere made it feel tomblike. I took a look around, but Baz wasn't hiding behind a keg and there was no way he could squeeze himself into the old dumbwaiter. It was a pretty boring cellar really, not spooky in the least. Still I turned and ran up the stairs as fast as I could, shutting the trap door with a slam.

When my heart had resumed a normal beat, I rang Flora. 'I just tripped over some weird piece of equipment in the cellar. It looks a bit like a vacuum. Did Baz book a tradie without telling me?'

'Not that I know of, hen,' she said. 'You'll have to ask himself.'

'I would if I could find him.'

'Is he still no' there?' A note of alarm had entered her voice, which worried me since I'd seen Flora evict drunk punters who weighed at least twice as much as her without so much as dislodging a false fingernail. 'I'm making some more calls, and when I get hold of that man, he's in danger of getting his guts ripped out.'

I almost felt sorry for Baz, but I was glad I had Flora on my side. I locked up the Phoenix and drove to my place. I was grabbing a clean shirt off the clothesline when Bunny's younger brother Timmy emerged from his caravan. His eyes had that glazed, staring-at-a-computer-for-twenty-hours-straight look.

Timmy was a nineteen and struggling to break into computer game design. He had some kickarse technology in his little caravan. In fact, that's pretty much all he had in there apart from a mattress on the floor and a microwave. On seeing him, it occurred to me he might be able to help me identify the machine I'd found in the pub's cellar a lot quicker than the council internet.

'Come in and I'll do a quick search for you,' he said.

'If you're not in the middle of some weird cyber battle with half-naked elves.'

Timmy blushed sweetly. 'I've paused it.'

Timmy was actually a cute little package: slim but not skinny and kind of tall with a good head of fair, wavy hair and dark blue eyes. As a gamer, he desperately needed some tuition about the finer points of social interaction with the opposite sex. I was pretty sure I was one of the only women Timmy talked to—apart from Bunny and maybe his 'Mummy', a cringeworthy title I couldn't believe anyone actually used outside of an Enid Blyton novel. As usual the caravan was a shambles of half-empty Coke bottles, cans of deodorant, sci-fi paperbacks and gamer magazines. Timmy was Bunny's younger brother by eight or nine years. They'd been brought up in a divorce and remarriage scenario and hadn't lived in the same house when they were younger. Apparently not all blond people have a perfect childhood.

Timmy had moved in with Bunny after falling out with Mummy, who sounded like a narcissistic nightmare, just quietly, but I didn't ask too many questions. In return Bunny and Timmy didn't quiz me on my own somewhat unusual upbringing. It got tiresome to explain.

I recited the serial number and he typed it into a search engine.

Timmy was easy to impress. 'How did you remember that?'

'Bartender memory. It just takes practice.'

His computer finished its search in record time. 'A ground scanner,' he said. 'Looks like it's for doing ultrasounds of the ground. You know, to see what's buried under there.'

'I've just found one at my uncle's club.'

Bunny and Timmy neither understood nor appreciated the Blues, but they liked Baz, especially when he came around and made his famous Cajun pizza.

'Is he renovating? He might be looking for pipes or cables or something?'

'I can't find him right now to ask him. But thank you, Timmy. You're sweet to help.' I gave him a hug. Bunny and Timmy weren't big touchers so by the time I let Timmy go he was flaming red. 'Have you heard from Bunny lately?'

To the best of my knowledge Bunny was somewhere in Africa using her medical skills to treat starving babies and victims of torture. It was a mystery to me how she worked in the midst of such human suffering without being sucked down into despair and madness. She still came across like she'd stepped out of a *Famous Five* novel, albeit one with lashings of proof alcohol rather than ginger beer. Timmy, on the other hand, was naïve in a way that said, 'I've spent my entire formative years playing Super Mario Brothers.' It was sweet, but ultimately annoying. He'd improved slightly since getting a few hours' work a week at a new cafe on Smith Street called the Black Possum. I'd skilled him up on the finer arts of making coffee and he was showing some promise as a barista. And he no longer said 'LOL', which was a huge blessing because it made me want to slap him.

'I got a text from her the other day,' said Timmy. 'A touch of cholera, but she's okay.'

I could see I wasn't going to get much more out of Timmy in the way of comfort or conversation, so I decided to leave him to his microwaved pasta.

When I got back to work, there was no one in sight except Brucie and I realised that I'd forgotten to go to the newsagent to pick up the newspapers.

'Where is everyone?' I asked.

'Phil started vomiting.' Brucie grimaced. 'It triggered a psychosomatic outbreak. Some people are such drama queens. But look—' He waved a shiny rectangular device in my face. 'My iPhone has arrived. It cost a thousand bucks, but it's so beautiful!'

I'd never seen Brucie look so happy, but a thousand-dollar phone was definitely not something I was contemplating for my future. Mine hadn't even cost a hundred and since I kept it on minimum credit it was almost useless. 'Who really needs a phone that fancy?'

Brucie gave me pitying look and I made my way back to my desk wondering when exactly I had started feeling so old.

CHAPTER SIX

The next day, as I made my way to work, the hot air balloons were all gone from the skies. Instead I saw four magpies. Not a good sign, according to Uncle Baz: 'One or two are okay. But if you get a whole mob then there's definitely bad news coming.' No surprises there. Everything about Yarra City Council had been bad news from the start.

I stopped at the newsagent and was making my way out with as much of the PR department's newspaper order as I could fit in my bicycle's basket when I spotted Sue Day drinking a coffee on a nearby bench while wrestling with a copy of *The Age*. Reading newspapers in the wind is a skill I'd never bothered to master.

'Hi Brick. Can you believe the news?' she asked as she batted the paper into submission. 'What an idiot!'

For a heart-stopping second I thought she knew something about the mayor's mysterious post-mortem move, but then I saw the front-page headline, flapping in the wind: FREEWAY FANATICS FRONT UP FOR FIGHT. It was another freeway protest.

A section of Sue's newspaper flew off. 'It's just the sports pages. Who cares?' she said, before changing her mind and grabbing the errant pages. 'Actually, I should care. What can you tell me about the premier's AFL career? Was he really any good at football?'

I was happy to sound knowledgeable for a change. 'Errol Grimes started out playing for Fitzroy, which has been underdog team pretty much since the days when my Uncle Baz was playing in the Reserves. They're the league just below the A league.'

'We do have football in South Australia,' said Sue. 'It's not just churches and serial killers.'

I'd obviously hit a nerve, so I continued quickly. 'Everyone thought Grimes was the next big thing. Then he switched clubs and started having injury problems. The rumour was that he was throwing games—like a betting scam type of thing.'

'Any truth in it?'

'Well, by this stage he'd left Fitzroy to play for the Melbourne Demons. But I don't think anyone could prove anything.'

'It didn't hurt his political career?' Sue asked but continued without waiting for an answer. 'What am I saying? It's probably how his political career got started. Still, he's in good shape for a politician. Usually they get really fat.' She held out her folded paper for me to have a look. The photographer had captured a look of unconcealed aggression as the premier barged past a picket line. I could see the footballer player in him. The hard man. It gave me an involuntary shiver.

'You okay? You suddenly went pale. I hope you're not getting that flu that's going around.'

'Just lack of sleep.'

'Wait until you have kids. I don't think I've had three consecutive hours' sleep in five years. If I couldn't have caffeine, I'd kill myself.'

When I got to my desk, I had more than three hundred new emails waiting, but none of them appeared useful. For some reason the PR team was copied into emails from all the other departments. It was probably part of Gail's attempt to make her fiefdom look like an indispensable cog in the wheels of bureaucracy, but whatever the reason, it mainly resulted in a lot of emails about leaf blowers and other equipment I neither understood nor cared to know about. I was about to attempt a mass delete when I got a cold prickly feeling.

I looked up to find Councillor Hugo Clark standing in front of my desk. As usual he was wearing an ill-fitting suit, which only emphasised his bulk.

'Can I help you?' I did my best impression of a person in the middle of doing something terribly important.

He produced a sheet of paper. 'I noticed you PR people haven't put out a media release about me taking over as chairman of the Development Consent Committee. What's your name again?'

'Brick Brown.' I avoided looking at his eyes and instead focussed on his beard.

'Weird name.' His mouth pulled into a sneer. 'You were taking photos at the mayor's memorial. I'll need to see them so I can tell you which ones of me you can use. I want you to delete the others. I have to protect my image.'

'The camera card crashed,' I lied, hoping it would get rid of him quicker. 'I lost all the photos. Sorry.'

He grunted as he threw his piece of paper on my desk. 'See that this release goes out today.' He turned and left as quietly as he'd arrived, leaving behind a strong scent of aftershave over body odour.

Gingerly I picked up the piece of paper. It was a barely literate spiel about Hugo Clark being the brightest spark at the council since the late, great Dickie Ruffhead, along with a thinly veiled hint that Mavis DuBois hadn't been up to the job, having only won it in the first place because she was a silver spooner whose grandfather was a war hero.

Gail would flip her lid if I put this out as a media release so I didn't quite know what I should do. My first impulse was to file it in the bin. But then I didn't want to give Hugo an excuse to come and see me again.

I typed out a couple of sentences, slapped on Hugo's official council photo and sent it to Sue. She was the only person likely to report on it anyway.

I was wondering what to do next when my computer coughed up an urgent email from Gail. I'd never been so glad to hear from her. As far as I could tell, Gail wanted me to draft a policy on the parking inspection department's usage of Myspace. This immediately struck me as strange, since I very much doubted that any of the parking inspectors had even heard of Myspace, and at any rate, Brucie had told me that Facebook was going to put Myspace out of business within a year.

I could see what Gail was up to. She liked to create unnecessary tasks for people as a passive-aggressive way of getting back at them for some perceived transgression. I had to suspect this assignment was punishment for Mitch Mitchell's visit to the council meeting. She'd obviously expected me to bar the door and not let him in.

I'd had to draft a policy once before as punishment for the phone call incident. The final document was ridiculously wordy and impenetrable. This was then passed around various department heads so they could make unnecessary additions, before being filed somewhere in the mysterious policy department and never seen again. The exercise had taken me weeks and left me none the wiser as to how the wheels of governance actually worked. Now it seemed I was about to relive the painful experience while probably alienating the parking inspectors in the process. I'd never owned a car myself, so I didn't bear any grudges against the grey ghosts, as Baz liked to call them. Rather, I saw them as the agents of vengeance against all the car drivers who'd nearly knocked me off my bicycle because they were too lazy to check their mirrors.

I often saw the council's parking inspectors coming and going. They were easy to spot, since they no longer wore grey but eye-shocking hi-vis, and I'd found they were a cheerier bunch than most of the other council employees, maybe because they spent their working day outside instead of stuck in a fluoro-lit office with grey decor and—if you were lucky—a plastic fern. I knew they had a locker room off the underground carpark, so I went down the stairs and knocked on the door before entering. It had a fridge and a microwave, but no sink or kettle, an old brown vinyl couch, a couple of chairs and a table with a scrappy pot plant in the centre. All the furniture looked like it had come from a hard-rubbish collection and, notably, there was no computer in sight.

'Can I help you?' said a gravelly voice behind me.

I turned around to see one of the inspectors, scooter helmet in hand. His name badge informed me that he was called Denis. Strong, sun-tanned legs poked out from his shorts beneath a solid round belly. He certainly looked like he could handle himself against any irate parking ticket recipients.

'Hi ... Denis?'

He nodded, confirming he hadn't borrowed the shirt.

I introduced myself. 'I'm Brick. From the PR department.'

A closed look moved over Denis's face—a look that had become familiar to me over my short time with the council. I'd discovered that the general sentiment was that staff from the PR department were prone to sticking their noses into everyone's business, messing everything up and then quitting or going on stress leave before the problem could be rectified. Denis probably saw the same look when he told people he was a parking inspector.

'This isn't about the ticket paper again, is it? Because I was on leave when that all happened.'

'It's nothing to do with that,' I said quickly. 'I just have to update some policy information—you know, routine stuff that we do every so often.'

Denis still looked wary.

'I thought it would be easier to come and see you guys in person rather than send you an email. After all, you're all out and about so much, I can't imagine you check emails that often.'

'We have to go into accounts if we want to do that and you know how funny they are about outsiders,' said Denis. 'I don't even know why IT bothered to give us email addresses. Any important information generally gets posted on the noticeboard. It might be old-fashioned but we find that it works pretty well.'

He pointed to a noticeboard next to the fridge that featured shift rosters and, more intriguingly, a rogues' gallery of repeat parking violators. I did a quick scan and wasn't surprised to see one Phoenix regular featured in the 'spitters and shitters' section.

My short chat with Denis had already given me enough information to ascertain that a Myspace policy for parking inspectors could be written on a beer coaster and still hit all the bases but I knew Gail wouldn't be satisfied with anything less than twenty pages. In the meantime, however, it had occurred to me that parking inspectors were potential goldmines of useful information: they were out on the streets all day watching people's comings and goings and surely some people would chat to them, if only in an effort to get out of a parking ticket. There was a good possibility the inspectors would be aware if something unusual was going on in the neighbourhood of Baz's club. I took a punt on Melbourne once again being smaller than one would think.

'Hey, didn't you play football?' I asked. 'You might know my uncle Baz Brown, he owns the Phoenix on Brunswick Street.'

'Baz. Sure, I know him,' he said, dropping the rabbit-in-the-headlights look and giving me a slightly chipped grin. 'I'm a league man myself, but Baz mentored one of my sons who switched over ... you know, to Aussie Rules. Bit of a shame job, but we got past it in the end. The boy still supports the Maroons in State of Origin.'

I nodded knowingly.

'So you're Baz's niece, well, what do you know?' He didn't comment on the difference between Baz's and my skin tones, a sure sign he had a similarly multifaceted family. 'How is the old bugger?'

'Pretty good,' I lied, 'all things considered. There's always the danger of live music venues being closed down due to complaints by residents.'

'You don't have to tell me. My youngest's in a band and he's always going on about it. Course, he's not the jazz kind, more your death metal, so I can't totally blame people for complaining. If the wife hadn't bought us some noise-cancelling headphones we'd both be stone deaf by now.'

I was willing to gamble on Denis as an ally. As long as I don't fancy a person, I'm a pretty good judge of character. 'You haven't seen anything weird going on around the Phoenix, have you? I imagine you guys are always up-to-date with what's happening out there on the streets.'

Denis smiled and took a carton of iced coffee out of the fridge. 'Nah, I haven't seen anything dodgy. But I haven't been over there for a little while—that's Joe's patch. I can ask him, if you like.'

'That'd be great.'

Denis looked pleased to be appreciated for once. 'If you're really keen to catch Joe, he always has lunch at the Blue Oyster about now—you know, it's in one of the lanes just off Brunswick Street?' He picked a filthy-looking mug up and poured the dregs of its previous contents into the sad-looking pot plant. 'Dicing with food poisoning if you ask me,' he said, as he poured his iced coffee into the cup. 'He's a bit of a funny one, but he gets the job done. Take all types, hey? Want some iced coffee?'

I decided I was lactose intolerant.

I had no burning desire to return to my cubicle. There was a chance that Gail was somewhere in the building, and I wasn't in the mood for an encounter. I decided I'd go and see if I could find this Joe, the 'funny' parking inspector.

I'd heard of the Blue Oyster but had never actually been inside it. It was a weird little cafe with an extremely eclectic menu and an even more eclectic decor—even by Brunswick

Street standards. Outside, it looked like any of the other Fitzroy cafes that had cropped up in the laneways lately. Inside, it looked like random furniture from a boot sale had been painted with leftovers from a fire sale and then thrown around the room by a group of children with anger issues. The waitress was a goth—judging by her make-up—but was dressed in a pink 1950s diner–style dress with a purple apron.

There was one customer and judging by his parking inspector uniform, it was Joe. Like Denis, Joe was large, but more wide than high. In his hi-vis shirt he could have been mistaken for the sun of a minor planet. His hair was about one centimetre away from being a buzz cut and a bright platinum blond, but it was offset by incredibly long, dark eyelashes.

'Joe? Denis told me I could find you here,' I said, holding out my hand in greeting. 'I'm Brick Brown from the council's PR department.'

'I know who you are.' Joe shook my hand. His skin was super soft, like a baby's. 'I go to the Phoenix jam sessions sometimes. I saw you there the other night. You probably don't recognise me in my work clothes.'

It was true, I did tend to identify some of our punters by their clothes. Like Baz, who always wore black with coloured braces, many of our regulars had a certain outfit they wore every day of their lives.

'You want a coffee?' he asked. 'This is the only place in Fitzroy I'll drink them.'

'Good, are they?' I was prepared to indulge coffee snobbery if it was the best way to get him onside.

'Nah, it's pretty crap—they only use goat's milk, and I think this goat must have had mastitis. But it's the only place that's definitely not mafia-owned.'

I was beginning to see what Denis meant by 'funny', but I thought of Baz and ordered a short black. Up close, I realised the waitress wasn't a goth, she was severely unwell. Maybe she'd drunk the milk.

Joe smiled, revealing a sunny set of white teeth. 'I take it you've got a parking ticket problem?'

'No, I ride a bicycle mostly.' I sipped my coffee warily after the waitress had plonked it on the table, slopping half of it out. 'This has nothing to do with council, actually. I was just wondering if you'd seen anything strange going on around the Phoenix lately. I was there last night and it was closed, and I haven't been able to track Baz down. I'm a bit worried something ... unusual ... might be going on.'

Joe paused before answering, as if sizing me up. 'I wouldn't tell just anyone, Brick, because, you know, it's dangerous. But I think something's about to go down in Fitzroy.'

'What do you mean?' My immediate thought was a mafia war—as disagreements between local crime gangs were dubbed by the tabloids, who loved nothing more than a good mob killing. Things had been relatively quiet since the 1990s, when various mafia hitmen gained a lot of media attention by being extremely stupid. These days the mafia types spent less time in Carlton and more time in Crown Casino or the strip clubs on King Street.

Joe looked around as if someone might be listening, even though we were now the only people in the cafe; the waitress had probably gone somewhere private to have a quiet vomit. 'Gene from the record store next door to the Phoenix might be able to tell you more,' he said in a low voice. 'I suggest you go and talk to him. But don't talk to anyone else. Loose lips and all.'

I thanked Joe for his time and he smiled and winked. With a sudden flash I remembered him belting out 'California Dreaming' in a dress, heels and beehive wig.

CHAPTER SEVEN

Gene's shop had sprung up next door to the Phoenix around ten years back. I suspected Gene was actually squatting in the warehouse because it was otherwise derelict, and he deflected any attempts to find out more by claiming he had sporadic deafness from when he was a roadie for AC/DC in the summer of 1974. This was especially concerning since Baz sometimes hired him to mix sound for gigs at the Phoenix.

Gene's shop catered to record collectors of the most extreme kind. Decor was strictly band posters from all eras. Otherwise it was scuffed tables topped with stolen milk crates full of records. Thanks to Baz, I've visited many such record stores and they are invariably run by collectors who are so obsessive they're no longer capable of holding down a regular day job. Baz had been collecting rare Blues 78s since the 1960s and would frequently bore the pants off people with the tale of how he found a Blind Joe Reynolds 78 in a skip outside a radio station in Bermagui in the early 1970s. Gene had long straggly hair of mostly a dirty grey colour. He also had a grey complexion that rendered him somewhat corpse-like. Together with his pale eyes—often shot with red—he had been known to scare small children. As well as looking like the Unabomber, Gene was a committed conspiracy theorist. This led him to be somewhat trying company, especially when he'd had a few beers. When sober, he'd bore you rigid with his in-depth knowledge of Bon Scott's tattoos. Gene had an exact replica of one on his right bicep. When drunk he tended to want to talk about Harold Holt's whereabouts. Gene was convinced he'd once spotted him at a bar in Goa.

I hadn't seen Gene since I'd started working for council and I felt a bit guilty. He was a weirdo, but he had a good heart and had done me a big favour about a year back. I'd asked Gene to order in a rare Albert King LP for me, as a birthday present for Baz.

'Are you sure you still want to buy it?' Gene had asked when I went to pick it up. 'Because I can find another buyer, if you're hard up for cash.'

'No, I'm good,' I'd said, pulling two fifties out of my wallet.

'It's just that your boyfriend was in here earlier. He was trying to hock some records. I couldn't help noticing that they were Baz's. When I mentioned it, he said he was selling them for you because you were having some, uh, difficulties.'

My stomach had dropped. 'What?'

'Don't worry, man. I figured he'd nicked them off Baz—he was stoned off his tits. But I bought the records anyway. I'll get them back to Baz.'

I was stuck for words. Not only had Jack stolen from my uncle, he was dumb enough to try and hock some of them at a store next door to my uncle's place. And he'd tried to blame me for it! I spent the next forty-eight hours visiting every other second-hand record dealer within a twenty-kilometre radius. It turned out Jack had only gone to Gene with the records no one else would buy. I wiped out my savings buying back as much of Baz's collection as I could find.

Baz was forgiving, despite his love for his record collection. 'Sugar, when a person's in the grip it's like they're possessed. There's nothing they won't do to get another hit, and there's nothing you can do to help them until they want to help themselves.' Baz had a habit of running a hand down his face, as if wiping off sweat, even on the coldest of days. 'I know you're angry, but you've got to cut your losses.'

'But you were good to him—you booked him for gigs even though he was pretty shit as saxophone players go, and he broke into your flat and stole from you.'

'Brick, bub, I'm a Blackfella who grew up Australia in the fifties,' Baz said, kissing me on the head. 'Not to mention I've worked in the music industry for nearly half a century. If I held onto every shitty thing that's been done to me the load would be so heavy I wouldn't be able to get out of bed in the morning.'

I pulled up outside Gene's shop, but I could see from the car that it wasn't open: the lights were off and there was a handwritten notice tacked to the front door. I hazarded a guess that it said, 'Back in 10'—although Gene had been known to leave similar signs on the door for weeks at a time. We'd sometimes get irate record obsessives looking for him in the bar. But like the saying goes: even a broken clock tells the right time twice a day. I'd give him half an hour and see if he turned up.

It was a blustery, grey day and the passing people were all wearing black and looking depressed. I cruised around the community radio stations to keep myself amused while I watched people trying to parallel park. A young couple were having a lovers' tiff outside a nearby cafe. She obviously worked there, judging by the waitress uniform of black jeans, Doc Martens and a tight-fit T-shirt with an ironic slogan. What had gone wrong in their romance? Was he too needy and clingy? Was it his brown corduroy trousers? Had she been flirting with the handsome barista I spied at the coffee machine?

Twenty minutes later there was still no sign of Gene, and I'd realised I wasn't the only person staking out the area. Thirty metres down the street, someone sat in a black Mercedes with tinted windows. Every so often the window would slide down with smooth German efficiency and a cigarette butt would be flicked out. The flicker had a muscular tattooed arm and a two-pack-a-day habit by the looks. I remembered Joe's warning. Was this why Baz had closed the Phoenix? Was he being hassled by someone? Or was the person in the Merc a coincidence? I made note of the car's number plate, thinking I could run it past Joe.

When the half-hour was up there was still no sign of Gene and I needed to go to the loo. I didn't want to attract the attention of the Merc lurker by going into the Phoenix, just in case it was the object of their surveillance. Instead I decided to risk the wrath of the nearby cafe's staff and sneak in for a pee without purchase. I darted into the cafe, charging straight past the tables and out the back door to the loo. Like Baz's flat above the Phoenix, many Fitzroy cafes had toilets off courtyards. I peed quickly and ran back through the cafe so the waitress couldn't pull me up for not being customer. I shouldn't have worried. She was so busy flirting with the barista I could have run through there naked without attracting attention.

I was about to dash back to the car when a flyer on the inside of the cafe's glass door brought me up short. 'Missing cat: Answers to Barry.' The photocopier used for the flyer was of such bad quality that it was hard to be sure that the blob in the picture was indeed a cat. I'd have to take the flyer's word for it. I paused to read the rest of the notice. *Last seen in Brunswick Street. Black with notes of grey.* I didn't recall seeing any strange cats around the other night, and believe me, if there'd been one, it would have found me. I was memorising the phone number, just in case Barry the cat turned up at the Phoenix, when I spied a figure stopping at the door to Gene's shop. It was Mitch Mitchell. I watched him knock on the door of Gene's shop and then peer through the security grilles on the windows.

The Mercedes driver was also showing interest in Mitch's arrival. The car window was down and I could see the outline of a large man with short hair and designer sunglasses.

Mitch Mitchell took one last look through the windows of Gene's shop then moved on. I took a moment to pull my hair back into a tight bun and secured it with a hair band, shoved my sunglasses on my face and crossed the road to follow him at a safe distance.

Mitchell ducked into a grimy hole-in-the-wall tobacconist but emerged again quickly and went to the next shopfront— a 24-hour chemist popular with methadone users and doctor shoppers. I lingered in the doorway of a warehouse selling cut-price designer clothes. Mitchell came out of the chemist and moved down the block to a community radio station (inspiring memories of a late-night DJ I'd once dated) and then popped into the legal aid service office (memories of several lost afternoons there with the same DJ).

After that he visited one of the old dive cafes that had been there since the dawn of time and then a swanky new one that had probably been there since last week. After that a 7-Eleven—a fluorescent blight on the landscape, but handy when you needed milk at 2am.

I ducked for cover in the doorway of a small bar that had also cropped up in the last few months. Inside, there were a lot of shiny new accessories. The girl behind the bar looked pretty shiny too. So shiny, in fact, she resembled a blow-up doll that had been lightly covered in Vaseline. I pretended my phone had just rung and lingered at the door as if I was trapped in a conversation with someone I hated, all the while looking through the glass to the street, to see where Mitchell was headed next.

Mitchell emerged from the 7-Eleven and I nearly dropped my phone when I saw the Mercedes pull up at the nearby tram stop. The large man got out and in two steps was man-handling Mitchell in a menacing manner while the boot of the Merc opened automatically. I got the distinct impression the large man was about to bundle Mitchell into it. In broad daylight. On Brunswick Street.

The man hadn't counted on a busload of shoppers suddenly appearing and blocking his progress. Coaches regularly brought shoppers to Brunswick Street from the outer Melbourne suburbs, lured by factory outlets and trendy designer stores. These perm-loving ladies were bargain hunters who shopped with ruthless efficiency and they didn't take kindly to a Mercedes being parked in their way. They were on a tight schedule.

Mitchell didn't hesitate. He lurched sideways, bumping roughly into several of the women and hooking one of them by her handbag strap.

She reacted immediately. 'Bag snatch! Bag snatch! Grab him, Joyce!'

Suddenly it was like a rugby scrum. Shopping bags pummelled Mitchell from all sides, and the Mercedes departed with a squeal of tyres. I left the calm of the shiny bar and waded into the melee.

'Hold it, ladies!' I yelled as loudly as possible. 'He's an epileptic. He wasn't trying to steal your bag, I promise! Give him some air. Please!'

The ladies contented themselves with a few last swipes and when it was ascertained that nothing had actually been stolen, they charged off in the direction of Smith Street.

The contents of Mitchell's bag were strewn across the footpath and Mitchell was slumped on the pavement, possibly unconscious, so I hastily picked up his wallet and laptop and shoved them back in his bag. Then I started picking up the various bits of paper that had also spilled out. Thankfully, passers-by gave us a wide berth.

I was just chasing down a piece of paper before it ended up on the tram tracks when I turned to see Mitchell back on his feet and heading my way. He snatched his bag from me in a less-than-grateful manner.

'Not following me, hey, sweetheart? Either you're my biggest groupie, or you're a stooge. Who are you working for?'

'I'm not following you.' Up close I could see blood oozing from a cut on his chin. I retrieved a wad of paper napkins from my handbag and offered them to him. The napkins were quickly soaked with blood. 'But I saw the guy in the black Merc. He looked dodgy and I wanted to warn you. No need to thank me for picking up your things; it's not like anyone would have stolen them. You might need some ice for that. I can get you a slushie from the 7-Eleven?'

'You're a regular Florence Nightingale.' Mitchell put his bag under his arm and charged off down the road, the bloody napkin still jammed to his chin.

Whatever Mitch Mitchell was up to, it appeared he'd pissed off more people than just my boss. I wondered if Joe the parking inspector was indeed hinting that a mafia war was brewing. Maybe that was the story that Mitch Mitchell was chasing. It occurred to me that maybe that was the reason Baz had gone to ground as well.

I remembered the envelope of cash I'd found in his drawer. Was it possible he was mixed up in some mafia-type shenanigans?

I was not feeling good about it.

CHAPTER EIGHT

The council car was still parked in the loading zone when I returned. The council was responsible for towing illegally parked or dumped cars so I'd figured they wouldn't tow one of their own.

The black Mercedes was nowhere to be seen, but there was no sign of Gene at his shop either. Rather than return to work, I decided to make further use of the council car. Although I didn't know Gene's surname—I doubt even Baz knew it—I had dropped him off at his house once. He and Baz had gotten into a particularly boozy session sparked by John Lee Hooker's death. Baz still had his Datsun back then, but he was too drunk to drive and even though Gene was too drunk to walk, he still managed to grope my left breast when I lifted him out of the car. After that I dumped him in his front garden and left him to sleep it off under a row of agapanthus. In typical bizarre Gene fashion, he later told me to forget I'd ever been there and not to reveal his address to anyone, under any circumstances—even torture. He said he had an ex-wife who was determined to get her hands on his collection of Bon Scott memorabilia, including a jar allegedly containing some genuine Bon Scott vomit.

Just quietly, I found it very hard to believe that anyone could have married Gene. The more likely story was that he was dodging debt collectors or the tax office—probably both. Either way, I was happy not to get caught up in Gene's weird world. I'd assured him his secret was safe with me, and I had indeed spoken the truth; his secret was so safe that even after twenty minutes of driving around Coburg, I still hadn't managed to find the house again. Too much had changed in the intervening years. I drove around aimlessly for a bit longer, hoping to spot the agapanthus, but after thirty minutes of fruitless searching I gave in.

I arrived back at the office to find Brucie in a state of nerves.

'Where have you been?' he hissed. 'Eve the psycho HR manager has come back from long-service leave a week early. She thinks someone might have raided the stationery cupboard without filling in the correct paperwork.'

This news was delivered with the same gravity as disciples must have reported that someone had opened the tomb of Christ. To be fair, it was momentous. In my months working for council, I'd had to steal pens from the TAB and post-it notes from Grant/Gavin's drawer. It was lucky I was handy with a lock pick.

'Why is the HR manager in charge of the stationery?' I asked. 'Surely that's not in her job description.'

Brucie rolled his eyes. 'Practicality and despotism rarely come in the same package.'

On that intriguing note, a woman suddenly appeared at the doorway.

'Hello!' she exclaimed. 'You must be Brick Brown! What a funny name!'

I was dumbstruck. The woman looked like a shorter, plumper version of Gail. She was wearing the same kind of black trouser suit that Gail favoured and had an identical spiky blonde hairstyle, but whereas Gail rarely cracked anything resembling a smile, this woman was cheerful to the point of mania, with a high-pitched voice and a girly giggle. It was a confusing juxtaposition.

'Since you came on board while I was away, I've decided to extend your probation period to six months!' she exclaimed. 'Hope that's okay?'

She was gone before I had a chance to say that was definitely not okay. 'Does this at least mean we can get some new pens finally?' I asked Brucie.

His face was grim. 'I wouldn't get your hopes up.'

My mood plummeted from low to rock bottom. I needed to make a phone call but didn't want to do it in our open plan office in case Eve popped up again. I headed for the loos on the fifth floor.

Maybe because of the stairs, I think I was the only person who used the fifth floor bathroom—but they were the nicest loos in the whole of the council building. Somehow they had escaped the more recent renovations that had blighted the other floors and were vintage 1940s. There were beautiful old porcelain sinks and toilets in a delicate shade of pale green with tiling a shade darker, but still beautiful, and the acoustics were amazing. Walking into the bathroom was like a soft embrace for your ears. I settled myself down in a cubicle and then I rang Timmy at the Black Possum.

'Can I ask a huge favour?' I asked. 'I've got a number plate I'd really like to know the owner of. Any chance?'

Timmy seemed torn between being happy that I asked and scared. 'I'll see what I can do when I finish my shift here. But don't tell Bunny. I promised her I'd given up hacking.'

Uncle Baz often says you make your own luck. You just have to keep your eye on the ball and watch out for the cats who want to take you down. By cats, he means people. Over the years I've found that his advice is pretty sound—although sometimes hard to understand due to a fondness for Blues and/or sports metaphors. I believe in luck—whether it's good or bad—but I don't believe in coincidence. Mitch Mitchell had been nosing around near Baz's joint. He'd been looking for Gene at his record store straight after I'd been told to go and talk Gene and he'd nearly been kidnapped by a well-dressed thug while asking questions in the area. Finally, there was the fact that Mitchell had shown an interest in council's Development Consent Committee. Had these thugs had something to do with Baz's disappearance? My heart constricted.

I went back to my desk and searched my emails; a gruelling and time-consuming task, but worth it in the long run. The week earlier I'd been cc'd into an email that contained the agenda for the next meeting of the committee. The same committee that had recently lost Mavis DuBois as a chairman and gained Hugo Clark. I printed out a copy of the agenda and addenda, using the back of a random document I'd purloined from Grant-or-Gavin's filing cabinet. It was at least a hundred pages long. I took the printout to the fifth floor toilets to read more closely, but even with the calm environment I couldn't focus. How did they make these papers so boring? Then I found something: an item relating to a new apartment complex being built on Lot 22 on Brunswick Street. It was the old warehouse where Gene had his shop, next door to the Phoenix. I wondered if this planning application had anything to do with Gene's absence. Maybe he was on a bender. And maybe he'd taken Baz along with him. A high-rise next to the Phoenix would not be good news. How would we survive the dust and noise of a major building site?

I crept back to my desk and did an online search of the development company. It barely seemed to exist beyond a flashy web page. None of the links there led to any information at all. I rang Sue. Her newspaper, *The Melbourne Weekly*, was a vehicle for real-estate listings. Maybe she could give me the fast track.

'Sue, quick question: I've been having a look at the papers for the next development committee meeting. Have you heard of some developers called Brave New World? They're behind an application to build next to my uncle's pub.'

'No, I haven't heard of them,' she said. 'But I know someone who's an expert on everything to do with development.

I need to drop something off at his house, so if you pick me up from my office in an hour I can take you to visit him.'

'Who is this person?'

'He was the committee chairman before Mavis DuBois. But he's really, really nice. When I first started my job with *The Weekly* he was the only councillor who'd give me any information about anything; everyone else treated me like a bloody pariah. Unfortunately he retired about a year back after a stroke, but I know he still takes an interest. More than an interest: he's a complete obsessive for civic affairs.'

I agreed to pick Sue up from her office in half an hour.

'Do you think anyone will notice if I take the car out again?' I asked Brucie, who was tidying his desk in an uncharacteristic fashion.

'Eve's a bit preoccupied by the stationery heist,' he said, sliding me his key. 'She's calling people into her office one by one, but I think you're pretty far down her list. If you're back within two hours you should be okay.'

'Where are you on the list?' Brucie was being surprisingly collegial, so I thought I'd reciprocate with some moral support.

'I'm sure I was top of the list, but I haven't been Gail's longest serving PA in history because of my pretty face. If you hadn't noticed, Eve is obsessed by Gail and I am the gateway to Gail, as gross as that may sound. I may let Eve "save face" though and interview me anyway. I need some new highlighters.'

'Should I be worried?'

'Hell, yeah, girlfriend!' Bruce looked delighted at my concern. 'Who knows what some of those guys will say about you? Grant and Gavin will crack like eggs, and you could be a handy scapegoat.'

'Are you telling me Gavin and Grant are two different people?'

Brucie rolled his eyes. 'On the plus side, Eve is psychotically possessive of Gail and since Gail doesn't like you much, you're probably not a threat to her. On the other hand, Gail doesn't like anyone much. Not even Eve. It's all a bit fucked up, but that's Eve for you.'

'I am never going to get my head around the office politics thing.'

'You don't know the half of it, sweetie. Wait until you've been here as long as I have.'

'I thought you'd only been here eighteen months.'

'That's what I'm saying.'

I headed back down to the parking garage, hoping that I could survive eighteen months. At this stage even another eighteen weeks was looking unlikely.

I extracted the car from the basement again and set a course for Sue's office, where she was waiting outside, holding a cheery bunch of gerberas and a large coffee.

'Thanks, Brick, my car's at the mechanics,' she said as she jumped into the passenger seat. 'I've been feeling so guilty for not dropping in on Otto Weber earlier. He had a nasty fall a few weeks back and I've been meaning to go and see him. That's why I've got the flowers. The coffee's for him, too. He loves a good coffee. Sorry, I should have got you one as well.'

She directed me westwards and once we'd crossed the ten-lane nightmare that is Flemington Road—while simultaneously swotting off a man who wanted to clean our windscreen—we were in the quieter tree-lined streets of North Melbourne. I parked in the loading zone of a nice-looking pub a few doors down from the address Sue had given.

'I know Otto used to be a councillor, but he's really a lovely old bloke—although very chatty. I think I've heard his entire life story,' said Sue as we arrived at the door of a modest terrace fronted by a garden bed of wild-looking rosebushes. 'He bought this house fifty years ago when he started work as a clerk with the public service, back in the days when people could afford a mortgage on a single salary. His wife died a few years back, but he's got a bunch of daughters. I think one of them has moved in to look after him. But like I said, he knows everything there is to know about Melbourne's planning codes. Completely obsessed by them. That and football. That's how he had his accident—adjusting his aerial during a football match.' Sue pointed to an aerial dangling at a jaunty angle.

'He fell off his roof? Jesus.' It was the kind of idiot thing I could imagine Baz doing.

A woman of about forty answered the door. Sue held forth her offering of flowers and the coffee and introduced us as representatives from council sent with a get-well gift.

'Come on in,' said the woman. 'I'm Romy. The youngest daughter. Dad's probably told you about my divorce. He seems to have told bloody everyone.'

'Yes, I was sorry to hear,' Sue said as we entered the hall. 'How's your father doing? We don't want to disturb him if he's resting.'

'No, he's up. Well, he's not exactly up, but he's awake. I'm sure he'll appreciate some company; he says the game shows are driving him crazy. Actually, he's driving me crazy, constantly asking me to change channels for him.' She ushered us towards what looked like the lounge room. 'I should warn you, though. The medication is making him very up and down. He seems fine one minute, confused the next, and he dozes off a lot, but wakes up again quickly. The doctor says it's to be expected, considering the extent of the head injury. We're just lucky he survived at all.'

Otto Weber's lounge room was vintage-1960s-meets-hospital-ward. He was laid out in one of those trolley-type beds, a mirror contraption above it allowing him to watch an old TV set in the corner. No remote control.

'You've got some visitors, Dad,' Romy called as we entered the room.

Otto didn't turn in our direction—even if he'd wanted to, the amazing metal contraption around his neck connected to a halo with spikes attached to his skull prevented it. I forced a smile and tried not to look too closely.

'Hi, Otto,' said Sue. 'We thought we'd come by and see how you're doing. Everyone on council's been asking how you are.' It was a lie, but a fairly harmless one. 'And I brought you a coffee, too. I know how much you like real coffee.'

'Young Sue, is it?' His voice was surprisingly loud and strong. 'Romy will put those flowers in a vase. My poor roses will be suffering, but I don't want Romy to prune them— she gets carried away. I think it'll be a while before I can do any gardening again.'

'Well, definitely no more climbing ladders,' Sue said as we sat down on the doily-covered couch.

'Don't worry about that. I hadn't been up a ladder for years. I must have been into the plonk to even try it,' he said. 'I can't remember the accident at all. And I've lost my memory of the two weeks leading up to it, including the entire preliminary finals, which is a bit of a bugger. I'll have to buy one of those video player things so I can watch the North Melbourne games again.' He paused and his eyes flicked in my direction. 'Who's this pretty lady with you, Sue?'

'This is Brick Brown,' said Sue. 'She's working in the council's PR department.'

'Well, I won't hold that against you dear,' Otto boomed jovially.

'And you might have heard of her uncle, Baz Brown. He used to play football.'

'Ah yes, Basil Brown. He played a few games for Fitzroy, didn't he? He wasn't a bad player at all.'

Romy returned with a pot of tea and a plate of biscuits on a tray commemorating North Melbourne's 1977 premiership. I hadn't seen an Iced VoVo in quite some time.

'I didn't even think Dad had a ladder,' Romy said. 'But I've asked the neighbours and it's not theirs, so he must have bought one. God knows how you got it home, Dad.'

'I don't remember buying the ladder either,' said Otto. 'It's an odd feeling, having all these blank bits in my head. Very strange.'

He stopped while Romy held his coffee, complete with a straw, up to his lips to let him take a sip. 'But strangely, I think the knock's actually made some bits of my memory better. I'm really good at these quiz shows that are on the telly. If only I could sit up properly, I think I could go on one and do really well. A lot of the people they have on these shows are idiots—have you ever watched one? Yesterday there was a woman who thought Gough Whitlam was a kind of cheese. What are they teaching in schools these days?'

'Maybe you can audition when you're better,' his daughter said. 'God knows you could use a new lounge setting.'

Otto's couch looked about as vintage as Baz's, but the room had more signs of a woman's touch: embroidered cushions, silk flowers in a crystal vase, a hand-painted picture frame showing a younger-looking Otto with a group of women who, judging by the resemblance between them all, were his late wife and his daughters.

'So how are things at council, Sue, since Mayor Dickie kicked the bucket?' Otto's eyes gleamed. 'I only wish I could be there. I hear the mayoral election could have more entrants than the Melbourne Cup. I'm almost tempted to try my luck, but—'

'But your daughters would put you in a home,' Romy said.

Sue took to the cue to move the conversation in the right direction. 'That's not the only shuffle going on. Mavis

DuBois just decided to give up your old position on the Development Consent Committee.'

'What?' Otto nearly choked on the sip of coffee he'd taken, forcing Romy to jump back up to wipe his chin with a tissue.

'She'd been wanting me to step down for years,' he said when he'd regained his composure. 'I think she would have bought me a first-class ticket on the *Queen Mary* to get me out of the way. Not that I'd have taken it, I'd miss the football too much. Maybe in the off season.'

'She needs to nurse her sick mother, apparently,' I said.

'What? She hates her mother. And I don't blame her. Everybody hates Winsome DuBois. She's one of those old-money, high-society types—likes to sit on the boards of art galleries and then complain about any art that's too interesting. So, who's going to replace Mavis on the committee?'

'Hugo Clark.' I braced myself for more coughing, but thankfully this was less shocking to Otto or I think Romy would have asked us to leave.

'Hugo Clark, hey? That's interesting.' Otto closed his eyes as if in meditation. 'I think someone needs to keep an eye on Hugo Clark. He was a bit too chummy with Dickie Ruffhead for my liking, and with me laid up here like a shag on a rock, those mongrels on the committee have just the opportunity they've been waiting for. They'll sneak through some ridiculous car parking proposals while they think I'm not watching.'

'That's partly why we're here, Mr Weber. We were planning on going along to the next committee meeting.' I pulled the paperwork out of my bag. 'I happen to have the agenda here. Maybe you'd like to have a look at it. If it's okay with your daughter.'

Romy shrugged. 'Just try not to get too worked up, Dad. I don't want you to split your stitches.'

I held it up for Otto to view. 'I'm particularly interested in this Brave New World Property Group that's bought the site next to my uncle's pub. It's an old warehouse that's been practically derelict for years, except for a run-down record shop. Who's this Brave New World? Have you heard of them before? I did an internet search but couldn't find out anything.'

'I'm not surprised. It's a shell company.'

'What's that?'

'It's a company that's used to hide assets for another developer—the kind responsible for half the high-rise apartments without enough car parking springing up across Melbourne. Then they expect council to come up with all the infrastructure to support it. And the shops will all be leased to those American chain stores that can't make coffee to save their lives. Melbourne used to be a place that knew coffee, if nothing else.'

'He's had to give up wine, but I couldn't make him give up coffee,' said Romy. 'I don't know how he gets any sleep.'

'Sleep?' Otto snorted. 'Who needs sleep when you're stuck in bed all day? I just wish there were better game shows to watch. Whatever happened to *Pick a Box* with Bob Dyer?'

I had no idea who Bob Dyer was, let alone what happened to him, I just wanted to get Otto back on track. 'So, who *is* behind Brave New World developers? Do you know?'

'I do happen to know,' said Otto. 'A friend told me. A friend who's since passed away. I'm not sure it's safe to tell you.'

I wasn't sure if Otto was paranoid, a la Gene, so I decided to drop the subject and return to the committee.

'So does this committee have the power to stop a developer from going ahead with a plan if they've already bought a site?'

Otto looked happier answering this question. 'If the proposal isn't up to scratch or if the plan contravenes the zoning requirements, yes. For example, you can't build an industrial-purpose building like a factory in a residential area and vice versa. Without an exemption, of course.'

'And how do people get an exemption?'

'There's an application process.'

'Is there the possibility of corruption?'

'Absolutely! I remember one time—' Otto had looked very animated but suddenly looked confused. 'Who was that? Romy ... do you remember? Around 1985?'

'Don't get yourself worked up, Dad.'

Otto's eyes closed for a long moment. I thought he'd fallen asleep, but after a moment he started up again: 'I was happy that Mavis DuBois took over after I stepped down. I was worried it would be Dickie. He was as crooked as a dog's hind leg.'

'Can you tell me who owns the shell company behind the proposal to build next to my uncle's pub?' I asked again.

'You're not the only person to ask me about that company.' He paused. 'Bad days, indeed, real bad …' His voice faded.

'Please, I'm really worried for my uncle.' I felt my eyes welling up. 'I'm starting to think that someone wants him out of his pub. I don't have parents, you see. My uncle is basically it.'

Otto's eyes softened. 'I was orphaned young myself— that's why I came to Australia back in 1955. I barely knew any English. It was a bit of a gamble, but when you're young, eh?' He sighed. 'I'll tell you, but keep it close to your chest.' Otto paused, allowing Romy to give him another sip of coffee. 'It's a shell company for Dave Mullett.'

'Who?'

'Shady Dave Mullett, they used to call him. And "shady" sums him up pretty well. There's not a lot of black and white evidence of criminal activity but there's a large grey area in some of his dealings. He always manages to wriggle his way out of any actual prosecutions by having a lot of expendable business partners that he can drop like a skink drops its tail. I remember when one former business partner washed up in the Yarra River in the 1980s. Apparently he'd decided to take a late-night swim without his teeth or fingertips. They identified him by the serial number on his pacemaker.

'Of course, Mullett's rarely seen in public these days. Probably scared someone will try and shoot him—or throw something at him. Did you see that photo of the premier on the front of the newspaper the other day? Those freeway protesters have pretty good aim. Do you think it was dog poo or human?'

'Dad! Do you mind?' Romy swatted her father affectionately.

Otto laughed and then coughed. 'When I was a younger, I had dreams of taking down the likes of Dave Mullett. But I was just a little fish, and I had my family to think about.' He cleared his throat. 'I do have a small collection of information, or rather it's a big collection: boxes and boxes. When I finish writing my history of the North Melbourne Football Club, I may start on that. But not while Mullett's alive, that's for sure.'

I saw Sue's interest was pricked. 'If you ever want to show someone your collection, I'd be happy to take a look.'

'Oh no, Sue, too dangerous. Especially for a mother of young children.' Otto's voice was beginning to fade again. 'I squirrelled things away for years. The archivist was drunk half the time, so I hid them in plain sight. It works for zebras—except the unlucky ones. There's always one unlucky one. I was going to show them to my friend, but ... he was an unlucky zebra in the end ...' He trailed off and looked confused.

Romy caught my eye and I cottoned on to her meaning.

'We'd better go, Sue. Let Mr Weber rest.'

We thanked Otto, although he seemed to have drifted into a nap. Romy saw us to the door.

'I do hope he'll be back to his old self soon,' said Sue.

'Me too.' Romy's eyes filled. 'You know what parents are like: they drive you crazy for years and then suddenly you realise they won't be here forever.'

* * *

When I got back, the office was a ghost town. Brucie was the only person left on the second floor.

'Where is everyone?'

'They're up with accounts on the fourth floor, trying to work out how much sick leave they have left. I told you about the Gail effect. Well, this is the Eve effect. Together they're like the perfect shitstorm.'

'How come you're still here?'

'Party drugs and phone upgrades. I need to afford them,' he said, continuing to type furiously. 'Plus I used up all my sick leave going to a rave fest last year.'

'Yeah, well, I need to afford food, so they're stuck with me as well.' I sat in my cubicle and started surfing the internet to find out more about Dave Mullett. There was no shortage of information. His career was well documented and made for interesting—but disturbing—reading.

According to an in-depth piece I found on a financial website, Shady Dave had pulled himself up by his boot-straps. Mullett's ticket out of Melbourne's slums was his marriage at twenty-one to the daughter of a small but pros-perous Collingwood builder. He took over the business at twenty-five when his father-in-law was incapacitated by a workplace accident. With some high-risk venturing, he had moved into major development interests by the time he was thirty. He was now one of Australia's richest men.

It made me an uneasy to know Dave Mullett was from Collingwood, a stone's throw from Fitzroy. I was also disturbed to read that at one time he'd been on the board of the Melbourne Football Club. It wasn't during Baz's time playing VFL, but it was still a little too close to home.

My phone beeped as a text message arrived. It was Timmy. *Car registered to Brave New World Corp. Hope that helps.* The two-dots-and-a-bracket smiley face did nothing to ease the news about the black Mercedes that had been tailing Mitchell and/or staking out Gene's shop. It was more like a kick to my already upset stomach.

By all accounts, Shady Dave Mullett was a ruthless bastard and if Gene was on his bad side then it was bad news. I hoped Gene hadn't dragged Baz into something.

CHAPTER NINE

There seems to be an unwritten law when it comes to venues for bureaucratic meetings: they must be ugly, with no windows to the outside world. Maybe this is because bureaucrats are bottom dwellers, using baffling procedural systems and mangled language to cloak their hidden agendas. The Development Consent Committee meeting was slated to be held in a back room of the council's ground floor that had walls painted in varying shades of murky green, giving the impression of being trapped at the bottom of the sea.

My problem was going to be my absence from the second floor, especially since this Eve character had started prowling the halls. I needed a plan and, with the benefit of continued insomnia, I came up with one. I arrived on the second floor early and typed up a draft of my parking inspector Myspace policy—or rather, I copy and pasted it from various past policy documents. Hopefully it would be enough to keep Gail off my back. When Eve arrived (8.30am on the dot), I made sure she noticed me by asking if I could put in a stationery order. She issued me with a form which she then returned to me three times, saying I hadn't done it correctly, before reluctantly issuing me with two ballpoint pens, a notepad and a pack of manila folders. Post-it notes were deemed unnecessary for me at this time. 'Some things have to be earned, Brick. Let's just wait and see if you make it through your probationary period first.' She smiled at me during our whole exchange, but it didn't reach her eyes. 'And you might want to rethink your choice of work attire. It looks a bit tighter than is appropriate to the office environment.'

I was wearing a black skirt that covered my knees and a stretchy black top. Admittedly my clothes were fitted but they were hardly skintight. I got a small amount of passive-aggressive revenge when I found Eve's council ID swipe card on the floor in the ladies' loo. I pocketed it, having been warned by Brucie that security required at least twenty pages of paperwork and 'at least fifty fucking working days' before they'd replace a lost swipe card.

I made my way downstairs to the Development Consent Committee meeting to find Sue was already firmly planted in the first row of plastic chairs, notebook and pen at the ready. I plopped myself down next to her and saw she was really doing a sudoku. A table was set out for the committee members, along with a screen and projector for the all-important PowerPoint presentations.

'Hey, you made it,' I whispered. 'Wonder boy turn up yet?'

'No sign. Maybe he won't show.' Sue didn't look up from her sudoku. 'That would really piss me off, since I promised my husband I'd have sex with him if he dropped Jake off at daycare this morning.' Sue's marriage was based on a barter system.

'After what I saw yesterday, he'll be here,' I said, hoping to buoy her mood.

She put down her pen. 'What did you see?'

'Well … I was on my lunchbreak,' I lied, 'when I just happened to notice a certain "acclaimed journalist" being roughed up by a man in black, if you know what I mean.'

Sue's nostrils flared. 'Tell me more.'

I opted not to tell her about the attempted kidnapping as I doubted Mitch Mitchell had called the police. 'There's not much more to tell. Mitchell got out of there as quickly as possible.'

'Maybe he will be too scared to show his face here this arvo. It sounds like there's someone out there who's not afraid of playing hardball.'

'Exactly. And the same could go for you and me. I think we should tread very softly.'

'I'm hearing you, don't worry. As much as I want to break a story that would allow me to tell my creep of a boss where to shove his real-estate pages, I'm also very fond of my limbs and would like to keep them unbroken.'

'What kind of story are we talking about here?' I asked.

'Well, fraud immediately springs to mind,' said Sue. 'Then there's bribery, corruption. The development industry's pretty well known for any of the above. And big money is involved. Big, big, *big* money, and dodgy, dodgy, *dodgy* people.'

My sinking feeling returned with a vengeance, although it hadn't really gone far since I'd first realised Baz had done a disappearing act. Was it somehow tied to a new building next door, being built by this Mullett character?

'While I was waiting for you, I noticed something else interesting.' It was Sue's turn to try and cheer me up. 'Your favourite councillor, Mavis DuBois, is here—and I think she's in disguise. Don't turn around!' Sue grabbed me just in time. 'I didn't recognise her at first. It looks like she's cut off her hair! And she's swapped the Sarah Palin look for Alaskan lumberjack.'

Sue handed me a compact so I could pretend to check my lipstick and I caught a glimpse of a woman in the back row wearing a moth-eaten baseball cap and flannel shirt.

'Who's Sarah Palin?'

Sue sighed. 'Your ignorance astounds me. But don't you think it's odd that Mavis is here, since she's given up her place on the committee to Hugo?'

I didn't have time to answer. A door opened and a group of suit-wearing folk filed in, among them Hugo Clark. I scrunched down on my chair, not that Hugo had any reason to take notice of me, but his attention had been diverted to someone behind me. Sue's audible intake of breath indicated it was Mitch Mitchell, and this time the temptation to glance back was too great. Like Mavis, his appearance had changed since the council meeting—the beatnik beard was gone—but it didn't look like he was attempting a disguise. He still had the messy bed hair and penetrating eyes, but he had an additional black eye and a general 'fuck you' aura. The public seating was now about eighty per cent occupied. Mitchell slumped down on a spare seat in the back row.

There was a tingling sensation in my stomach, like a bear awakening from a winter hibernation. I got the distinct impression this man was going to cause me trouble. And that kind of trouble was the last thing I needed. I tried to distract myself by looking at the other people who were shuffling in the door.

'Who are all these people?' I whispered to Sue.

'The non-suits will be people who have objections to stuff. I recognise a few of them. They object to just about everything, kind of like a hobby.'

Some of the audience did look eccentric, including one wearing a hat made from an intricately folded newspaper.

'Is that guy in the paper hat one of the objectors?'

'No, I think he's homeless. He's probably just after a free coffee and a place to sit down for a while without getting moved on. The suits will be the ones trying to get buildings approved. Sometimes there are other reporters here, but I think it's just me and Mitch today.'

'Well, if he's trying to keep a low profile, I don't think he's succeeding,' I said.

A very large man wearing black appeared in the doorway, briefly eclipsing the light from outside as he entered. I couldn't be sure, but he looked very like the man from the black Merc. He was big, muscled and tattooed, wearing a well-cut suit, designer sunglasses and sporting designer stubble.

Sue was trying to look nonchalant but I could sense her building excitement. I, on the other hand, had had two espressos on top of a sleepless night and knew that Mitchell had recently come very close to being driven off in the boot of a car. My heart rate was rapidly reaching warp speed. I locked my eyes forward and prayed that this whole venture was not going to end with us cornered in a dark alley.

The meeting got underway with a distinct lack of pomp and ceremony. There weren't even microphones for the committee. I was having trouble following proceedings over the palpitations coming from my chest. I could only hope Sue was having more luck and would catch me up later.

* * *

After three hours, my panic had been mitigated by the intense boredom that only bureaucratic procedure or Test cricket can bring. I was at the point of nodding off when I heard Hugo Clark say, 'Proposal for Lot 22 Fitzroy.'

I dragged myself back to consciousness.

'Is anyone here from Brave New World Property Group?' he asked.

The man who stood to take a comfy chair at the important table could best be described as slick, from his hair gel to his pinstripe suit and the gold man-bracelet decorating his right wrist.

Slick cleared his throat a little. 'Yes, I'm Brendan Jones from Brave New World Property Group.' He fired up his laptop and began outlining the benefits of this twenty-first century, state-of-the-art commercial opportunity that was presenting itself on the 'most depressed, depraved and scruffy block' in Fitzroy.

I risked a glance back at Mitch Mitchell to see his reaction to Slick's presentation. Again he wasn't taking any notes, but Slick definitely had all of Mitchell's attention. In turn, Mitchell seemed to have the mafia stooge's attention. The mountain had managed to squeeze himself into the chair closest to the door. It would have been comical if he hadn't looked like he could crush a man's skull like a pomegranate. I got the feeling that this meeting ending in tears would be a best-case scenario for Mr Mitchell—it was looking increasingly likely that he'd be lucky to end up in an intensive care ward.

I forced my attention back to the proceedings. Slick was gesturing meaningfully to the PowerPoint slides. I scanned the people sitting in the comfy chairs. There were eight men and one woman, all in dreary business suits of grey and navy, watching Slick earnestly. Town planners, bureaucrats and pencil pushers.

My eyes were drawn to Hugo Clark, jammed into the chair at the end of the table. His face was inscrutable as always, but when he looked in my direction cold spread all the way to my toes. I quickly dropped my eyes back to my notepad.

One of the suits at the table started asking question about car parking. Slick's bracelet gleamed as he brought up the appropriate slide in his PowerPoint presentation—a golden ray of light in the greyness of the surrounds. I could see that the only woman on the committee appreciated the manly way in which he handled his clicker. I could hardly blame her, given the impotent environment in which she spent her days: blueprints and car-parking spaces; it was almost worse than working in PR. Were all so-called real jobs this boring?

'I have a question,' said Mitchell from the back row after Slick had finished giving his company's views on providing adequate parking. (Half a car park for every unit—because not everybody drove, did they?)

Hugo turned his bulk towards Mitchell. 'We haven't yet opened the meeting to the floor.'

Mitchell took absolutely no notice. 'My question is, Mr Jones: Why is Dave Mullett using Brave New World as a front for this development?'

A moment of silence followed as Hugo Clark wrestled himself out of his chair, his eyes darting to the man in black. 'You are out of order, Mr Mitchell.' Hugo Clark didn't shout but his strange husky voice was menacing. 'Keep quiet or you'll have to leave.'

A few taut seconds later, Mitchell sat down, although his body language made it clear he wasn't giving in. The ball was in the committee's court. Was one of them going to take the bait or were they going to stick with procedure? My bet was on the latter. The committee wouldn't like being told how to run things by some smart-arsed journalist, especially one who looked like he'd woken up next to a gutter after being bashed in the face by the gutter's violent associate. And I was right. Stony expressions dominated.

A five-minute break was called so everyone could recover from the disruption—or more likely, so that the disruption could be forcibly removed.

By now, even the homeless guy in the paper hat was hip to the fact that something interesting was going down. Everyone was staring at either Mitchell or the large man standing menacingly next to the door.

'Sorry,' I whispered, as I pushed Sue as hard as I could and sent her flying into Slick, knocking his laptop onto the ground with a crash.

CHAPTER TEN

'Stand back, give her some air,' I said, batting away the people who'd rushed in for a closer look. 'She must have forgotten to take her pills.'

After a few moments, Sue fluttered her eyelids as if she was regaining consciousness. 'What happened?' she asked, wanly. I was glad that Sue was a better actor than me.

'You said you were having a heart attack.'

She sat up in a shaky fashion. 'I'm feeling much better now. I'm probably just pregnant again.'

'An ambulance is on its way,' said one of the suits.

'Brick, could you take me to the ladies?' Sue leaned on me heavily as I helped her to her feet. 'I'm sure I'll be alright. I don't think I need an ambulance now.'

We made a beeline for the ladies' toilets, Sue clutching my shoulder. 'Did it work?' she whispered. 'Did he get away?'

'I didn't see—I was distracted by your acting. You're surprisingly good.'

We pushed open the door to the loo. It was empty.

'I hope they cancel the ambulance,' said Sue as the door closed behind us. 'Can you ring and check? I'd hate to get billed for it.' She handed me her mobile phone. 'I am actually busting for the loo though. Three boof-headed babies have shattered my pelvic floor.'

She pushed open a cubicle door, then stood there frozen.

'What's up?' I asked. I moved towards her and saw that there was a man sitting on the toilet seat.

Mitch Mitchell. He lifted a finger to his lips.

Voices just outside the toilet door jolted us into action. Sue grabbed the mobile phone from me and shoved me into the cubicle. I practically landed in Mitchell's lap, upsetting his balance and sending him flying into the wall. I heard the door open.

'Are you sure you're okay?' came a woman's voice.

'Yes. Please don't trouble yourself. I've just cancelled the ambulance,' she said. 'I had the feeling I might be pregnant again and that seems to clinch it. My colleague will take me home. She's just using the loo.'

'I won't be a second,' I called out, hoping it would help get rid of the woman. With Mitchell balanced again, I turned around so my feet would be facing the right way if they were visible under the door.

'Well, if you're sure,' said the woman.

'I'm sure,' said Sue. 'You get back to the meeting. It sounds like you've got a lot to get through.'

The door shut again and there was silence. I realised one of Mitchell's hands was digging painfully into my shoulder.

There was a knock at the cubicle door. 'She's gone, but let me just check outside for that thug in the black,' Sue whispered. 'Stay in there a little longer to be sure.'

I heard the door open and close, leaving Mitchell and me alone. 'Hello again,' I said awkwardly, wondering whether it was too late to look professional and offer him my hand to shake. 'I'm Brick Brown. We seem to be bumping into each other a lot.'

Mitchell still looked on alert, but less so than a minute earlier. 'I guess thanks is in order, Brick Brown. But I have to wonder why you'd help me out.'

'Did it ever occur to you that you're not the only one who has questions about what's going on in Brunswick Street?'

'Why would that occur to me? Developers seem to have carte blanche with Melbourne in general. Your council, for one, seems to have just bent over and dropped its pants. No one takes the slightest notice as long as it keeps making them money.'

'Yeah, maybe that's because the developers have people who are prepared to deal with anyone who gets in their way. That guy in the black suit can't be far away. How are you going to get out of here? In the boot of a luxury German car?'

His hand went to the cut on his chin. It had a few stitches in it, explaining the shaved beard. I heard the door open again and Mitchell's hand clapped over my mouth. If he was trying to keep me quiet, he'd missed the mark. I felt like I was being smothered and nearly screamed.

'Don't worry, it's me,' hissed Sue, and Mitchell let his hand drop.

'What's going on out there?' I asked. 'This toilet is getting claustrophobic.'

'I think the building's safe, but the big guy is parked right out front in a black Mercedes. I don't know what we're going to do.'

'We?' I asked, still a bit thrown by being almost smothered. 'He's not looking for us. We can just stroll right out.'

Sue looked shocked. 'Brick! We've got to help Mitch. What happened to mateship?'

'Glad to hear someone's on my side,' said Mitch Mitchell, emerging from the cubicle.

Sue held out her hand. 'I'm Sue Day, by the way. *The Melbourne Weekly*. It's one of those free newspapers that no one reads. I'm so honoured to meet you. I see you've already met Brick.' Her eyes were bright with excitement. 'Listen, I've got an idea to get you out of here,' she said. 'Do you reckon you can get out the window?' She pointed to a dingy little window high up on the wall, propped open to let some breeze in. 'I can bring my car round to the alley.'

Mitchell and I looked at the window.

'Well, can either of you think of a better idea?' Sue said.

We couldn't.

'I think I can do it,' said Mitchell. 'You go get your car, Ms Day. Ms Brown here will have to help me get up there. If I'm not out in five, drive off or they might get suspicious.'

Sue practically skipped out of the bathroom. Mitchell grabbed the wastepaper bin and put it down in front of the window.

'Wait,' I said. I ran into the cubicle and grabbed the feminine hygiene disposal unit. 'These things are much stronger than that piece of crap, and taller. I'll hold it steady and you climb up. Then if you can get over the sill I can push you out.'

Mitchell didn't look impressed at being told what to do, but he complied, after first letting his leather coat fall onto the floor.

'Can you take that out for me? I won't fit with it on.'

His took off his shirt as well to reveal a worn-looking T-shirt that he had underneath. Through the fine cotton, I could see he was thinner than I'd expected. Maybe he could really make it through the window.

He clambered up on the bin, as I struggled to keep it vertical. 'I can just reach.'

With upper-body strength I wouldn't have credited him with, he pulled himself up. His head disappeared out the window and he eased his arms out one by one. I braced myself against the wall and put both my hands up under his right foot. Finally he was out. I heard a thud that I hoped was him landing without breaking any bones. I rolled up his jacket and shirt and shoved them in my handbag, smoothed down my hair and tried to look as nonchalant as possible as I exited the building. Sue drove up a second later and I got in the front seat, guessing that Mitchell would be scrunched down in the back.

'Did they notice anything?' I asked. 'I was too scared to look.'

'No, I think we got away with it. But we're not home and hosed yet.' Sue drove off at a remarkably sedate pace. Only her hands, clenched on the wheel, revealed she was feeling the tension.

'How are you staying so calm?' My hands were shaking so much I could hardly do up my seat belt.

'I've driven from Melbourne to Adelaide and back with three screaming kids. More than once.'

We cleared the block and Sue started to speed up.

'Where should we take him?' I asked. 'Where will be safe?'

Sue went through an orange light. 'I don't know. But if I don't get home by five, Shane will divorce me. He's got a work dinner tonight—his national manager is in town.' She frowned. I wasn't sure if it was concern for her marriage or annoyance at the prospect of being left out of the action.

'You should drop me off as soon as possible.' Mitchell popped up in the back seat, giving me a start even though I knew he was there. 'No sense putting you in any more danger. But I can't go to my place. They know where I live.'

After seeing the size of the stooge in the black Mercedes, I certainly wasn't going to volunteer Bunny's place as a hideout.

'I know. Turn left here,' said Mitchell. Sue did as commanded.

Fifteen minutes more of crazy twists and turns followed as Mitchell barked directions while craning his neck to see if we were being tailed. There would be no way we could outrun them if they found us. Sue might be a good driver, but her ten-year-old family wagon would be no match for a top-of-the-range German car.

Mitchell seemed satisfied that we were safe and sank back into the seat. His directions became less intense.

We hit Sydney Road and were immediately trapped behind a tram. I gazed out the window, surprised to notice it was a beautiful Melbourne afternoon—cool but with sunny skies and the trees a vibrant green with their spring leaves.

The tram started moving again. We overtook it and Sue turned back into some side streets. After a few minutes we went past the old brickworks, soon to be apartments; then there was the old tram switching depo, soon to be apartments; and finally, as we reached Coburg, there was Pentridge, the former high-security prison, already apartments, with more under construction.

'If I hadn't known the world had gone mad, that one clinched it,' said Mitchell. 'Turning the old Bluestone College into luxury apartments. And I can't believe they turned the gates into a display office. What do they display? Which hardened criminal might be buried under your patio?'

'They've dug up all the bodies,' said Sue, speaking over her shoulder to Mitchell. 'At least, that's what the sales rep told me—so it could be complete bullshit. I did a four-page spread on the apartments a while back. They're pretty plush, but still, I wouldn't be moving my family in there. It'd take more than a smudge stick to get rid of those bad vibes. Kids are particularly vulnerable to poltergeist activity.'

I looked out the window. We were now deep in the back streets of Coburg where I'd been the day before when I'd tried unsuccessfully to find Gene's house. After all the excitement I suddenly felt very tired.

Mitchell asked Sue to pull over at a decrepit bungalow set back from the street. It looked like it was straight out of central casting for a crazy hermit house. The front garden was untamed to the point that one tree looked like it might engulf the front porch. But it was the nature strip that caught my eye. A row of agapanthus shone with purple and green magnificence in the sunlight. Mitchell had taken me to the exact place that had evaded me on my last visit to Coburg. My tiredness left me in an instant.

Mitchell got out of the car and leaned on the driver's side window. 'Thanks, Sue Day. I owe you one.'

Sue blushed like he'd just asked her to the Year 12 formal.

'Wait!' I said, opening my door before Sue could take off. 'I've been looking for Gene, too. There's something I need to ask him.'

For the first time in our short acquaintance, Mitch Mitchell dropped his arrogant smirk. I used the moment to gesture for Sue to go and she took off down the street.

I had no idea of Mitchell's agenda, but for some reason it had converged with my own. He'd led me to the very person who was most likely to have knowledge of Baz's whereabouts.

CHAPTER ELEVEN

Gene's face appeared behind the front door's fly wire and again I found myself roughly grabbed by the arm to be dragged through Gene's front garden.

'Quick, let us in, Gene,' Mitchell hissed.

Gene looked over his shoulder, then let us in the house.

'Are you alone?' Mitchell asked.

'Of course,' Gene whispered. He hustled down the corridor past several closed doors and into a larger room at the rear of the house, closing the door to the corridor. I got the distinct impression he *wasn't* alone in the house, but I didn't want to give too much thought to his domestic situation.

The house's crazy hermit look was even more pronounced in the interior. Every single wall was lined from floor to ceiling with shelves and the shelves were jam-packed with records—LPs, 78s and 45s—catalogue cards sticking out at regular intervals. Although Gene seemed unable to organise a piss-up in a brewery—even if all the brewers were AFL players who'd just won a country premiership—there was obviously another side to him when it came to cataloguing music.

'Sorry to come to your house, Gene, but I had to think of something fast,' said Mitchell.

'Uh, well, anyone fancy a drink?' Gene shuffled off into what I presume was the kitchen, although I glimpsed through the swinging doors that it too was lined with records. Mitchell followed him, sending me a glare that said 'stay out'.

I used my moment alone to do a quick reconnaissance of Gene's dimly lit lounge room. As well as more shelves and more records, there was an old-fashioned rotary dial phone on a surprising tasteful side table. A scrawl on the message pad next to the phone caught my eye. I could swear it was Baz's handwriting, so I stuffed the pad into my handbag just as Gene and Mitch returned from the kitchen bearing some scary-looking liquid in a couple of old Vegemite jars. Gene probably wouldn't even notice the message pad was missing.

Mitchell handed me a jar. 'I don't want to seem ungrateful for your help, Brick Brown, but I think it's best if you drink up and get out of here.'

'What? No. I need to talk to Gene about something.'

'Go ahead and talk, then.'

'It's kind of sensitive. I don't know if I want to mention it in front of a journalist.'

'I'm perfectly capable of keeping things off the record,' he said.

'Off the record—that's funny,' said Gene.

We both glared at him.

I took a sip from the jar. 'You haven't been at your shop, Gene. And I've noticed a strange car parked there.'

'There's some bad shit been going down in the old neighbourhood. There's been threats, man. Threats.' Gene's eyes looked wilder than usual.

'What's going on? Is Baz involved? Has he been threatened by someone?'

Gene's eyes went to Mitchell, which was good because I was hoping he'd be able to offer me a more coherent explanation.

'You realise she works for the council, don't you, Gene?' Mitchell gestured at me with his jar.

'What? No, Brick works at the Phoenix.' Gene seemed to wink at me.

'Gene. It's true. I am working at the council. Remember? You told me they'd put a chip in my shoulder, the same way they do for cats?'

'Just trying to cover for you. I wasn't sure if he knew.' Gene could sometimes surprise me by being canny.

'So that's why you're so interested in Mullett's plans? The Phoenix. Are you Barry Brown's wife?'

'His name's Basil Brown,' I said. 'And he's my uncle. Only just as you turn up on the scene asking questions, it seems that he's gone missing. I'm worried that something bad might have happened to him—and I'm even more worried now I've seen the kind of goons who seem to be after you and Gene.'

'Your uncle?' Mitchell didn't look convinced. 'Well, I guess that explains why you're called Brick.'

I didn't see how, so I concentrated on drinking my beer. It tasted like piss from a cat that was undergoing chemotherapy—but it had a kick like a mule in full health and my shattered nerves needed some kind of medication.

'Gene, do you know where Baz is? I'm worried absolutely sick.'

'I haven't seen him for a week or so.'

I tried to look Gene in the eyes to see if he was lying, but it was hard because his eyes went off in crazy directions at the best of times.

'Do you swear?'

'On my mother's grave, Brick. I don't know.'

'Your mother's not dead. You told me she lives in Ballarat.'

'Same thing.' He winked again, or it may have been a twitch. 'I tell you what, Brick, if I hear from Baz, I'll find some way to send you a message. I've just got to lie low, if you know what I mean? I think my shop is being watched.'

'How are you involved in this?' I asked Mitchell, hoping he might shed some light on things. The development meeting hadn't told me much at all, except I hated meetings and I didn't want to be killed by mafia thugs.

'Well, as you may have gleaned, billionaire property developer Dave Mullett is behind the company that is planning to build a huge fuck-off building right next to your uncle's pub.'

'I got that much,' I said, annoyed at the patronising tone. 'The question is,' said Mitchell, 'why is he using a shell company to buy it? And how did he get the whole block rezoned for residential use?'

I gave an educated guess. 'Dickie Ruffhead? Or Mavis DuBois? Or Hugo Clark?'

'No doubt Dickie was a part of it, but I think it goes even higher up the food chain.'

'It's the tunnel, man.' Gene sloshed some liquid from his jam jar in his agitation. 'They've wanted to tunnel under there for years, take the freeway from east to west.'

I rolled my eyes. 'People have been talking about an East-West tunnel for decades. I can't see it ever really happening.'

'I don't know, man. That new premier Errol Grimes—he seems pretty set on the idea. He probably wants something named after him, like the Bolte Bridge.'

The mention of the Bolte Bridge made me shudder. It carried a huge freeway running over the river, docklands and scrubby, vacant land. The kind of place where mafia shootings were known to take place and stolen cars were found burnt out and trashed. 'If a tunnel is in the offing, why would Mullett want to build a giant apartment block there? It would have to be torn down as soon as it was finished.'

'Maybe he just wants a big payout when the government acquires land for a tunnel. Or maybe he wants to build another crap tower filled with crap apartments. Either scenario would make him money. It's a win-win for him, but it doesn't change the fact that the people of old Fitzroy are going to cop it. I need to get to the bottom of this, Gene. If you're holding out on me … These are very dangerous people we're dealing with.' Mitchell smiled in a way that reminded me of Gene: ever so slightly unhinged. 'And the way they're tailing me, I know this exposé is going to blow some minds!'

I had the sudden urge—enhanced, no doubt, by the powerful homebrew—to beat Mitchell over the head with any object I could lay my hands on. 'Fuck your exposé! Uncle Baz raised me as if I were his daughter and I don't want him killed by ... by—' Luckily the rumble of a large car pulling up outside interrupted me before I could start blubbing to a hack who would probably use it for 'colour' if Baz's body was pulled out of Port Phillip Bay.

Gene heard the car too (proving his hearing was fine) and reacted with unusual alacrity.

'I'm not expecting anyone,' he said. 'Quick, go out the back door and into the shed. There's a tunnel from there to the street.'

A tunnel? Jesus Christ! I couldn't imagine council would give out permits for that kind of thing, but I didn't think it was a good time to bring up planning regulations.

Gene thrust an old Dolphin torch at us and we piled out the door and into a back garden that matched the front for its intensity of flora. A machete would have been more useful than the torch. By the time we made it to the shed, I had half a tree and what felt like a small possum in my hair.

The shed was made of asbestos sheeting and looked about to be completely devoured by the surrounding jungle. Inside it became apparent that Gene had a hobby other than music. Evidence of dope cultivation was all around, most notably in the row of halogen lights hanging from the ceiling. It went a long way to explaining Gene's paranoia, not to mention the bloodshot eyes.

The entrance to the tunnel wasn't immediately obvious, obscured by rows of pot seedlings balanced on some old planks of old wood propped up on bricks. From the entrance a ladder went down about three metres. Mitchell held the torch while I clambered down—not so easy in a tight skirt.

Inside, the tunnel looked like Gold Rush–era mine, braced as it was by rickety wooden beams. I was glad the torchlight meant I couldn't see the construction too clearly.

After stumbling along for about twenty-five metres, the surface underfoot changed to what felt like some kind of concrete sewer. I was trying not to gag when Mitchell stopped, sending me thumping into the back of him.

'Any danger of a warning me if you're going to stop suddenly?'

Mitchell ignored my complaint. Light was filtering through a manhole above—our way out of this dungeon. 'We seem to have found a rope ladder of some kind,' he said. 'You'll have to go first, so I can push you if necessary.'

I wished it wasn't true, but I knew I would indeed need a push. I also wished I wasn't wearing a skirt and tried to remember if I was wearing decent undies, but the morning seemed a very long time ago.

The manhole cover was obviously not a much-used getaway, as it was very hard to budge. When I finally levered it up, I peeked around as well as I was able while balancing on

Mitchell's shoulders and trying to grip the rope, which was slimy with mould. At least I hoped it was mould.

Several undignified moments later I'd broken a fingernail and lost what was left of my dignity. The manhole came out in a laneway. That was good—we could clamber out without having to worry about being run down by a ten-tonne truck.

I scrambled out, hearing a disturbing rip as I did so. It seemed Eve had been right about my skirt being too tight. I could feel that I now had a split all the way up the back to my waist and my undies were well and truly exposed.

Seconds later, Mitchell emerged.

'Should we go back and check on Gene?' I asked.

'Better not risk it.'

'Well, what should we do?'

Mitchell brushed off a speck of dirt from his otherwise spotless clothes. 'I don't think *we* should do anything. I think *you* should go back about your business as usual, although you might want to fix your skirt first.' He peered around at my bottom. 'The less you know about what I'm going to do, the better. Can I have my jacket back?' He held out a hand expectantly and I reluctantly retrieved his leather jacket from my tote. He shrugged it on and was gone before I had a chance to even yell after him. Well, actually, I did have a chance to yell, 'You dickhead!' but as usual with dickhead types, he wasn't listening.

I didn't want to call a taxi to come and get me. A taxi driver had once bragged to me that he was an informant for the mob. I didn't really believe him at the time, since he'd also said that he had supersonic hearing that could detect speed cameras. But there was no point taking a chance. Hanging out with Gene, even for a short time, had made me paranoid.

Mitchell had forgotten to ask for his shirt back, so I tied it around my waist, then walked back to Sydney Road and caught a tram. The only upside of looking like a homeless person was it might keep any ticket inspectors at bay.

I took out the notepad I'd found beside Gene's phone. Some phone numbers with a US code were scrawled down and I assumed they belonged to record dealers. I flipped a few more pages and froze. There, in familiar careful lettering, was a message: *Gene, your mum wants you to call and says this is her number in case you've forgotten.* The message was in Baz's handwriting, but since Baz wasn't the clerical type, there was no date or time. It could have been written yesterday or five years ago.

Next I took out the notebook I'd lifted off Mitchell when I bumped into him in the tunnel. I was amused to note that it was one of those old-fashioned flip-over ones used by reporters in movies. I was less amused to find out that— unlike me—Mitchell really did know shorthand. I couldn't make much sense of most of it. Only dates, numbers and names were decipherable. I continued scanning and an entry caught my eye: *Margaret, St Bernadette's, 42 Cedar Street, Moonee Ponds. 10am Fri.*

Margaret was one of the names I'd found in the list on Baz's desk. Maybe this had something to do with Baz's disappearance. Had he been doing some investigating himself? Maybe Mitchell was on the same trail.

Even though he was as arrogant as he was annoying, Mitchell seemed to be extremely talented at ferreting out information. I suppose you'd have to expect that from a hot-shot journalist—although according to Sue, you'd be surprised at the number of journos who couldn't even use a phone book these days. Already Mitchell's investigation had parallels with my own: he'd led me to the committee meeting and he'd led to me to Gene. I decided then and there that if he had a meeting with someone called Margaret, then I would go along, too. I would follow his every move if it brought me any closer to finding Baz.

The only fly in the ointment was my nine-to-five job with council. I was going to need a ruse to explain a certain amount of absenteeism from the workplace while I stalked Mitchell, especially now Eve from HR was hovering around the office like a spy drone.

When I got home I checked the letter box just in case there was a postcard from Baz. He was only person I knew who still sent them. But there were just the usual takeaway menus and one lost-dog notice. A black lab called Brownie. I wondered if Barry the cat was still at large. As if on cue, the three stray cats that were currently mooching off my hospitality appeared. I really needed to find them new homes. I poured out some dry cat food and then headed to the bathroom.

After a hot shower and an intensive shampoo I looked less like an extra from a zombie movie. My skirt was ripped beyond redemption, however, and my body felt a little creaky after the strain of the day's events. It had been a long while since I'd done any rope climbing. In my school days, Phys Ed was one class almost guaranteed to be spent smoking behind the shelter sheds.

Just the thought of nicotine sent a rush of longing through my body, even though I'd kicked my smoking habit cold turkey five years ago. There was no point rummaging through the drawers—being a doctor, Bunny had never bought a packet of cigarettes in her life and only cadged them off other people when drunk. Timmy only ate carcinogens in the form of extremely burnt food. I decided I'd have to settle on peanut butter toast and the dregs of a bottle of port that was lurking in the back of the pantry.

Once safely in my pyjamas with my dinner on my lap, I rang Sue and filled her in on my plan. The wheels were in motion.

When I finally fell asleep, I dreamt I was at back at Baz's flat again. I was sitting in the courtyard loo, frozen, afraid and unable to move as I listened to footsteps slowly coming closer and closer. Finally the door creaked open to reveal a woman standing there. She was my age, with dark hair and sad eyes, wearing a long coat and high heels. She looked like she was trying to tell me something, but when she opened her mouth, black liquid came out, spilling over her hands like oil.

CHAPTER TWELVE

I arrived at work extra early the next day. Once I'd ascertained Gail wasn't in her office, I shot off an email telling her about the great PR opportunity I'd dreamt up for the parking inspectors: a warm and fuzzy 'day-in-the-life' piece in Sue's newspaper *The Melbourne Weekly*. I said it was an excellent way for the newspaper to make reparations for its cruel and malicious—forget that it was utterly factual—story about the parking ticket paper stuff-up.

It was all totally beyond my job description, and I knew Gail would pitch a fit. But I also knew that Gail wouldn't read the email for at least a day—possibly three days, and maybe even a whole week. By then it would be too late for her to do anything.

The upcoming mayoral election had made her even more scarce than usual. Brucie said she was busy frequenting any fundraisers held by mayoral candidates in an effort to do some all-round sucking up so whoever won the election would already know how hard she worked and how important she was in the scheme of the council. Whatever the reason, Gail's absence made for fairly happy days in our little section of the office. Plus it meant she couldn't harass me about the parking inspector policy she'd asked me to draft.

I then wrote another version of the email which made it sound like the project was Gail's idea and I sent it to Evil Eve, Brucie, Gavin and Grant, and all of accounts, just in case. I hoped it would be enough to cover my own absence from the office.

My target for the parking officer lovefest was Joe. I wanted to pump him for more information—particularly regarding the black Mercedes I'd seen outside Gene's shop. I only had to track down Joe and then tell Sue where to meet us. We could probably knock over the photos and interview in an hour, and that would leave me with the rest of the day free to stalk Mitch Michell.

A quick confab with Denis informed me that Joe was cruising the streets of Fitzroy. I rang Sue and we arranged to meet at the Blue Oyster. By this time Brucie had arrived at his desk, but last night's party pills must have finally worn off. He was having a catnap with his head on his keyboard. I borrowed his key for the pool car, grabbed my bag and was about to head off when my office telephone rang. This caused the eternal dilemma of 'will I answer it, or will I let it go to voicemail?' I decided to answer it since I didn't know how to retrieve the office voicemail and I was too embarrassed to ask Brucie for help.

'Hello, PR department,' I said, hoping it would be a wrong number.

'Hello, is that Brick Brown?' The booming voice was unmistakably Otto Weber.

'How are you today?' I asked.

'I'm still as useless as a handbrake on a Holden. That's why I've rung. I wonder if you could do me a favour.'

I wasn't really in the mood, but I couldn't say no to a sweet old man.

'Keep it hush-hush, dear, but I've got some boxes of papers I wonder if you could help me with. I put them in the council archives. I knew no one would find them there, it's a total mess.'

'I can't help you find them today, Mr Weber. Maybe next week?'

'No, leave them there, love. I'm telling you because you struck me as someone I can trust. I'm an excellent judge of character. I want someone to know about the boxes. In case I drop off the perch.'

'You'll be back on your feet in no time, I'm sure,' I said with as much false confidence as I could muster. So much for being trustworthy.

'Well, I survived the bombing of Dresden as a little tacker, so here's hoping. But just in case, the boxes with my documents have a sticker on them. A green sticker with an X on it. Did you ever watch that TV show *The X-Files*? Whatever happened to that show?'

There was a pause during which I thought he'd fallen into one of his microsleeps, but he suddenly piped up again. 'Did you find your uncle yet, love?'

'Not yet.' I felt my throat closing up. 'But I'm sure he'll turn up soon.'

'That's the spirit, dear, stay positive. I saw him play, you know. Those were the golden days of football—before it became big business. Simpler times.'

* * *

Half an hour later I arrived at the Blue Oyster cafe. I ordered a black coffee from the goth waitress—who was looking marginally healthier—and took an outside table to keep a lookout for Joe. It was a one-hour parking zone so I was sure he'd be by at some stage. There was a stiff breeze blowing leaves and assorted rubbish around, while the fast-moving clouds made it sunny one second, gloomy the next.

I grabbed a copy of Sue's newspaper as it blew past and leafed through the real estate pages to the horoscopes. Not knowing my actual birthday, I was at liberty to select whichever one I liked best on the day. *Aries: You are entering a new phase in your planetary cycle*, said Melvin the Mystic Maven. *Prepare for a revelation of earth-rocking proportions, but beware of coincidences that may leave you cornered. Your colour this week is beige.* Apart from the beige thing, it sounded quite promising.

Sue arrived. 'Thanks for the idea for this day-in-the-life piece,' she said, flopping down and motioning for a coffee from the waitress. 'We needed some kind of filler since our self-help guru asked for a pay rise. Actually, he just asked to be paid instead of doing it for free. The editor told him to get stuffed. I've tried to do interviews with parking inspectors before, but the council would never let me. Said it might lead to vigilante attacks.'

'This parking inspector's pretty unrecognisable out of his uniform, so I think he'll be okay.' I hadn't told Sue about Joe's drag act in case she was tempted to mention it in her story. I didn't want to stuff up Joe's life if his hobby wasn't common knowledge. I hadn't been in PR that long yet.

Sue's coffee arrived. She downed it in one gulp, winced slightly, and then I could see that it was time for me to be interrogated. 'So,' she said, indicating to the waitress that she was ready for a second shot. 'What happened after I dropped you guys off yesterday? You weren't very forthcoming on the phone.'

When I'd rung Sue to tee up the parking inspector yarn, I was too tired to deal with a third-degree interrogation so I'd hinted it wasn't safe to talk, as if my phone was bugged.

'I promised I wouldn't say too much,' I said, hoping her hero worship of Mitchell might curb her probing. 'The house you dropped us off at belongs to a source. All Mitchell would say was that the building next to my uncle's club had been rezoned recently, under suspicious circumstances.'

I thought I'd managed to placate Sue, but I was mistaken. Her second coffee arrived and she stirred it happily as she leaned closer to me. 'So ... what else happened?'

'Nothing. I went home.'

'Are you going to see him again?'

'Not if he can help it.'

'What if he *does* want to see you? Don't you think he's sexy?'

'Yes, he's very sexy, but so were all the useless musician types who've stuffed me round and cost me a heap of money. I've decided that celibacy is the way to go for me. I'm going to try to do a year.'

'That's what I said after baby number one and then I was pregnant again before she was six months old.'

I was grateful to spot Joe striding up the street, ticket machine in hand. He waved cheerily, seemingly oblivious of the panic his appearance was causing: our waitress, for one, made a mad dash for a car.

'Denis told me you were out looking for me. How's it going?'

I introduced Sue to Joe and he sat down. After her coffee infusion, Sue was raring to go with the interview. 'Is it true that you have certain targets that you have to meet each day? Or could you go a whole day without writing a single ticket?'

'I can't reveal any trade secrets,' Joe said. 'Or if I tell you, I'll have to kill you.'

I laughed obligingly, although I wasn't entirely sure if he was joking.

Sue continued in professional journalist mode, asking him to describe a usual day, an unusual day and the most unusual excuses people have used in an effort to avoid parking fines when they catch him just as he's about to slide the ticket under the windscreen wiper.

She scribbled in her notebook furiously. 'Is there a lot of burnout in the profession?'

Joe smiled again, revealing his beautiful white teeth. 'Nah, you'll find people actually stay in the ticketing profession for quite a long time. If you can handle being treated like a pariah while in uniform then it's a pretty good wicket. Lots of fresh air. I could never work behind a desk.'

I waited for Sue's inevitable trip to the loo—'Two coffees and I'm peeing for the rest of the day. With my wreck of a pelvic floor, what was I thinking?'—before I brought up Baz. 'So, have you been near the Phoenix lately? I haven't been able to get in touch with my uncle. I even spoke to Gene, but he wasn't making much sense. You know what he's like.'

Joe looked at me in a peculiar fashion. 'I haven't been over there this week. I've been stuck at this end of Brunswick Street, on Beemer duty.'

'Have you noticed a big guy driving a black Mercedes at all. Number plate 1NC-1FT?'

'I might have … but I wouldn't want to be quoted on that, if you catch my drift. There are some people it's not worth ticketing, not if you like your teeth. And my teeth cost me a crapload of money.' He stopped to stroke the arm of my green jacket. 'Nice coat,' he said, 'is it designer?'

It was an obvious ploy to change the subject, because my jacket was from an op shop and in no way trendy. Joe had revealed as much as he was going to let me know.

When Sue returned we headed for the street to take a nice sunny picture of Joe out patrolling past the expensive cars and latte drinkers.

'The camera loves you,' Sue said, clicking away. 'You should be a model.'

'I've heard that before, darling,' replied Joe with a wink.

CHAPTER THIRTEEN

With the parking inspector photo spread firmly in the bag, I was free to drive the council car over to Moonee Ponds to see if Mitchell turned up for the appointment I'd learned about from his notebook. More famous for the Moonee Valley racetrack, I'm not sure if there were any actual ponds in Moonee Ponds. There was, however, an impressive clock-tower, pleasant shopping strip and nice brick suburban homes a mere seven kilometres from Melbourne's CBD.

I arrived at the address in Mitchell's scrawled notes. The orange brick units looked like a supported-living complex. I knocked gently and the door was answered by a robust-looking woman in her seventies. She was wearing sensible brown trousers and a twin-set, her grey hair cut short. 'Sister?' I enquired, noting the gold crucifix around her neck. 'I'm Mitch Mitchell's research assistant. He's running late, but he asked me to meet him here. My name's Brick.'

'Come in, dear. Nice to meet you.' The woman scooted backwards in her wheelchair to allow me entrance. 'I've got MS,' she said, tapping the wheelchair. 'It's a real bugger. Cup of tea?'

The sister whizzed into her kitchenette and I followed. 'Mitch didn't have time to brief me fully. Am I right in guessing that you're a religious sister?' I looked around the sunny but austere unit.

'I was once upon a time. But I left, so you don't have to call me sister. Margaret is fine,' she said as she filled the kettle. 'I still believe in God, and I would have liked to have stayed working for the church to try to make it more relevant, but it wasn't to be. Sorry, I'll get off my hobby horse.'

She was spooning some tea into a cheery red teapot when the doorbell rang again.

'That'll be Mr Mitchell now. Would you get the door for me, dear? I'll have the tea ready in a jiffy.'

I swung the door open with dramatic flair and was gratified to watch a look of annoyance cross his features.

'Mr Mitchell, we meet again.'

'Indeed. You seem proficient at stalking.'

'That's because I'm your research assistant, as I've told the good sister. Ex-sister,' I said. 'I'd suggest you back me up or I'll tell her I'm chasing maintenance money for our three children and she'll think you're a shmuck.' I gestured for him to enter just as Margaret emerged from her kitchenette with a tray balanced on her lap.

Mitchell got straight down to business once we were perched on her plain brown couch, sipping tea. 'As I said on the phone, I'm interested in the old St Bernadette's Convent. In particular, the events leading up to it being sold to Dave Mullett.'

'Well, as you probably know, the orphanage was closed down in the 1980s and after that the buildings weren't really being used much at all. The church decided to sell it, which of course they're entitled to do. The only thing was that some of the community—myself included—thought it should have been sold to people who intended to preserve the historic building. It really was such a lovely building. The gardens too. So lovely.

'It was founded in 1860, although the Coburg grounds were built a fair bit later when it became part of the Josephite Order. The founder was a pioneer of early Melbourne. She used to look after the women who'd fallen on hard times during the Gold Rush. Women didn't have a lot of options in those days if their husband died or beat the living crap out of them. When the convent went onto the market, Dave Mullett started sniffing around. He wasn't as rich as he is now, but he was certainly on the way up. He was ripping down buildings all over Melbourne to make way for hideous monstrosities.'

Margaret set down her teacup. 'I couldn't bear to think of the buildings being destroyed, so I got involved with a local heritage network. We tried to get the building protected with a heritage listing. But of course the wheels of government move so slowly and Mr Mullett was in a hurry so the network needed to get the community's attention quickly. I was a bit headstrong back then and I organised an event which ended up making it onto the news all around the world. It's so long ago now that I can admit I was pretty proud of my efforts. But my superiors were not pleased. There was talk of excommunicating me, can you believe it? With all the outrageous child abuse we've now found was going on at the same time? Sorry, I've gotten off topic. It just makes me so angry!' She added another spoon of sugar to her tea and stirred. 'But to get back to the Coburg Convent— blind Freddy could see that Dave Mullett had a wrecking ball poised to strike the second he had his hands on the convent. But it was up to the board to make the decisions.'

'And who was on the board at that time?' Mitchell asked.

'The usual bunch of men with very little imagination beyond the dollars. There was a school interested in buying the convent, but of course they couldn't offer as much money as Dave Mullet.'

'But isn't the Catholic Church rich? What did they need the money for?' I asked.

'I think it was more a case of someone's pockets being lined,' said Margaret.

'Any idea whose?' asked Mitchell.

'Well, from memory there was one board member in particular who favoured the Dave Mullett proposal.' She paused for dramatic effect—a Catholic isn't a Catholic unless they like dramatic effect. 'Our late mayor, Mr Dickie Ruffhead.'

Mitchell raised his eyebrows, but I got the impression it was to humour the old lady. He'd obviously done his research and already knew that Ruffhead had been on the board. 'What I need though, Margaret, is any kind of proof that Ruffhead may have used undue influence regarding the sale.'

Margaret paused again. This time I sensed it wasn't for dramatic effect.

'I actually still have a lot of the convent's paperwork in storage,' she said eventually. 'I shouldn't have it, I know. But the convent was in a state of chaos at the time of the sale. The Mother Superior was in the early stages of what turned out to be Alzheimer's. I was afraid that the records might end up being dumped or burnt. There are some important documents there, you know, of the children who were put up for adoption. Quite a few people have come to see me over the years, wanting to find out about their parents or their children or siblings. A man came to see me just a few weeks ago.'

'How do people know you have these records?' Mitchell asked.

'A few people who are still part of the church know I have them. They're discreet. They don't want them destroyed either.'

'This man you mention, was he looking for information about a family member?' Mitchell asked, no doubt concerned for his scoop.

'He was looking for the children of an old friend—a woman who'd stayed at the convent for a time with her two sons. He said she disappeared, leaving the boys behind at the orphanage. This was well over thirty years ago.'

'Do you think the woman's sons were his own children?' Mitchell asked.

Margaret shook her head. 'Oh no, I shouldn't think so. I remember the boys, actually. They were identical twins, but one had been injured in a house fire and he had terrible burns on one arm. He'd needed therapy because the scar kept tightening up, so I often saw him in the infirmary. He'd cry so much we'd have to bring his brother in too. But I don't think this man could have been their father. He was Black. He said his father was a Black American, a GI posted to Australia during the war, and his mother was Aboriginal. Such a lovely man. A musician.'

My heart was beating fast. She had to be talking about Baz. Was he really looking for an ex-girlfriend? And did this have anything to do with his disappearance?

'How long ago was this, do you remember?' I obviously sounded a bit frantic because Mitchell looked at me strangely.

'About four weeks ago.'

I tried to cover up my sudden interest with a follow-up question. 'What happened to the twins? Do you know?'

'They were adopted, thank goodness. They needed more care and attention than the orphanage could provide.'

Mitchell was still watching me. It was an expression I'd seen before on Sue and Selena: the look of a reporter who'd caught whiff of a good story. He turned back to Margaret.

'Would you have any records from the sale of the convent as well?' he asked.

Margaret nodded. 'Probably. I took everything from that time. I haven't destroyed anything—not even the photos from the protest that created all the brouhaha. I didn't really understand the fuss. Nuns are just people—and I was wearing full body paint ...'

A mouthful of Earl Grey very nearly came out my nose. So that was why she was threatened with excommunication. The church really doesn't like its people to get naked in private, let alone in public. Paint or no paint.

'Have you got those files here?' Mitchell was so focussed on finding hard proof I don't think he'd even heard the sister's last comment.

'Goodness, no. Barely room to swing a cat here as it is. I've got them in one of those self-storage places. Not far away from here—I can give you the key. I'd go as well, but it's too hard to get around these days. I'm sure I can trust a well-respected journalist like yourself.'

Margaret retrieved a key ring from a drawer and put it in an envelope. 'It's just before the main road. Look for the sign: Vigilante Storage. I think it's a mistranslation. Let's hope so, anyway.'

'Did you come by car, Brick?' Mitchell tucked the envelope with the key in his pocket. 'My battery was flat. That's why I was a bit late—I had to find a taxi. Assistants do have their uses.'

'And if you come across those photos from that particular protest—'

'Don't worry, Margaret,' said Mitchell, cutting her off. 'We'll respect your privacy.'

'No. It's not that. If I were a prude, I hardly would have done it, would I? I just wondered if you could bring me back the negatives? I wouldn't mind making some copies. I'm writing a memoir. To be published after I'm gone, naturally.'

'Naturally.'

I returned the tray and cups to the kitchenette. It was a comfy little flat in which to live out the end of your days, but slightly impersonal.

'Margaret,' I said as I was leaving, 'I know you said there wasn't room here to swing a cat. But you wouldn't happen to like a pet cat, would you?'

* * *

It was only about a five-minute drive from Margaret's unit to Vigilante Storage. It was a grim-looking outfit with the feel of a pay-by-the-hour motel. This was partly due to the proprietor, Serge, who had two visible gold teeth and at least five gold chains snuggled in his ample chest hair. Since Margaret had given us the key, we were shown to the unit with a minimum of fuss and soon we were in a windowless, fluoro-lit shed. Yellowed storage boxes were stacked everywhere.

'Okay, research assistant,' said Mitchell, 'you may as well make yourself useful.' He pointed me towards a wall of boxes on the left side.

'What exactly am I looking for?' I asked as I lifted a dusty lid off a box.

'Anything that looks like board minutes or letters regarding the sale of the convent.'

'If money was being siphoned off, do you really think they wrote it down? I didn't think criminals left records.'

'You haven't heard of the Nazis then?' Mitchell grabbed a box, sending up a plume of dust. 'Just start checking files and pass anything business-related to me, then let me do the thinking.'

I didn't like his tone, but I couldn't help but notice he was looking a little shaky so I let it slide.

The first box I opened contained a mass of ageing manila folders, their cardboard brittle with age. It seemed they were files on the children who'd passed through the orphanage and contained faded photos showing the gap-toothed smiles and bad haircuts of kids who had gotten a raw deal early in life. The boxes were labelled with letters of the alphabet and dates, which went up to 1985. With a sideways glance to check Mitchell was preoccupied, I scanned through the wall of boxes for L.

Before I was adopted by Baz, my name was Brick Lane. Apparently I'd been named after the lane where I was found; no doubt someone's idea of a joke. I didn't really think I would find anything, but my heart was still beating strangely fast. Over the years I'd toyed with the idea of finding out more about my origins, but I'd always come up with some reason to put it off. Deep down, I knew I wasn't living in a Dickens novel and that there was very little chance of me ever discovering the identity of my parents. And perhaps I didn't want to discover their identity. I had a parent who loved me. I had Baz.

I opened the box and started rifling through the files to scan the names. When I saw 'Brick Lane' scrawled on a file in old, faded ink, I felt sick. My hands were shaking as I drew the folder out of the box. Was it about me or was there more than one kid with my name? Maybe Brick Lane was a well-known dumping ground for unwanted children. Already I could feel that it was a slim folio, so I took a breath and opened it.

It was empty. Completely empty. My breath came out in a weird juddery exhalation. Why would there be a folder if there wasn't anything in it? The only explanation was that the contents of the folder had been removed. This was turning out to be a very strange day, although I'd had a few strange days in recent weeks.

'Have you found something?'

I jumped to find Mitchell standing right behind me.

'It's nothing.' I hastily shoved the folder back in the box. 'I just thought I saw a file about someone I know.'

'We're not here to pry into the affairs of people you know. We're here to find out about the sale of the orphanage.'

I was glad my skin tone was resistant to blushes. 'You're not very pleasant. Has anyone told you before?'

'Frequently.' Mitchell smiled in a patronising manner.

'Well, have *you* found anything?'

'Not yet. But this filing cabinet is locked, which makes me curious.' In the corner of the room was an ancient-looking filing cabinet with boxes stacked all around it. 'None of the keys from Margaret work. I tried already.' Mitchell wiped his forehead with the back of his hand. He was starting to look shaky again, like an alcoholic in need of a drink.

'Let me have a look at it.' I examined the filing cabinet. Its lock was a standard mechanism. Baz had a similar one in his office and he frequently misplaced the key. I took out my lock-pick kit and in less than a minute the cabinet was open.

Mitchell hesitated, then did a quick inventory. 'Bingo. It looks like a bunch of correspondence between board members from the days before email.' He rubbed his forehead again. 'It's going to take hours to go through. But I think I need to get some fresh air first.'

I looked around. The room was rather like a prison cell. I remembered he'd been kidnapped and held hostage and I realised why he was so testy. 'Maybe we should just take the stuff from the filing cabinet, go through it somewhere else and bring it back later. I'm sure Margaret wouldn't mind. These boxes of photos need going through too, to find the ones she wanted.'

Mitchell agreed and we carted the boxes to the car before driving back to Margaret's unit. I was still annoyed at Mitchell's bossy attitude, but he didn't seem to notice. He was too busy checking the rearview mirror every thirty seconds as if we were in a seventies cop show.

Margaret had no problem with us borrowing the files and insisted we keep the storage unit's key until we'd had time to look through everything. She'd call us if she needed it.

Mitchell was suitably gracious, for a change. 'You're a gem, Margaret. I'll return these boxes as soon as I can. And … um … I haven't found those photos for you yet, but I'll drop them off too.'

'So what's our next move, Mitchell?' I asked as we headed back to the council car. There was no way I was letting him out of my sight until I understood the reason for Baz's visit to Margaret.

'What do you mean *our* next move?'

'I mean, I helped you get these files and I want to know what's in them.'

'You didn't help me, Brick Brown. You stole my notebook and I'd like it back. But if you want to make it up to me, I could use some help going through all these files.'

I was suspicious at this sudden change of heart, but I was going to have to take my luck where I could find it. 'So where to then? Do you still think you're being followed?'

'I haven't noticed anyone following me today,' he said. 'I took a cab here to be safe. I didn't really have a flat battery; I actually don't have a car.'

'Where shall I take you then?'

'I don't have a place either. I was staying at my father's old flat, but I think I'm being watched.'

'Fine. We can go to my place.'

Mitchell's gratitude was not overwhelming. 'You obviously think that Margaret's recent visitor was your uncle.'

'No flies on you.'

'Any ideas who your uncle was looking for?'

'None.'

'Any old girlfriends spring to mind?'

'My uncle's not Miles Davis or anything, but he *is* a Bluesman,' I answered. 'I suppose I could ask one of his old mates. But I'd say Baz's visit to Margaret has nothing to do with Dave Mullett.'

'Who's to say they're not connected?' Mitchell seemed to be getting his energy back now we were out of the suffocating confines of the storage unit. 'Doesn't it strike you as odd that your uncle, whose club is next door to a building Mullett is hell bent on redeveloping, has gone missing after going to see a former nun who may have some information about Mullett's past shonky dealings? I'd say there's a connection for sure.'

Was there a connection? I was almost afraid to make it in case it meant Baz was in serious danger. 'But what if the vital information has been removed from these files?'

'Then there's a good chance it was removed by your uncle. In which case we need to find him.'

'What do you mean "in which case"? That's the only reason I'm putting up with you.'

'And I thought it was my good looks and charisma.'

CHAPTER FOURTEEN

It was after six o'clock by the time we got back to my place, and it seemed that Melbourne wasn't quite done with winter. It was gloomy, dreary and cold.

We needed somewhere to put the boxes of papers, and the lounge room with the heater in it was the obvious choice. We moved the dining table out of the poky, useless dining room that was generally used to park bicycles and set it up in the lounge room to give us a space to work on. Then I put the gas heater on full blast and made some coffee.

Mitchell insisted on switching on the TV news, but unless it had a newsflash on Baz's whereabouts, then I wasn't really interested. I thought I'd take the opportunity to ring Baz's old friend Mick O'Toole and see if he knew anything about Baz's visit to Sister Margaret. He'd known Baz since his first days in Melbourne when they both played football for Fitzroy.

'Any word from Baz, yet?' I asked when Mick came on the line.

'No.' Mick sounded tired. 'Don't tell me you haven't be able to find the old bugger either?'

'Not yet. But I want to ask you something. Do you remember Baz ever having a girlfriend with identical twin sons? We're talking more than thirty years ago—before he went to the US.'

'Geez, that was back in our footy days, love. We were good-looking roosters back then,' said Mick. 'Baz was playing guitar at nightclubs most nights—they were the only places allowed to serve alcohol after six back then. Hard to believe now. And we spent a fair bit of time at the Phoenix. It was still run by Pascoe and his old lady, and he'd run an illegal casino some nights, with grog on the sly. I think Pascoe's old lady had a bit of a soft spot for Baz. Of course, Baz and me weren't allowed near the nice girls. I was too Irish Catholic and Baz was too Black. I remember Baz once had five shades of shit beaten out of him over some girl. Pardon my French.' Mick paused, his raspy breathing amplified by the phone's tinny receiver. He was a two-pack-a-day smoker. 'Come to think of it, when Baz came back from America after all those years, he *was* looking for someone. Because I'm Catholic, he asked if I could help him. She'd stayed at one of those homes run by nuns, you know, for girls in trouble, and I put him in touch with my cousin. She was a nun herself, once upon a time. At the time I'd thought Baz had some bastard he was looking for. Pardon my French.'

'Was the woman Betty Jones?'

'No, I remember clearly that he was looking for a girl called Delilah, because it was like the Tom Jones song. *Why, why, why, Delilah?*' he sang.

Delilah. It was another of the names I'd seen written on the paper in Baz's office.

'He went to see a former nun called Margaret the other week.'

'Yeah, that's my cousin. Margaret.'

'Do you think Baz had been looking for this woman and her kids all this time? Since he came back from the US?'

'Maybe he's just going soft in the head.'

I really hoped Mick was right. Better soft in the head than dead. I relayed Mick's information to Mitchell, who'd helped himself to the packet of Tim Tams I'd been saving for a special occasion or PMT, whichever came first. I was surprised to see one of the stray cats sitting on his lap. This particular cat had turned up about the same week I moved into Bunny's house. It had a tendency to slam its head violently into doors, furniture, the TV, people—so I'd named it Head-butt. Perhaps it had been a goat in a former life.

'Anything helpful on the news?'

'Can hardly call it news, it's all about the bloody Spring Carnival at Flemington bloody Racecourse. As if horse racing were the most important thing in the world right now.' Mitchell offered me one of my own biscuits. 'Even the bloody premier of bloody Victoria has nothing better to do than dress up like a bloody dandy and gamble on horses. If I was part of that nutty freeway protest gang, I'd throw myself in front of a horse like a suffragette—that's how you get attention in this country. Mind you, that freeway protest mob did get quite a lot of media coverage with the poo projectile they hit the premier with the other week. Impressive aim.'

I took advantage of his rant to regain ownership of the Tim Tams and was in the process of hiding them in the vegetable drawer when an item on the TV news caught my attention.

'... Authorities are seeking to identify a man who was killed this afternoon in a hit-and-run incident in Melbourne's inner north.'

My breath caught in my throat. I slammed the fridge shut and ran back to the TV in time to hear the man's description: aged in his seventies, Caucasian appearance. It didn't sound like Baz.

I went back to the kitchen and made us double-shot coffees while Mitch divvied up the boxes for us to sort through. He assigned me to a box containing a jumbled mess of photos. I sipped my coffee as I flipped through the photos: rows of kids lined up in formation, squinting above frozen smiles, hair brushed, knees scrubbed, but still with that shabby, second-hand look. Where were the kids in these photos now? Dead? In prison? Living the Aussie dream in the suburbs, creating the families they'd never had as children?

I was well into the third box of photographs before I found something. There in the front row—pride of place— were two little boys who looked like the same child twice over. I'd always found identical twins fascinating, if a little creepy. These twin boys were cute, but I can't say they looked happy. Grim would be a better description: their little mouths set in identical lines. The only difference I could see between them was that one had extensive scarring on one arm.

'I've found some twins. Take a look at that,' I said, holding the photo out to Mitchell. 'Does it look like that kid's been burnt?'

'Yeah. I'd say so. Saw a lot of that in Afghanistan.' He squinted closely. 'Are there any names for the kids in the photo?'

I turned the photo over, but it was blank. 'No names, no date. So what's our next move?'

'Well, my next move is to analyse these documents. Unless you have a degree in property law, I don't need your help.'

After that putdown, I was only too happy to give Mitchell some peace and quiet. I reclaimed the Tim Tams from the fridge and went to have a bath. It had been a long and grimy day and I did some of my best thinking in the bath.

Since it was raining, I put some bubble bath in the steaming water; I wouldn't need to save the water for the pot plants. Melbourne's residents and their gardens were still scarred by the drought years. I barely remembered a time when people could water their gardens with impunity.

I lit a candle, switched off the light and pressed play on a portable CD player that was on the bench—my favourite Billie Holiday compilation. My voice, though adequate for back-up vocals, was too light for the intensity required to fully carry the Blues. 'Give it another decade,' Baz used to say. 'Sometimes a voice takes time, like a good whisky.'

Or a heroin habit, in Billie's case, and that seemed a pretty high price to pay. I removed Billie Holiday and looked around for something more cheery. My eyes fell on a meditation CD I'd found in Bunny's collection, a gift from her father in Byron Bay. It involved a woman whispering and the sound of waves in the background, which sounds creepy but was strangely soothing. I put in the CD and pressed play before sinking into the bath. The hot water was a welcome relief to my muscles, still recovering from the rope-climbing episode.

I was also exhausted due to disrupted sleep. I'd had night terrors my whole life, but they worsened during periods of stress. The dreams were confusing collages of places that were strange and yet familiar—and people whose faces were blurred when I tried to look too closely. I didn't need to see a specialist to know that the dreams were probably due to my early childhood—the time before I was adopted by Baz.

In general I had a good memory; it was probably how I made it through Year 12. When it came to my past, however, my memories were blurry, as if viewed through water on a windowpane. And some parts of my early life were blank altogether, like I'd shut them behind a solid door. I didn't know if these memories were gone forever or if they were buried somewhere inside my head.

I took a deep breath and searched for my earliest memory of Baz. I had the sensation of being pulled into a river: submerging, losing breath, feeling pressure around me and something moving—a current carrying me. Then I saw myself as if from above. I was no longer in the bath, instead

I was a child again and I was sitting on the couch—the same couch Baz still had in his flat. I was sitting next to a woman.

There was a tugging sensation and I found myself pulled down into my child self. I became aware of the sounds around me. The woman next to me was weeping. I looked at the photo of Lionel Rose—his arms raised in the ecstasy and exhaustion of victory—then I looked back at the woman next to me. I could see the delicate swirl of her ear, adorned with a pearl stud earring. I could feel the woman's anxiety. It came off her like waves, like radio static. A man came into the room with a plate of biscuits. He gave me one. It was pink like my dress and I tried to eat it quietly; I didn't want the man to notice the crumbs in case he got angry. This man didn't get angry, though. He was nice. He didn't ask me to speak. He gave me another biscuit. My adult self recognised the man as Baz, and a wave of warmth washed over me ... and then I was back in the bath.

A bump on the window roused me from my reverie. I looked at the window, expecting to see the outline of one of the cats, but instead I saw a shadow that was way bigger. In under five seconds I was out of the bath and in the loungeroom—just enough time to grab a towel to preserve my modesty.

Mitchell had been joined by Timmy and they both looked somewhat stunned at my sudden and wet appearance.

'Am I interrupting something?' Timmy asked.

'I think I just saw someone out in the garden. Was it you?' I asked, wishing I were the kind of person who kept a bathrobe handy.

'Uh, no. I've been in here about ten minutes. I was wondering what Mitch Mitchell was doing in your lounge room.'

Cripes, even Timmy knew who Mitchell was. I didn't realise I'd been so far out of the loop.

'Yeah, we were thinking of ordering pizza,' Mitchell said.

'Did you just hear what I said?' I asked, outraged that these men were more interested in pizza than in protecting a defenceless—and some would say attractive—woman who was dressed in only a towel. A small towel at that.

'Are you sure you saw someone?' asked Timmy. 'It's pretty dark out there.'

'No, I'm not sure. But it would be nice if one of you men were concerned enough to check it out.' My tone conveyed that their status as 'men' was in doubt.

Mitchell didn't look about to budge, so Timmy decided to assert his manhood. Our garden's not that big so it only took him about thirty seconds.

'I can't see anyone. It must have been Head-butt, he's butted the side gate open again,' he said as he returned. 'Man, it's freezing out there.'

The cold blast of air reminded me that I was soaking wet and wearing only a towel.

Mitchell was looking at me as though he didn't need reminding. I retreated to my bedroom and hastily pulled on a tracksuit. When I returned to the lounge room, Timmy was on the phone ordering pizza.

Timmy and food. You'd think he was still growing. I was often just tucking into dinner when I'd look up and find him staring in pitifully through the glass door like one of the cats. Actually, the cats don't so much look pitiful as accusatory. I'm not sure why that is, but it may be because they're basically just mini psychopaths with fur. Head-butt's the exception to the rule, but only because he's so stupid.

Over pizza and beer, Mitchell and I gave Timmy an abridged version of our adventures. I said I was helping Mitchell with a story he was researching—mostly the truth. Mitchell also seemed happy to keep Timmy in the dark, and Timmy, bless him, was a trusting soul.

'So you're looking for these twins now they're grown up?'

'They could potentially help us, yes,' said Mitchell.

'I have some software that might be useful. It's one of those freeware apps, just for messing around. You put in a photo of a kid and you're supposed to be able to see what they'd look like grown up.'

Mitchell and I looked at each other.

'It could be worth a shot,' he said.

Timmy looked pleased to have been given a project by Mitchell and darted out the back door to his den with half a pizza under his arm. I was left alone with Mitchell, wondering if I should offer to call him a taxi, but then I gave in to the same urge that let Head-butt get a paw in the door.

'You can stay in my housemate's room if you like. She's overseas. Just don't touch the aquarium. There's a snake in there.'

'Uh, thanks.' Mitchell was begrudging in his gratitude. 'I was a bit afraid of taking all this stuff home. Someone broke in the other day and turned the place upside down.'

'Doesn't that make you concerned for yourself?'

'No. It only confirms that I'm onto something. And I take my laptop with me everywhere, so I didn't lose anything. But I'd hate to lose Margaret's files.'

'Well *I'm* worried ... I'm worried about what it means for my uncle.'

'How is Baz your uncle? Through your mum or your dad?'

Just when I was feeling a bit sorry for him, I remembered he was a journalist with a different agenda from my own. 'He's my uncle through both sides if you must know,' I lied. 'We're all inbred, like the royal family. Why did you come back to Australia? I gather war zones are your speciality. Was it a woman? You don't strike me as the type.'

Mitchell gave a rare smile. 'Are you trying to ask if I'm gay or single?'

Before I could think of a witty—and slightly sexy—comeback, Timmy came bursting back in.

'Am I interrupting?'

'No, you're not interrupting,' I sighed. 'What are you, a stuck record?'

'What's a stuck record?'

I went and flicked on the kettle on again. How could Timmy make me feel so old? There was less than a decade between our ages.

'I take it you've got something,' said Mitchell.

Timmy handed Mitchell a few printouts. 'Well, I tested out the freeware app on a picture of me first and it wasn't too inaccurate—hairstyle aside—so I put in the picture of those twins and this is what I got.'

I looked over Mitchell's shoulder. The black and white images looked somewhat like a police photofit.

'Thanks, Timmy,' I said. I could see by his excited-puppy stance that he was just dying for a pat on the head.

'Yeah, thanks, man.' And of course, a pat on the head by a man was worth more than anything I could offer.

'I can't say I recognise them immediately,' said Mitchell. 'Although there is something slightly familiar. I'll have to check through my files and do some comparisons.'

'Maybe we should do an internet search for any newspaper stories about reunited twins,' I suggested. 'If they were put up for adoption then they could have been split up as children. People love stories of twins being reunited.'

Mitchell looked at me through narrowed eyes. 'That's actually a good idea.'

'I can do that!' said Timmy and he was back out the door to his caravan.

'He doesn't sleep at night,' I said. 'We may as well make use of him. I, on the other hand, need my beauty sleep.'

There was a moment of weirdness between us. Or maybe my months of celibacy were clouding my ability to judge a situation. It had been some time since I'd been alone with a man late at night. And after all, Mitchell and I had just had pizza together—and some beer. It was almost like a date. Better than most dates with the average Australian male.

'I mean alone—I'm going to bed alone. I'm not hitting on you. Don't worry.'

'I didn't think you were.'

I should have shut up while I was ahead.

I went to bed and set my alarm for 5.30am. Mitchell was using me as a safe base for now, but he might do a midnight flit if he could find somewhere else to stay. Then I settled under the doona with my hot water bottle. It wasn't as hot as I'd like, but I hadn't wanted to go back into the kitchen to the kettle after making such an idiot of myself. I had to settle with water from the hot tap in the bathroom.

The rain outside was turning into a storm, the wind rattling the windows. Hopefully the bad weather would keep any potential housebreakers away. I was still worried that someone had been nosing around earlier.

Finally I resorted to an old paperback to put me to sleep—a copy of *Oliver Twist* that looked like a leftover from Bunny's school days. I was around a hundred pages in when I eventually dozed off, only to dream I was being pursued through the back streets of Fitzroy by a horde of ragged children with evil intentions.

As was the way of dreams, I ducked into an alleyway and their little feet went pattering past. I hoped the dream would end there, but for some reason I felt drawn to continue down the dark alleyway, which became narrower and narrower, and just as I decided I would turn around and run back into the light, I became aware of heavy footsteps. Someone was following me. I shrank into the shadows and saw the figure of a tall man approaching but I couldn't make out his face in the darkness.

I woke with a start to find it was five in the morning and I was desperate for the loo. I pulled a large jumper over my pyjama top, slipped my feet into my tattered ugg boots and ventured out into the corridor. The door to Bunny's room stood open and her semi-bald teddy bear mocked me from where it was perched on top of the pillows. The bed had not been slept in; I'd been right to suspect Mitchell would be out the door at the first opportunity. I should have rigged a fishing line trap at the front door to wake me up.

I braved the frigid bathroom and then decided to make myself a hot Milo. As I opened the door to the lounge/kitchen area I was hit by a wall of warm air. The heater was still on, as were all the lights, and there was Mitchell, asleep on the couch. Head-butt the cat was sprawled on his chest.

I picked up a half-empty packet of pills that was lying on the floor near the couch. It seemed I wasn't the only person having trouble getting a bit of shuteye. The pills were on prescription, too—the good stuff—made out to Muggerdich Mitchell. No wonder he called himself Mitch. I smiled and then I checked Mitchell was breathing before turning off the heater. There was no danger of him freezing with the cat on him, although Head-butt did have a drooling problem.

Mitchell actually looked quite sweet asleep. The frown lines that made him look overly serious, if not downright hostile, were softened. He looked less arrogant—even likeable. I made my cup of Milo and used it to swig down one of Mitch's pills. Then I turned out the lights and went back to bed for another forty winks.

The next thing I knew it was nine o'clock. I'd had three hours of dreamless sleep, but rather than feeling refreshed, it had left me fuzzy-headed and dry-mouthed. I stumbled to

the kitchen to find Mitchell frowning at the coffee percolator as it bubbled on the stove.

'Good morning.' I brushed past him to fill a glass with
water from the tap. I took the grunted reply to mean that he
wasn't a morning person.

I plonked the bread and Vegemite on the bench and
started making toast. 'What kind of a name is Muggerdich?'

'Armenian.' The percolator finished hissing and he poured
himself a short black. 'My mother was from Armenian
stock.'

'Sleep well?'

'I think your cat peed all over me.'

'It's drool, and it's not my cat. It just turned up here one
day and wouldn't leave. Help yourself to toast.'

Mitchell put a couple of slices of bread in the toaster.

'So, what's our next lead?' I asked. 'Find out anything last
night?'

'No, I get a feeling someone might have been through the
boxes before us and removed certain documents.'

'Maybe Timmy will come up with something,' I said.

'He was just in here. No luck.'

I wasn't really surprised. 'Those twins probably wouldn't
be able to help us in any case. They look pretty young in the
photo. Five years old at most.'

'You'd think they'd remember something about their
mother,' said Mitchell.

'They may have memory issues, especially if they've been
through a traumatic incident, like a fire.'

'You have a degree in child psychology, do you? Is that
why you're working in PR?'

I decided to ignore Mitchell and make myself a coffee since he hadn't been gracious enough to offer me any.

'Where would your uncle put something if he wanted to keep it safe?' Mitchell asked as if he hadn't just insulted me.

'In his office desk. But there was nothing much in there.' I didn't mention the wad of cash. 'And he still has an old safe from back when banking was more of a hassle. I think he still uses it to keep his rare 45s.'

'Well, let's go and take a look then,' said Mitchell. 'Can we get into it?'

'Sure, I have a key to Baz's place. But you might want to take a shower first—wash off the drool.'

* * *

I was nervous about going to Baz's flat again in case we found something awful, but it looked unchanged since my previous visit. Baz's safe was screwed into the floor in the linen cupboard. I didn't know the combination so I ran through the birth dates of various Bluesmen. Lead Belly did the trick—20-01-1888—although, like my own birthday, it's unlikely to be accurate. (Don't get Baz started on the subject of Lead Belly unless you've got a few hours to kill.)

Mitchell didn't look so much impressed as suspicious. 'This really is your uncle's place, isn't it? Is there a photo of the two of you around here somewhere?'

'What are you implying?'

'I'm just saying, you seem to know an awful lot about burglary.'

'A misspent youth,' I said as I pulled open the safe's door. 'And a bunch of dodgy ex-boyfriends. As well as being raised in a pub. I'm also deadly at pool, darts and accounting software.'

Inside the safe was a box of 45s, as predicted, but also some manila folders. Mitchell handed me them to look through and a quick flip revealed they were insurance papers and other boring documents.

'Why would these boxes of old photos be here?' He passed me a couple of pictures.

'That's Baz's mum—he hasn't got many photos of her, that's probably why they're in here. It's a fire safe.' In the picture, Baz's mum looked very young, her dark hair styled in a 1940s Veronica Lake wave, her light eyes smiling as she held an old-style microphone. It looked like a publicity shot from her singing career.

'Is that Robert Johnson?' Mitchell showed me a faded black and white card featuring a dapper-looking hepcat with a saxophone.

'No, that's Baz's dad. He does look a bit like Robert Johnson, now you mention it.'

'Do you recognise this couple at all?' Michell held out a picture of a man and a woman. They were sitting at a table in the Phoenix, but they were looking at each other, rather than at the camera. I recognised the woman.

'I *have* seen her before. When I came by here the other day, there was a box of photos out on the coffee table and there were some pictures of her in it. She was singing with a band. It was labelled Betty Jones, 1962.'

'Here's another one of her holding a baby—a blonde baby.'

I looked at the photo of the blonde woman smiling down at a chubby infant. 'It's only one baby, not twins.'

'Take a closer look. This photo has been cut in half and look at that—another child's foot there, so the kid could be one of a pair.' Mitchell continued nosing through the safe. 'Let's check these negs too, there could be something among them. Hopefully they're not skin flicks.' He pulled out several packets of film negatives and held them up to the light. 'I'd almost forgotten what negatives looked like in this digital age.'

I took the negatives and had a look myself. 'It's just a bunch of guys having a jam session.'

Mitchell thrust another photo under my nose. 'Who's this?'

It took a moment for me to focus and then I felt like the air had been sucked from my lungs. 'That's me!' I grabbed the photo for a closer look. It was definitely a photo of me as a child. I was sitting at the bar of the Phoenix with a glass of what looked like lemonade. Next to me was a pretty young woman who I didn't immediately recognise.

I had never seen this photo before and yet Baz had it stashed away in his safe. Why hadn't he shown it to me? I realised that my heart was beating very fast and loud. I turned over the photo to read Baz's written notation. *Brick and Nora, 1991*. My blood was causing a rushing sound in my ears. I knew at once that this Nora was the woman from my dream. The woman in the high-heeled shoes.

I realised my breath was coming in pants and I thought I was going to vomit. Then my vision faded out.

CHAPTER FIFTEEN

I opened my eyes to find I was lying on the floor in the
corridor with a cushion under my head. For a moment I just
stared at the ceiling. The paint was discoloured and peeling.
Like the Phoenix, Baz's flat was in need of a spruce up.

I became aware of Mitch sitting next to me. He was fan-
ning me with a manila folder, but when I tried to sit up,
I felt dizzy again. I lay back down and kept breathing as
deeply as possible.

'Just stay there for a minute,' said Mitchell. 'You can't fall
lower than the floor.'

Ain't that the truth, I thought, as I ran my hands over my
face. My forehead was damp with sweat, although Baz's flat
wasn't in any way warm.

'Do you want a cup of tea?' asked Mitchell. 'Or something stronger?'

I tried blinking my eyes to see if it would make me feel more alert. 'There's some bourbon in the kitchen.'

He held up a mug. 'What you think I'm drinking?'

I leveraged myself gingerly up into a sitting position and Mitchell helped me take the two steps into the living room where he deposited me on the couch. Then he went into the kitchen and returned with another mug of bourbon.

'This'll fix you up.'

I doubted it, but I took a big swallow anyway and relished the burning in the back of my throat.

'I was going to ask whether you could be pregnant—but the way you're necking that down makes me think it was something else.'

'There's no getting anything past you.'

'Do you want to talk about it?'

'With a journalist who's mixing prescription drugs with alcohol at ten in the morning? Are you kidding me?' I took another mouthful.

Mitchell left me to my mug for a minute while he continued looking through some papers. 'Looky here,' he said, removing a document from the sheaf. 'I think it's your uncle's will.' He squinted at it more closely. 'Congratulations, you're getting the record collection. That could be worth a few bob.'

'I don't think my uncle's will is any of your business.' I tried to grab the document but he stood up, out of reach.

'But he's not leaving you the Phoenix, I see.' He handed me the will and disappeared back into the kitchen.

My eyes were slow to focus, but then I could see it there in black and white: *I leave the Phoenix to Delilah Russell, if she is still living and can be found, or any children or grandchildren that she may have, if she is no longer living.*

The ringing in my ears was back, along with the dizziness and nausea. 'Who the fuck is this Delilah Russell?' My voice came out as a croak.

'I don't know.' Mitchell had returned from the kitchen with the bourbon bottle. 'But your uncle also has her birth certificate in his safe.'

He handed me another document. It was indeed a birth certificate for a Delilah Russell. Born to a Daphne Russell in Melbourne in 1960. No father named.

'It looks to me like your uncle may have had a daughter,' said Mitchell. 'I assume by your rather extreme reaction that you didn't know.'

I shook my head and accepted another hit of bourbon. In 1960 Baz would have been still in his teens—but of course, that was old enough to father a child. If he did have a daughter born in 1960, where was she now? Was that the real reason he was going through the records of St Bernadette's? Why had he never told me about her? And why was he leaving her the Phoenix?

I looked back at the will, scanning further down the paragraphs. *And if Delilah is dead and has no living issue, then I leave the Phoenix to Beloved 'Brick' Brown, formerly known as Brick Lane.* The words stung. Baz knew how much the Phoenix meant to me, but he'd never told me about his will.

I turned away so Mitchell wouldn't see my face.

'Brick Lane, hey? That makes more sense. You gotta love parents with a wacky sense of humour.'

Suddenly I didn't care what Mitchell thought any more. 'My parents didn't name me Brick Lane. It was a sick joke by a social worker, most likely. Brick Lane is where I was dumped as a baby. My parents abandoned me. They were probably junkies.'

Mitchell seemed speechless for once, then his expression softened. 'It could have been an admin error. Never attribute to malice that which can be adequately explained by stupidity. You already found out about my real name. And I'd managed to keep that one under wraps for years.'

I sipped my drink silently and let Mitchell keep talking.

'My parents were going to name me Darren, for reasons unknown. But my dad buggered off from the hospital and went straight to the pub to get royally pissed, leaving Mum getting stitches after a two-day labour. As a result, my mother decided she should have full naming rights and she called me after her favourite grandfather. It was the beginning of the end for their short but shitty marriage.'

I think the bourbon had begun to work its magic. I tried to imagine how Mitchell's life would have panned out as a Darren. 'That makes me feel a little better.'

'Glad to be of service.' He patted my hand. 'And in other good news, there's nothing here that looks like it came from Sister Margaret's stash, so your uncle's in the clear as far as stealing documents from a former nun who stole them from a convent. Bad news is we need to go back to the storage unit for a more thorough look.'

Strangely the thought of a defined task—even a boring one—cheered me up.

'I can drive your car if you're still a bit wobbly,' Mitchell offered. 'I'm only slightly drunk.'

'It's not my car—it belongs to council,' I said after finishing my bourbon. 'And if we get stopped by police, I'm going to say you stole it.'

We arrived at the self-storage facility to find Serge's wife was on duty, wearing even more bling than her husband. Judging by the jewellery on her right hand alone (which looked like it could finance a Rolling Stones tour) people were hanging onto way too much stuff these days. We unlocked the padlock to Margaret's storage bay and the roller door rumbled as Mitchell lifted it up.

'You start on that pile and I'll start over here.' Mitchell was no longer as relaxed as earlier and I wondered if it was the storage facility's lack of windows affecting his mood.

'How am I suddenly your lackey?'

'Investigative journalism is about research. If you want to find your uncle, then you'll help me out.'

'What exactly am I looking for?'

'I'll look for anything relating to board business. How about you look for any files relating to kids who could be twins. I'm still curious as to who your uncle was looking for and whether it has anything to do with his alleged disappearance.'

* * *

Five hours later and I wished I'd thought to bring a chair with me. My hands were filthy from handling dusty boxes and my knees were bruised from kneeling on the concrete floor while I thumbed through a million ancient files, looking for kids with the same surname. There were a surprising number of kids with the same or similar surnames—but none of them also had the same birth dates.

After two hours I'd popped out to get us both a coffee—double shots to keep us awake—but it didn't make the afternoon any more bearable. It was six o'clock before we'd made it through the whole lot and we had nothing to show for it but filthy hands and clothes and a few paper cuts. The dust had also given me a runny nose.

We stopped at a takeaway pizza joint on the way home and Mitchell bought a six-pack from a nearby bottle shop. We each cracked one open while we sat on the edge of the bluestone gutter and waited for our order to be ready. It had been a strange day and it was jarring to see people going about their normal lives as if they didn't have a care in the world. The pizza joint had a gelato counter and a father was negotiating cones for three little girls ranging in size from small to tiny.

'I've got to say I've had more fun afternoons,' I said, taking a sip of beer.

'Not all leads pan out but the secret is not to be deterred.'

'So, what's next?'

'I'm still curious to know who used to own that building next to your uncle's club. The one where Gene has his shop.'

'Can't Gene tell you?'

'Believe me, I've asked him multiple times and either he doesn't know or he isn't telling.'

I was glad to hear I wasn't the only person who had trouble getting information out of Gene. 'How did you even meet Gene in the first place?'

Mitchell finished his can of beer and cracked another one. 'I used to collect records when I was younger but I gave up when my mum died. I was living out of suitcase for years and had nowhere to store any stuff.'

It made sense to me that Mitchell had been a music collector. They were usually intense, driven individuals. But I'd never met a collector who'd kicked the habit before. 'Why did you come back to Melbourne?'

Mitchell looked uncomfortable. 'Bloody HR got into my managing editor's ear after the Afghanistan incident and insisted that I take a break. Occupational Health and Safety bullshit.'

'Is this what you consider taking a break? We are literally sitting in a gutter drinking cans of Melbourne Bitter. I hear some people like to sit by a pool and drink cocktails.'

Mitchell rubbed his eyes. 'My father died while I was in Afghanistan. I couldn't make it back for the funeral, on account of being held hostage. But this "break" from work gave me a chance to come back and sort out his flat, and all that stuff.'

I watched the young father doling out ice-cream cones to his daughters. 'Were you and your dad close?'

'We'd just started getting closer. My parents divorced when I was a baby, like I said, and I hardly ever saw my dad after that. He was an old-school newspaperman—if he wasn't at work, he was at the pub.'

'Is that why you became a journalist? Because of him?'

'In a way, I guess. At first I wanted to show him I could be a better journalist—a foreign correspondent and not some shitty hack who worked for the same newspaper for thirty years. But that's when we reconnected. He would email me, commenting on articles I'd had published, and after my mum died we starting talking on the phone every week. He was a nice guy, really. Just a shit husband.'

Mitchell pulled a packet from his pocket, lit a cigarette and took a drag. 'He was working on a major investigation piece before he died. It was an investigation of Dave Mullett.'

A cold prickle ran down my spine. 'How did your dad die?'

Mitch paused again, his shoulders stiff. 'He was killed in a hit and run. They never caught the driver. The car had been stolen and was found burnt out.'

I thought of the man in black who'd tried to bundle Mitchell into the boot of his car. 'Do you think it was an accident?'

Mitchell turned back to me. His eyes were the colour of Coca-Cola. 'No, I don't think it was an accident. Not long before he died, Dad told me he'd found a source who had some iron-clad, documented proof of illegal dealings between Mullett and all three levels of government. But when I went to pack up his flat, his computer's hard drive had been removed and all his notebooks were gone. Not just the recent notebooks—all of them.'

'Did he have a back-up copy of anything? What about his editor at his newspaper?'

Mitchell laughed, but not in a happy way. 'After more than thirty years working there, Dad had been forced take a redundancy. The newspaper had changed hands and the new bosses said he had to either retire or go to the subs desk. Newspapers are dying a death by a thousand cuts. Dad was going freelance on this one—his final story and a "fuck you" to the newspaper's new owners.'

'Did he tell anyone who gave him the information about Mullett?'

'No. If Dad's source had told him to keep it confidential, he would never have betrayed that trust. Like I said, he was old school.'

'When you say source, what do you mean?'

'A whistleblower, an informant of some kind. Possibly someone working for Mullett or working for government. Maybe even someone who knew him a long time ago.'

It suddenly occurred to me why Mitchell was interested in helping me find Baz. 'You think it might have been my uncle?'

'Your uncle lived in the same neighbourhood as Mullett in the 1960s. Both had football connections. I believe Mullett knew the man who owned the Phoenix prior to Baz. Mullett and Baz may well have known each other.'

'Why didn't you tell me this earlier?' I'd thought Mitchell was using me for cheap labour and a place to set up office; I hadn't realised he was actually using me to get information on my uncle. Any sympathy I'd begun to feel for him disappeared as quickly as a band's complimentary drinks rider.

'I thought you were just humouring me and now you're confirming that my uncle may be in serious danger?' My voice was rising in an alarming fashion, but I didn't seem to be able to control it. 'Because if something bad has happened to Baz, I don't know what ... I don't know how ...' I hadn't stuttered for years now, but I could feel that I was going to if I kept speaking.

Mitchell put down his beer, leaned over and gripped my shoulders. For a moment I thought he was going to shake me. 'I don't know anything at this point. I could be totally wrong. I am probably totally wrong. Maybe I do just need to bugger off to Bali and drink myself into a stupor.'

I looked back at the gelato bar. The littlest girl had just dropped her ice cream and a wail was forming. 'I don't think Baz was your father's source, Mitchell, but I have met someone who says they've been keeping information about dodgy developers for years. Decades, even.'

I told him about my recent encounter with Otto Weber and how he'd mentioned that he'd been collecting a dirt file on the mayor and other characters.

Mitchell sobered up immediately. 'Where does this Otto character keep this information? At his house?'

I chewed the inside of my lip, wondering if I was betraying Otto's trust by confiding in Mitchell. 'He used to be a councillor. He told me he'd hidden some documents in the council's archive department, but who knows if they'll still be there. Anyone could have removed them.'

'You work at the council, or so you've led me to believe. Do you reckon you could get us into this archive department?'

With the tone he was using, I didn't think it was a good time to tell him about my previous break and enter. 'Maybe I could get us in there.'

Mitchell crunched up his empty beer can and threw it at a bin, narrowly missing one of the little girls, who was leaving the gelato bar with a fresh ice-cream cone. Her father shot us a dirty look.

'I'll grab the pizza. We can eat on the way.'

CHAPTER SIXTEEN

By night the council building loomed in splendour under artful lighting, like the Acropolis. I didn't dare park in the loading zone. There was definitely CCTV outside the building and I didn't want Eve to find out I'd been driving the pool car after hours. I parked two blocks away and we walked back, trying to look like we were just out for a casual stroll. As we reached the building, I wrapped a scarf around my head while Mitchell made do with a hoodie pulled low over his face.

It had occurred to me that it might be a dumb idea to use my own swipe card to enter the building, so I tried the one I'd found in the toilets. Either Eve didn't know it was missing or she hadn't reported it yet, because the door clicked open.

'There might be some cleaners around, so we'd better look like we belong here,' I said. 'The archive department is on the third floor.'

We took the stairs in case the lift had CCTV. When we got to the third floor, Mitchell assessed the door. 'That's an old-school lock—the swipe card's not going to work.'

'Not a problem.' I took out my lock-pick kit and put my pen torch in my mouth. But just as I was about to set to work, Mitchell grabbed my hand.

'Are you sure you want to go ahead with this?' he asked. 'We are kind of crossing a line here.'

'I won't tell if you don't.'

A few seconds of manipulation and the door clicked open. The room was fluoro-lit and as ugly as I remembered it from my previous visit.

'God, it smells like something died in here! There must be a rat problem.'

It did smell, but not as badly as I'd expected.

'And the lights are on,' said Mitchell. 'Is that normal?'

'I think they're always on,' I said. 'So much for green initiatives. Or maybe it's to keep the burglars away.'

We closed the door behind us and assessed the vast sea of shelves, each one stuffed with box files in varying shades of dirty yellow.

'All he said was that he'd labelled his boxes with a green sticker with an X drawn on it,' I said. 'Although I warn you, he is a bit confused due to his injury. So this could be a wild goose chase.'

'You start over there and I'll start here,' said Mitchell, pointing.

I trudged down the alphabet. I'd spent the whole day elbow deep in files. This was obvious karmic payback for not doing any of my own filing since I started work at council. Or maybe it was karmic payback for deserting the mayor's body when I found him. Then an idea occurred to me. While I was here, I may as well have a little look for any file relating to the Phoenix, as was my original plan when I accidentally found the mayor.

I knew the lot number, so I walked along a shelf that was in a vague numerical order. I could see what Otto meant about the archive department being an absolute dump. Boxes at the bottom of shelves were collapsing under the weight of things stacked on top of them. Some boxes looked like they'd disintegrate at the slightest touch.

I made my way deep into an aisle and found a shelf of boxes labelled with lot numbers. Things weren't exactly in order, but suddenly there in front of me was a box file labelled *Lot 20 Fitzroy* and below it in brackets *(The Phoenix Hotel)*.

I turned and looked for Mitchell, but he was nowhere to be seen. I removed the box from the shelf as quietly as possible. Then I exited the archive room and took the box down the stairs to the second floor, where I shoved it deep under my desk.

I was about to head back to the archive department when I noticed that the door to Eve's office was ajar. Perhaps the

cleaners had left it open. Gingerly, I nudged the door with
my toe and it swung open slowly to reveal the world's most
pathologically orderly office. Eve's monitor was dark and
her desk was bare, apart from a framed photo of Eve and
Gail, possibly taken at a Christmas party—I have to say
that Gail looked very drunk. I couldn't resist some further
exploration. I walked over to her desk and opened a drawer
to find it was similarly barren. Then I noticed a tray on
the top of the filing cabinet. The manila folder lying there
caught my attention, since it had my name on it. Inside was
my job application, my interview assessment, my terms of
employment. But lastly in the folder was a memo from Gail.
It was an official warning. Due to my transient lifestyle I
always used the Phoenix as my postal address, so if they'd
posted it to me, I hadn't received it yet. It accused me of
leaking sensitive information to a member of the media in a
deliberate attempt to embarrass the council. Gail must have
finally read the email about the parking inspector profile
piece.

The news was strangely shocking. I knew Gail didn't like
me, but I didn't think she'd try and fire me. I felt my lip
tremble, even though it was a crappy PR job working for a
crappy council.

I dropped the folder back in the tray and returned to the
archives department. I could hear Mitch moving and opening boxes. Perhaps he was opening every box, shelf by shelf.
It would take all night at this rate. A better strategy would
be to try and think like Otto.

I considered the scant facts. I knew that Otto loved the
North Melbourne Football Club, so I checked under A for

Arden Street. No luck. Then I remembered what Otto had said during our brief phone conversation about *The X-Files*. I headed down the stacks to the end of the alphabet.

The Xs, once I found them, were actually larger than I'd anticipated. It was obviously the dumping ground for everything that defied category. And in council business, there was a lot that defied belief, let alone categorisation.

Then a flash of green caught my eye. There was a box with a small green dot sticker, and the sticker had an X scribbled at its centre. I opened the box up and pulled out a wad of papers, and was just about to examine them more closely when a prickly sensation came over me. I put down the box as quietly as possible and tiptoed towards the next row of stacks. Just as I exited the row, the shelves fell behind me with an ear-splitting crash. I froze, heart thumping. Was Mitchell trying to kill me? Or was someone else here? I crouched down low and made my way up past the aisles, peering into each one.

I found Mitchell in H–J. Either he'd decided to have a snooze or he'd been hit on the head with a blunt object. I knelt down for a better look, now certain we were not alone. There was no blood, but Mitchell was lying in a pool of drool rivalling anything Head-butt could produce.

'Mitchell!' I hissed, giving him a shake. I didn't think he could have been bashed to death without me hearing anything, and sure enough, he let out a guttural 'mfff'. Then I heard movement behind another stack.

It must be true what they say about fear giving you extra strength, because within five seconds I'd managed to pull Mitchell to his feet and push him towards the emergency exit. We fell through the metal door onto the fire escape and immediately a fire alarm began blaring. The ear-splitting racket seemed to trigger Mitchell into action—maybe it was his war correspondent training. He set off down the fire escape stairs at speed.

When we reached the bottom of the fire escape I looked up to the door through which we'd emerged. No one had followed us. Maybe the alarm had scared them away, or maybe it was the sirens I could hear approaching. Mitchell and I needed to get away quickly or we were going to have some explaining to do.

I looked down at my hands, surprised to see that I was still clenching the few papers that I'd been holding when the shelf nearly squashed me. I shoved them in my coat pocket just as a beat-up Kombi screeched to stop on the curb in front of us and a woman yelled, 'Get in!'

I made a split-second assessment that Mullett's goons wouldn't have traded their Mercedes for such a pile-of-shit van, so I shoved Mitchell aboard and climbed in as well.

'Drive it like you stole it!' I yelled, sliding the door shut behind us with a bang.

'I did steal it,' the woman said as she took off.

Luckily for me, Mitchell cushioned my impact as I was thrown across the vehicle. He barely seemed to notice, having possibly passed out again. Probably a blessing because the woman was driving like a maniac. I sat up to get a better look at her. It was Mavis DuBois, minus her beautiful hair. She now had a short spiky do that looked like a home job. She wasn't wearing make-up. Not even mascara.

'Mavis. What are you doing here?' I asked as I clutched the back of the driver's seat for safety.

'I need to talk to Mitch Mitchell, but he's a hard man to track down.'

I looked back at Mitchell. He was sprawled half off the seat. 'I think he's incapable of speech right now. He may even be unconscious.'

'Well, I'm not taking you to hospital,' said Mavis. 'It's not safe.'

'You'd better take us to my place then,' I said. 'If he gets any worse I'll call an ambulance.' I gave her my address.

Mitchell was still drooling a bit by the time we reached North Fitzroy but had at least regained enough muscle control to stand as we exited the van.

'I'll be in touch,' Mavis said. Then she drove away before I could ask what the fuck was going on.

As I unlocked the front door, I could hear the television and guessed that Timmy must be in the lounge room. Mitchell managed to stagger through the door, although he still needed support.

'I'll put you in Bunny's room,' I said, not wanting to explain Mitchell's ragged state to Timmy. I steered him through her bedroom door and pushed him unceremoniously onto the bed.

'Let me get your shoes off before you mess up the cover.' I started tugging off a boot while Mitchell continued making bizarre groaning noises—probably a complaint of some kind. I ignored it.

'What's going on here?' asked a woman's voice from behind me. 'Why is my bedroom better than yours?'

'Bunny! You're back!' I was relieved and embarrassed at the same time to see my friend and landlady standing in the doorway.

Bunny was looking very unimpressed. 'I got evacuated. The civil war escalated.'

'I hadn't heard.' I dropped one of Mitchell's boots on the floor. 'I've been a bit busy.'

'I can see.'

'Actually, it's a good thing you're here. This is Mitch Mitchell, and he's had some kind of—' I paused to think of the right word, '—turn. Could you maybe take a look at him?'

'He looks familiar,' she said, peering at his pale and sweaty face.

'Yeah, he's been on TV apparently.'

'And what have you done to him?'

'I haven't done anything. We were—' I was unsure how to explain. 'Mitchell's a journalist and I've been helping him research a piece he's writing about council. But you know how psycho people can get about council stuff. It seems that someone attacked him. I'm not sure if he got hit on the head or what. I just found him on the ground drooling and shaking and I haven't been able to understand a word he's said since. Except the occasional "fuck".'

Mitchell obliged me with a demonstration. 'Fuck!'

'Let me have a look.' Bunny peered in his eyes and ran her hands over his head. 'I can't find any bleeding. He actually looks like he's had an electric shock.'

This seemed to strike a chord with Mitchell, who began making ape-like grunts.

'I think he's agreeing,' I said.

'Could it have been a cattle prod or something like that?' Bunny asked. 'Or a taser? Were there police involved?'

'Not that I noticed. I didn't actually see it happen.'

'Well, I'd say it was a taser. He's probably got a mark on him somewhere.'

She tugged up his shirt and started checking his torso, ignoring his outraged spluttering, which got worse when she undid his jeans and pulled them down.

'There you go. There's the mark,' she said, pointing at his left buttock.

Sure enough, there were two red marks—but otherwise he was in good shape, I noticed.

'He should be okay in an hour or so, as long as he doesn't have a heart condition. If he has a heart condition he could die at any moment. Do you have a heart condition?' she asked, leaning close to his face.

'N-ughrgh,' said Mitchell.

'I think that was a no,' she said. 'Some sugary tea wouldn't be a bad idea. I suppose you can leave him here for the time being.'

'We'll get you some tea, Mitchell. Try and rest.' I was shouting at him as if he'd suddenly gone deaf. I don't know why.

Bunny and I retreated to the kitchen, where she crossed her arms and gave me her stern doctor look. For a tiny woman with a pixie haircut, she could be surprisingly scary.

'So what's the story with this guy?'

'No story. It's just professional. Doing my job,' I said, unwilling to meet her eye. There was usually no fooling Bunny.

'He's a bit sexy, bit scuzzy looking, nice bum. Definitely your type, I'd say. So how's the celibacy going for you?'

I tried to look outraged. 'There have been no shenanigans, I'll have you know, no funny business—not even flirting. So how was Ethiopia?'

'It was Somalia and it was busy. There was a measles outbreak in one of the camps so we had babies dying all over the place.' Bunny took a gulp of white wine from a glass the size of a goldfish bowl. 'Drink? I stocked up at the duty free.' I took this to mean she wasn't ready to discuss it in any more detail yet.

'Don't mind if I do,' I said, accepting an equally huge glass and drinking about half of it before remembered I was supposed to be making a cup of tea for Mitchell. I hastily put the kettle on.

'I can sleep on the couch if you want to leave your friend there,' said Bunny. 'He *is* looking a bit rough.'

'Thanks, Bunny. I don't think he's had much sleep lately. He's one of those driven types. But you sleep in my bed—you must be stuffed after your flight. I'll sleep on the couch.'

Fortified by the wine, I gave Bunny a run-down on the last few days' events—minus all the break-and-enters.

'So you're telling me that Dave Mullett is building a giant block of flats next to Baz's club and you think Baz has either been kidnapped or gone AWOL? Don't you think that's odd?'

'Very.' I refilled my glass. 'But Baz can be odd at times. He never mentioned he was looking for this old girlfriend.' I wasn't ready to tell Bunny about the possibility Baz was also looking for a daughter. 'Oh shit, I forgot.' I delivered Mitchell a cup of tea, but he had fallen asleep. I stopped briefly to check he was breathing normally.

Then I remembered the papers I'd shoved in my pocket. I took them out and laid them on the coffee table while Bunny poured more wine. There were various printed documents, along with some press clippings.

'Hey, I think that's an old picture of Dave Mullett,' said Bunny, picking up a clipping to take a closer look. To me the man in the photo looked like any nondescript white man in a bad 1970s suit. The caption read: *Businessman Dickie Ruffhead and Dave Mullett with his sons John and Ron.* The boys looked identical—except for a scar on Ron's arm.

I felt like a stone had dropped in my stomach. Were these the same boys from the orphanage? Had Mullett adopted them? It was the only explanation.

Bunny's jet lag kicked in and she staggered off to my bedroom to lie down. I couldn't see sleep coming easily myself, so I ran a warm bath and lit a candle.

As I soaked in the dim light, my mind kept returning to the photos of children from the orphanage. Rows and rows of children who'd been abandoned for one reason or another.

I'd once watched a documentary about the Foundling Museum in London. It was the former site of a charity home that raised babies who were dumped on its doorstep, a service created by demand: thousands of children were abandoned every year. If I'd been born in 1800s London, my foundling status would have been startlingly mundane.

The Foundling Hospital in London was practical, at least. If the mothers left an identifying item with their baby, they could come back and reclaim the child should circumstances allow. These 'foundling tokens' were catalogued and some survive to this day: a ribbon, a ring, a key, a button, a walnut shell. I'm sure most of the mothers had no real hope of reunion, but the tokens were a way to leave the child with something of their mother, some tiny scrap. But the tokens were never given to the children. Like me, they'd been left with no clue of their origins; no memento of motherlove.

At times I wondered what would have happened to me without Baz. With the advent of birth control and the single mother's pension, Australia's orphanages started running out of children. By the mid-1980s, the children's homes were all closed and foster care was the preferred way to deal with wards of the state.

It was rare in Australia these days for children to be abandoned anonymously, but my mother had done it to me.

I didn't usually dwell on a woman I was probably never going to meet. And who knows? She could have been just a girl when she left me on the street. I'm sure she had her reasons.

After my bath I took out the photo we'd found in Baz's safe, the one of me with Nora. She was young, late twenties maybe—about the same age as me now—and really quite beautiful, with delicate features and large, dark eyes. She had her hand on my head in a motherly fashion, a glass of beer and a cigarette in the other hand and a shy smile for the camera. She wore pearl stud earrings.

I was certain she was the woman I'd been with the first time I met Baz, when he'd fed me biscuits while she wept. This sad-eyed woman had bought me the pink dress—a new pink dress. She'd loaded my hair with conditioner and carefully removed the tangles with a comb. She'd read me picture books and played dolls with me. She'd loved me … and then she was gone.

I don't know how Baz organised the paperwork; we'd never discussed it. I realised a few years ago that he'd forged parts of it. He may well have paid someone under the table or done a favour for a mate with connections, but he took me in when Nora died and social services never bothered me again.

CHAPTER SEVENTEEN

It was several hours before I checked on Mitchell. He was now lying on his back, one arm flung out across the bed and the other folded over his chest. I took a blanket from the foot of the bed and was about to lay it over him when I realised his eyes had opened and he was watching me. I fought the urge to sit on the side of the bed and smooth his hair out of his eyes.

'How are you feeling?' I asked.

'I've felt better, that's for sure.'

I fetched him a fresh cup of sugary tea and the photo of Mullett from the file. I'm not sure which had more effect, but he sharpened up quickly.

'Where did you get this?'

'From a box in the archive room.'

He looked like a kid in a candy shop. 'Are you sure it's from your friend Otto's collection?'

'I presume so, but no idea really.'

'And this Otto character had an accident recently, you said?'

'He fell off his roof.' An awful thought rose in my mind. 'Do you think it's possible it wasn't an accident?'

'Extremely possible.'

'His daughter did wonder how he managed to get onto his roof in the first place.'

'It's possible he didn't fall off his roof at all.'

'There was a ladder, his daughter saw it. Although neither she nor Otto knew that he had a ladder.'

'Then whoever hurt Otto provided the ladder, which proves premeditation.'

'Is Otto still in danger then?' I asked, a cold shiver of fear prickling my skin. Otto was a sitting duck if anyone wanted to break into his house and kill him. It would be like *Rear Window* when the killer throws Jimmy Stewart out of his wheelchair, then out the window.

'I think they'd have finished the job by now if they were going to. But it definitely indicates that something rotten is going on at your council.'

'Of course something rotten's going on there. It's a council.'

Mitchell ignored me. 'I can't help feeling the mayor's death has some bearing on all this.'

'Do you think someone killed him and made it look like a heart attack?' I asked. 'Is that even possible?'

'No, Dickie was a heart attack waiting to happen. I'm surprised it didn't happen sooner. But there are a lot of people who are interested in taking his place as mayor.'

I remembered Mitchell's reaction to Hugo Clark at the council meeting. 'You think Hugo Clark wants to be the next mayor? Do you think he's dodgy like Ruffhead? I couldn't help noticing he doesn't seem that fond of you. Why is that?'

'That's because I've got some questions about Hugo Clark's resume. A lot of it appears to be fabricated. I rang him and asked him about it, but he was very defensive and threatened to ban me from council meetings, which I pointed out he's not entitled to do. He's trying to hide something.'

'But he couldn't be the person who attacked us at council. We'd have to have seen him. He's not exactly small.'

'He has access to the council building. He might even have keys to the archive department. And there were a lot of places to hide in that room. It was a total mess.'

'Maybe it was Evil Eve. She might have keys too.'

'Evil Eve?'

'The council's HR manager. I don't trust her one bit.' I didn't mention that I'd searched her office.

'Sounds a bit paranoid to me.'

I left Mitchell to his own devices and went into the kitchen to find something to eat. I was considering my options when my mobile rang. It was Flora.

'Any news from Baz, hen?'

'Nothing.'

'What's he like, giving us grief like this?'

I paused for a while, listening to Flora's raspy pack-a-day breathing.

'Flora, have you ever heard Baz mention a daughter?'

'A daughter?' Flora sounded as shocked as I had been. 'No, hen. Why are you asking?'

'I was sorting out some of his papers, and I found a birth certificate for someone called Delilah Russell. She was born in 1960 and her mother's name was Daphne Russell.'

Flora was silent for a long moment. 'I can't help you there. I didn't meet Baz until 1975.'

I hesitated before asking quietly, 'What about Nora? Have you heard of her?'

Flora seemed lost for words. 'I didn't know her well, hen,' she said eventually, 'but I heard about it when she died. To be honest, Brick, at the time I thought Baz was off his head to take you in. But I was wrong. He was exactly what you needed.'

'But how? How did he come to adopt me? Surely he had to go through some kind of government department?'

'Baz is no saint,' she said, 'and he may have done things that are not entirely above board … but he's always had a good reason. He's a good man, hen, and I could see you were attached to him. I made up my mind to stay out of it and not pry.'

* * *

The next morning, Mitchell seemed to still be feeling the effects of the tasering. It was eleven o'clock and he hadn't yet emerged from Bunny's bedroom.

'I wouldn't worry,' said Bunny. 'I imagine it's a bit like having electro-shock therapy. He's probably a bit sedated.'

'Wow. Do you think it'll make him less of an arsehole?' I asked hopefully.

'I don't know—it might be worth someone doing a study.'

I was just debating whether I should wake him when my phone rang. It was Sue asking me to meet her for a coffee. No doubt she wanted an update on Mitchell and me, and although I didn't really want to discuss my feelings in that regard, I did feel like getting out of the house.

It was one of Melbourne's blue sky days, perfect for cycling. I crammed my hair under a baseball cap and found my sunglasses and bike shorts. The great thing about riding a bike is that you can sneak down the cobblestone lanes of Fitzroy and Brunswick, although it can be a bit hard on the backside, depending on your bike's suspension.

I cycled past the Phoenix—to check it was still standing, at least—but I didn't dare stop. The events of the previous night seemed a bit like a fever dream, but I didn't want to draw too much attention to myself in case Mitchell was right about Otto being thrown off a roof by rampaging bad guys.

I skirted past the cemetery and then on past Princes Park, keeping an eye out for magpies who might want to dive bomb me. Joggers, cyclists and picnickers were everywhere, lured out by the good weather.

Cycling is a good time for thinking—as long as you're not on a major arterial road. On this day, I couldn't seem to stop thinking about Mitchell. It was very worrying. Obviously

I was attracted to him, I couldn't control that, but could I control my response to him if he made a pass at me? Or would I crumble and forget about my goal of being celibate for a year? And what was I even doing thinking about sex when Baz was still missing?

I arrived at the southern end of Sydney Road and wondered, as usual, when it had gotten so trendy. Renowned for its bridal shops, you could judge the rate of gentrification by the wedding dresses in the windows. Sydney Road used to be the place to go if you wanted to get married in fifty metres of blindingly white tulle; now there were designer dresses in tasteful shades made from natural fibres at prices higher than a honeymoon in New York, let alone five days at Kuta Beach.

Five minutes later I locked my bike up outside one the newer cafes. Sue was already at a table with a half-drunk latte. Her youngest glared at me from his pusher.

'Hey,' she greeted me. 'Jake and I were just in the neighbourhood and thought we'd catch up. Didn't we, Jakey?'

Jake couldn't talk, yet he conveyed quite clearly how unimpressed he was to be there.

'You can drop the act, Sue. I know you want to pump me for more information about Mitchell.'

'Well, yes, that was my plan, but then I got a phone call about Otto. He's had another accident.' Sue's lip trembled.

I'd felt warm from my ride, but now I was ice cold. 'Is he okay?'

Sue shook her head, tears beginning to spill. She shoved on her sunglasses. 'No. He's in intensive care at the Alfred

Hospital. They don't think he's going to make it. Romy's there now with her sisters.'

'What happened?'

'A hit and run. Romy said he got out of the house while she was asleep. She's absolutely devastated.' Sue blew her nose loudly on a napkin.

'How did he do that? He couldn't walk, surely?'

Sue moved on to a second napkin. 'I know, it seems unbelievable. But he always was a tough old bugger. He came to Australia alone at sixteen with nothing but the clothes he stood up in, you know. Same as my own grandpa. I hope they catch whoever did this and throw the bloody book at them.'

My thoughts went to what Mitchell had said about Otto's accident with the ladder. Had someone finished the job? Should I have warned him or his daughter? I felt sick.

'I've got some more bad news I'm afraid,' said Sue, still sniffing.

I froze. Was it about Baz? Had they found his lifeless body floating in the muddy waters of the Yarra River?

'I've had a tip-off from an old friend from uni who's working in TV these days. He says Selena McManus is cooking up a sting operation and it involves you.'

'Me?' I nearly spilled my newly arrived latte.

'My friend wanted me to give you the heads-up. He hates Selena. She's a total bitch to him.' Sue was beating around the bush, which was unusual for her.

'Why would Selena be interested in me?'

Sue paused to remove a semi-masticated packet of sugar from Jake's mouth.

'It's about you and the mayor,' she said. 'She's reckons you and he were having an affair. And he died while you were … you know … don't make me say it.'

'Oh my God,' I gasped. The horror was so intense, my ears started ringing.

'Of course *I* know it's not true,' said Sue, giving Jake another packet of sugar to shut him up. 'But he was a sleazy old bastard, and you are young and rather sexy—you know, your lovely hair, your boobs that haven't breastfed three babies—so it's going to look believable to the average bogan who watches Selena's show.'

The implication of what Sue was saying started to hit home. 'Oh, no! Is Selena going to try and ambush me?' Selena's current affair show loved footage of people blinking with shock as a camera was shoved in their face at a time when they were least expecting it. It was the last thing I needed—my schedule was already overfull. 'Shit, it'll be today, won't it? While I'm wearing bike shorts.'

Sue shook her head. 'No, I think you'll be safe until next week, with the Spring Racing Carnival and all. Selena always goes to Derby Day, Oaks Day, Ladies Day and the Melbourne Cup—all that social-climbing crap. But the horse races won't slow her down forever. The only chance you might have to shut her down is to get Mitch Mitchell on your side. He's got cred. And he hates Selena too.'

'What do you mean? Why does he hate Selena?'

'Well, rumour has it that she was the reason he came back to Australia.'

The news was just getting more and more disturbing. 'What? She and him were … dating?'

'Yes. She was covering one of those political summits—what a joke—and he was the one who was summitted.'

My coffee suddenly tasted extra bitter. 'Geez. I would have thought he'd have better taste than that.'

'Well, she is gorgeous. Actually, you two look a bit alike. Maybe Mitchell has a type.'

And to think I'd actually begun to like Mitchell. It was insulting that he might fancy someone like Selena and then make a pass at me. Selena and I might both have dark hair and similar builds, but our personalities could not be more different. Did this mean Mitchell was like so many other men who didn't look past the packaging?

'Obviously their liaison didn't last very long,' continued Sue, who'd cheered up a little from being the bearer of gossip. 'Selena turned up to the Brownlow Medal count on the arm of some footballer. It was basically a public humiliation for Mitchell—dumped by a dumb bimbo for a dumb meathead.'

The things you miss when you don't pay attention to the news. But I was glad to hear that I wasn't the only one who was a fiasco in the romance department.

'So have you seen Mitchell lately?'

Baby Jake took this moment to stop masticating his packet of sugar and start whining in such a high-pitched manner that the dogs tied to the pole outside yelped in pain.

'Um, no,' I lied. 'But if I do run into him again, I'll definitely ask if he has any ideas how to get Selena off my back.'

Sue picked a chunk of muffin up off the floor and attempted to shove it in Jake's mouth, much to his chagrin. He cranked the whining up a notch.

'I'd better go, before everyone's eardrums start bleeding. But I just wanted to warn you about Selena.'

I stayed behind to finish my coffee and clear up the sugar mess so the waitress wouldn't have to deal with it. Then I unlocked my bike and took off, worried that I'd see Selena lobbing towards me with a cameraman in tow.

It was a good thing I was on alert because it meant that I noticed immediately when a black Mercedes appeared not far behind me. I took a sharp turn down a laneway. Was I imagining things? Or was it the same Merc I'd seen casing Gene's shop? I cursed myself for cycling past the Phoenix. I'd thought they hadn't noticed me the day I tailed Mitchell, but maybe I was wrong.

I wasn't close enough to read the number plate, but I wasn't going to hang around. Adrenaline surged through my muscles and I pedalled madly over the ragged stones. The rattling jarred my wrists as I hung on for dear life. I heard a car screech to a halt on the street, and then power into reverse. It was going to follow me down the lane.

I'm usually a sedate Sunday cyclist, but I instantly transformed into a lycra lout, screaming at a family with two young kids to get out of my way as I exited the lane. My whole body was shaking—and it wasn't just from riding over the cobblestones. I churned through the gears and pumped as hard as my legs would go.

I barely braked for Sydney Road. Luckily the traffic was immobile due to a Sunday brunch traffic jam. I headed for the railway tracks which ran behind a row of warehouses and buildings. There was a bike path running next to the

railway line, but no road for cars. I took off up the path and
nearly fell off as I tried to turn around and see if anything
was behind me. My only problem would be the streets that
crossed the bike path and the train tracks—the Mercedes
could barrel up one and cut me off at the crossing.

I gritted my teeth as I approached the first crossing, keeping my eyes peeled. I saw a flash of black car a block away.
It was the Mercedes and it was driving parallel to me. No
doubt it would go down the next cross street and try and
head me off. I could turn around, but maybe they'd left a
thug off down there as well. My bicycle would be no match
for a large man with murderous intent.

Then I heard a train approaching. I could get off and
carry my bike over the tracks, but I wasn't certain my legs
would function again if I stopped pedalling. It was better I
just power on and try to ride across the tracks at the next
crossroads. Then the Mercedes would be stuck at the level
crossing until the train passed. They do it all the time in the
movies. However, movie stars aren't usually riding a second-
hand bike with an irregular service history.

My leg muscles were burning as I rocketed towards the
tracks, hoping this wouldn't end with me making the news
as yet another rail crossing statistic. By this time I was verg-
ing on Lance Armstrong speeds. I held my breath and hoped
I wasn't about to die as I propelled myself across the tracks.
The train crossing bells rang in my ears.

I think I saw my horror mirrored in the train driver's eyes
as I whizzed past. I hoped the poor woman didn't have a
heart attack. Then I was on the other side of the track—and

I was still alive. The Mercedes would be stuck behind the boom gates for several minutes, providing the driver didn't do an illegal zigzag after the train went past. And if they were prepared to run down a cyclist, then odds were on they weren't afraid to flout a few traffic regulations.

By now I wouldn't have been able to stop if I wanted to—my brakes weren't that good. I zoomed down another lane and made my way back towards the railway track, this time via a road I knew was closed to car traffic. Then I crossed back over Sydney Road—still pedalling like a mad woman—and into the labyrinth of streets on the other side.

It seemed I'd given them the slip for now, but they could still be cruising around looking for me. I stopped in a lane and threw up my coffee, my heart pounding violently in my ears as I retched. I considered leaving my bike behind and getting a tram home, but I was shaking too much to get my key in the bike lock and I didn't want to leave it unlocked or it would be stolen for sure. I decided it was just best to keep riding until I was safely back home.

CHAPTER EIGHTEEN

I returned home, still shaken from my near-death experience, to find Mitchell was back to his ordinary self—that is to say, he was in front of the TV news, tapping on his laptop, surrounded by bits of paper and drinking beer. He looked mildly surprised at the state of me as I staggered in.

'A black Mercedes just tried to run me down near Sydney Road.' I filled a glass with water from the tap and drank it too fast. My stomach roiled. 'I think it was that goon who tried to kidnap you on Brunswick Street.'

I pulled off my long-sleeve T-shirt in an effort to cool down and collapsed on a chair. My heart was still beating at a furious pace and I was drenched in sweat. Either I was very unfit or I was having a panic attack.

'Yeah, it sounds like one of Mullett's bozos. I hope they haven't followed you here.'

He disappeared from the room and I heard the front door open and close. Then he was back again.

'No, I can't see anything. And they're usually not subtle. You must have lost them. Well done.'

I thought Mitchell could have given me a bit more sympathy. I was still having hot and cold flashes when I thought of how close I'd come to being squashed by a train.

'I've been taking a closer look at those documents you took from the council archives,' he said. 'Any chance I could meet your friend Otto?'

I remembered Sue's news and I felt even worse. 'I just found out he was hit by a car last night—even though there's no way he could have been out walking.'

Mitchell finally stopped stuffing his face. 'Is he okay?'

'No.' I wiped my face with my T-shirt so he wouldn't see that I was close to tears.

'I'd say that clinches it. He was definitely Dad's source.'

I was upset, nauseated and near hysteria. I felt like yelling at someone. So I did. 'That's all you have to say? Otto's on life support! I've narrowly escaped being knocked off my bike and run over! And then there was what happened to us last night! If Mavis DuBois hadn't come along, I don't know what would have happened!'

'Mavis DuBois? The councillor with the war hero grandfather? What's she got to do with last night?'

'She was driving the Kombi.'

Mitchell actually put down his beer. 'What Kombi?'

'The Kombi that saved our arses—' I broke off, noticing his expression of utter confusion. 'What do you actually remember about last night?'

He rubbed a hand across his face and I heard the *crisk-crisk* noise of his stubble. 'It's a bit fuzzy, now you mention it.'

'Well, to give you a recap: we were in the council's archives department when you were tasered in the arse by person or persons unknown. We exited the building post haste, the fire alarm went off and then Mavis DuBois turned up out of the blue in a beat-up old Kombi and gave us a lift home.'

'Then what happened?'

'She refused to come in but said that she'd been looking for you and she wanted to speak to you about something.'

'Do you have a number for her?'

'Not on me—I could maybe find it at the office.'

'Uh, guys.' Timmy had arrived unnoticed and was scouring the fridge. 'There's been a Kombi parked across the road all night.'

I took a peek out of my bedroom window and, sure enough, there was an off-white van parked under a tree about thirty metres from our front door. I poured a strong coffee and ventured outside. The Kombi brought back memories of various cold and uncomfortable weekends spent at musical festivals with a boyfriend who fancied himself as a folk musician for a while.

I knocked softly on the sliding door. 'Mavis, are you in there? I've brought you a coffee.'

Her face appeared at the window. She was looking worse than the night before and more than slightly crazed.

'Do you want to come into the house? Mitchell's regained his senses—or at least, as much sense as he had before.'

The door slid open and the smell of unwashed human wafted out, once again bringing back memories. Mavis emerged and grabbed the coffee like it was a life buoy. I took advantage of her subdued state to lead her across the road and inside. Then I double-locked the front door and gently propelled her towards the bathroom.

'Help yourself to a shower. There are towels in the cupboard. I'll bring you some fresh clothes and another coffee.'

Mitchell was waiting expectantly in the kitchen.

'She seems kind of freaked out and from the aroma, I'd say she's been living in that van for a few days.' I poured another coffee and put in even more sugar. 'Has Mavis cropped up in any of your research?'

'Not as such. She's ambitious, obviously, but she seems to be on the level. Although her high-profile friendship with the premier does raise some questions about her integrity.'

'Everyone thought it was odd that she gave up her position on the Development Consent Committee.'

'Well, judging from her recent antics, I'd say she had some other reasons for stepping down. A mental breakdown, perhaps.'

Half an hour later Mavis emerged looking scrubbed almost red raw, but slightly less deranged. 'Thanks, I needed that shower. Whoever had that Kombi before me was a filthy pig.'

I sat her down and put some toast in front of her. 'So, Mavis, what the hell's going on? Why are you hiding out in a Kombi? This is Mitch Mitchell, by the way.'

'I know.' She practically rolled her eyes at me and I remembered why I'd never liked her much. 'I've been looking for him since he came to that council meeting. And I've been looking for you too, Brick, since you turned up to that development committee meeting. The address HR has for you is a Brunswick Street pub, one of those really dirty old ones where people go to score drugs. It was closed anyway so I was just parking out front of the council building, figuring I'd catch you when you turned up to work. It's a well-lit area. Safe to park in. But then you both ran out in front of me. What were you doing in the council building in the middle of the night?'

I thought I'd ignore that question. 'Why didn't you just ring Mitchell if you wanted to talk to him? His phone number's not that secret.'

'It's not safe. These days phones can be tracked in a second.' She was starting to sound like Gene.

'Who do you think is tracking your phone?' I asked carefully.

'It's a long story.'

'We've got lots of coffee and nothing better to do right now.'

Mavis's hands were still a bit shaky as she accepted another coffee top-up. 'My big mistake was getting involved with Errol,' she said.

'This is Errol Grimes you're talking about? The premier of Victoria.' I was glad Mitchell was there to stop me asking questions that made me look like an idiot.

'We'd met lots of times at various charity balls, the races,' Mavis said. 'We were part owners in a horse, you know how it is.'

Not wanting to interrupt, I nodded as if I too was a part owner of a racehorse.

'He started texting me,' she continued. 'And then we began seeing each other. But he said we had to keep it under the radar, for political reasons. Officially we were just friends. He said people were always out to make up rumours about him. At first I thought it was just your usual political paranoia and I was happy to take things slowly. I knew the media would have a field day if they found out about us, plus my mother is a nightmare, especially since my little sister produced the world's ugliest baby. You know what mothers are like.'

Once again I nodded, although I couldn't relate, lacking a mother—annoying or otherwise.

Mavis paused to blow her nose delicately on a tissue. 'Then I started realising something strange was going on. Errol has a secret house in Fairfield—it used to belong to his grandmother. We would go there to spend time together. It had very good security. But one day I happened to overhear a phone conversation. Errol was asking someone to dig into Dave Mullet's past—find some proof of illegal activity.'

'But I thought the premier and Mullett were mates,' interrupted Mitchell. 'He's always been the developers' best buddy, squashing all kinds of attempts to reform building legislation.'

'I think Mullett had some kind of power over Errol, like he knew something from Errol's past—something embarrassing. And that's not exactly Errol's thing. He likes to be top dog.

'Not long after that, I was at Errol's Fairfield house when a package was delivered. It sent him crazy. He started smashing things up. I had to go and hide in the bathroom. Then he drank so much he passed out and I found the package. It was a photo of Errol with a woman.'

'Did you recognise her?' Mitchell asked.

'No. And Errol looked a lot younger. Like in his football days.'

'Do you think someone was trying to blackmail Grimes?'

'I'm sure of it.'

'What did you do?' I asked.

'Like an idiot, I stayed there. Cleaned up his mess. When he came round he—' Her face began to crumple.

I gave her a clean tissue. 'He hit you?'

She nodded.

It was a while before she pulled herself together enough to continue. 'He said if I told anyone about this he'd make sure my career was ruined. A little while later I started getting anonymous messages. I think my phone was bugged. I was told to get off the Development Consent Committee or embarrassing pictures of Errol and me—you know, a sex tape, basically—would be given to the press.'

'Did they really have a sex tape?'

'Not with my knowledge, but it's not hard to do these days with hidden cameras, is it? And I didn't want to find out! I felt like I was being followed. It was all getting too much.' The wild expression was returning to Mavis's eyes. 'When Mitchell turned up at the council meeting I wondered if he might be able to help me. I went to the next development consent meeting hoping to get a quiet word with him, but he left before I got a chance.'

'I'd suspected Errol Grimes was doing Dave Mullett favours,' said Mitchell. 'But I didn't think there was black-mail involved. I thought it was just the usual top end of town looking after each other: back scratching, tickets to the horse racing and whatnot.'

Mavis looked exhausted so I told her she could have a nap in my room, but when I opened the door to check on her thirty minutes later, she was gone—via the front win-dow rather than the front door. And she'd left the window wide open.

I shut it and looked around. This wasn't an area where you want to leave windows open—you were liable to find your jewellery gone, even the cheap-shit jewellery I owned.

I did a scan of my room, but nothing seemed to have been disturbed, although I noticed that the photo of me and Nora wasn't where I'd left it on the bedside table. I looked under the bed to see if it had fallen there, but there was no sign of it.

'Mavis has flown the coop,' I said, returning to the lounge room where Mitchell was snacking on cold pizza. 'She climbed out the front window so we wouldn't notice.'

'Yeah? Can't say I'm surprised. She did seem a bit skittish.'

'Do you think she's telling the truth about Errol Grimes?'

Mitchell considered the question. 'I find that in cases like these you usually have to ask yourself how she'd benefit from making up a story like that.'

'I can't see a benefit. She's a nervous wreck. And she's cut off her hair, for crying out loud. She'd spent a fuckton of money on that hair.'

'Then maybe she is telling the truth. Or maybe she's gone batshit crazy. These are our options.' Mitchell absentmindedly patted the cat that had installed itself on the sofa next to him. 'What she said about the possibility of Errol Grimes being blackmailed by Mullett was interesting. Maybe I was on the wrong track thinking my dad was investigating a connection between Mullett and Dickie Ruffhead.'

The mention of Ruffhead brought back my guilt. Maybe it was because the poor demented cat trusted Mitchell, but I felt it was time to unburden myself. 'I'm going to tell you something., but you have to promise me that it is off the record. Way off.'

'It's not about UFOs is it?'

'I'm serious. It's about Ruffhead.' I paused, hoping I wasn't making a giant mistake. 'He didn't die at home, like everyone thinks. He died in the council's archive store. I found him in there.'

Mitchell nearly choked on a piece of pepperoni. 'What?'

'He was in the archive store. Where we were when you were attacked.'

'What were you doing in there?' He was looking at me in a strange way, his eyes still watering from the inhaled pizza.

'I'd picked the lock, it was a spur-of-the-moment thing … not important,' I said, aware of how dodgy I sounded. 'Anyway, the mayor was in there dead. I didn't want to explain how I happened to find him, so I left him there. I called my boss Gail and left an anonymous voicemail. I'm not sure if she even took it seriously, but somehow his body got moved and the official line was put out that he had a heart attack at home.'

'Are you sure he was dead? Maybe he was just having a nap.'

'He was dead as.'

'I guess that explains the weird smell in there.' Mitchell had put down the pizza like he'd lost his appetite. 'If what you say is true, then the mayor was probably killed there and moved later. Like what happened to this Otto fellow.'

'What do you mean *if* it's true?'

'Okay, it's true then. We should go back there and check it out again. If we can find some evidence, then the police can get forensics in there.'

'I'm not really keen to go back to the council building after last time.'

'Yeah, I hear you.' Mitchell shifted in his seat. 'I'd still like to know who got the body out of the building. I mean, we're talking about a large, public building in a well-lit street, not a little house in the suburbs. We just have to think. How would you get a body out the building without anyone noticing?'

'Rolled-up carpet?'

'Let me guess. You watched a lot of TV as a kid.'

'Do you have a better idea?'

'What's least likely to attract attention at council?'

'A wheelie bin, probably.'

'They'd still need some kind of vehicle to put it in. A truck or van, at least. Is there any CCTV outside council?'

'I'm sure there is, but I don't know how we'd access it.'

'Maybe Timmy could—'

'No.' I felt guilty enough about the hacking I'd already asked Timmy to do and I didn't want him dragged in further. I thought back to the days after I'd discovered the body. 'This is a bit of a long shot, but there's this old homeless guy called Morrie. I saw him a few times that week. He has a thing about writing down number plates. I saw him that morning. There's a chance he saw something.'

'Could we find Morrie?'

'He's pretty regular with his routine. That's why I noticed him near the council building—it was unusual. He's usually at the 24-hour supermarket on Smith Street or in the Fitzroy Gardens. There's a group of drinkers that hang there. Although he might be in hospital. Sometimes he gets admitted to the psych ward for a spell.'

'Let's check the supermarket, at least. We can buy some more beer.'

I found an old hoodie in an attempt at a disguise while Mitchell went for the baseball cap look.

'God, we look like a couple of junkies,' I said. 'We'll fit right in at the supermarket.'

I'd realised I'd left the council pool car parked in a back alley, so we got a taxi and reclaimed it before we headed to the supermarket. I thought I may as well make use of council perks while I still had them.

Supermarkets are dull places in general, but you could always rely on seeing something a little bit unusual at the Smith Street supermarket. We weren't disappointed. As we arrived we saw a young woman being evicted by a female security guard who was saying firmly—although not in an unsympathetic manner—that licking the watermelons was not appropriate behaviour.

'Tough night?' asked Mitchell.

The woman just sighed. 'We like to say when you're tired of this place, you're tired of life.'

'I wonder if you can help us,' I said. 'Have you seen a really old homeless guy who's always going on about his dog?'

'Morrie?'

'Yeah, Morrie.'

'Nah, not today. But he was in here yesterday. He's probably not far away.'

We thanked the woman and then went to purchase beer and snacks.

'Around here, the homeless are almost like celebrities. Everyone knows who they are,' I commented as we left the supermarket.

'We should tell all the young folk that. Isn't that the Gen Y dream? To be famous?'

'You're kind of famous. Isn't it nice?' I asked.

'It's never done me much good. Although it might have got me kidnapped that one time.'

We cruised down to the Fitzroy Gardens, parked and set off on foot. The grass held pockets of cool air as we passed the old grandstand, left over from the time when this was the home grounds of the Fitzroy Football Club.

'Geez, haven't been here for years,' Mitchell commented.

'I like it here. Peaceful. Of course, they're always trying to get rid of the homeless and the drunks. But I think they deserve some breaks.'

'Has Morrie lived around here a long time?'

'God, forever. Baz has a soft spot for him. Morrie was taken off his mum, raised in some god-awful institution, the usual Stolen Gen story. The same thing happened to all Baz's aunties. They were split up and raised in children's homes.'

'Is that why Baz adopted you?'

I didn't know the answer to that. I was starting to realise I didn't know exactly know why or how Baz had adopted me. But I was saved from any further speculation when we nearly tripped over a man sprawled on the grass.

'Watch where you're goin'!'

A couple more men were sitting in the bushes near the rotunda.

'We're looking for Morrie. You seen him?'

'Who's askin'?'

'I'm a friend. I'm not going to humbug him or anything.'

'Someone askin' for me?' A bush moved and out popped Morrie, fastening up his pants.

'Uncle. It's Brick, Baz's girl. I just wanted to ask you something.'

Morrie squinted at me, then smiled in recognition, revealing some stumps of brown teeth.

'Do you remember when I saw you outside the council building a week or so back? I gave you ten bucks.'

I could see from Morrie's expression that he did remember. 'Love, I've spent it. I can't give it back.'

'It's okay,' I said. 'It was a gift. I was just wondering if you saw anything strange happening at the council building while you were there.'

'Always something strange happening there! Those bastards stole my dog!'

'Your dog died years ago, Morrie,' I said gently, hoping to bring him back to the more recent past.

'Yeah! After those bastards stole it!'

I took a deep breath. Talking to Morrie was like talking to Gene. 'I think I can help you with that, Morrie. It would just really help if I knew if any trucks or vans pulled up at the council building while you were there. Can I have a look at your notebook?'

I was sorry to lie to an old homeless man, but I hoped that in the bigger scheme of things, I would be forgiven. Maybe I'd find a cat for him. One that didn't mind a transient lifestyle. Morrie gave Mitchell an assessing look as if judging whether we wanted to steal his notebook but then passed over the greasy, stained book.

I flipped through to the end, surprised by the neatness of his handwriting. It was old-fashioned but very even, almost like copperplate. Unfortunately, none of it made much sense. It was just lists of number plates, with no times or dates.

'Can you read my writing, love?'

'You've got beautiful writing, Morrie.'

'The brothers used to whack our knuckles with a ruler if we made a smudge. Course a whack on the knuckles was the least of our worries with that sadistic pack of bastards.'

'You've done a great job at getting the number plates, but unfortunately, I don't know what one I'm looking for. I just need to know whether a truck or van pulled up.'

Morrie's face lit up with one of his wide smiles. 'Why didn't you say? I remember one van, clear as day!'

'Why's that?' Mitchell asked.

'Because two people come out and put a dead body in the back of it!'

Obviously I hadn't been asking the right questions. 'How do you know?'

'Two people come out carrying it, wrapped up in plastic. Looked like men but I supposed one could have been a woman—they were wearing overalls so it was hard to tell. Overalls and face masks like they'd been painting ceilings, ya know?'

I stared at him, wondering if somehow he knew what we were trying to find out and he was playing a practical joke. 'You didn't think of reporting it to anyone?'

'Bless you, child. Who'd listen to me?' He laughed with delight at the thought, then broke off to cough up a blob of mucus.

Mitchell was still scanning the notebook. 'What's the number plate of that old bomb Mavis is driving? That was pretty whiffy.'

'IEZ 820,' I said without even thinking. 'Is it in there anywhere?'

He ran his finger down the columns. 'And we have a winner!'

'Maybe Mavis was involved in moving the mayor's body,' I said. 'She said she'd stolen the Kombi, but I don't know where from.'

'This story just gets weirder and weirder,' Mitchell said as he handed Morrie back his notebook. 'Many thanks, Morrie.'

I gave him our six-pack of beer as well and we bid him farewell.

'Baz grew you up right, love,' said Morrie as he shoved the six-pack under his coat. 'You'll get your reward in heaven.'

* * *

We bought a replacement six-pack and were halfway home when my mobile phone rang. The caller ID revealed it was Sue, so I felt safe to answer.

'Brick. I need some help. I was parked near the housing commission flats in Flemington and someone's let my tyres down.'

I really didn't want to go driving in the council car any more than I could help it, we were already pushing our luck, but I also couldn't abandon Sue. 'Can't Shane come and get you?'

'No. He's at his best mate's bucks night. There was going to be a stripper and everything, so he'll be too drunk to drive by now. Plus I don't want him to know I left the kids with our neighbour's sixteen-year-old and her pot-smoking boyfriend.'

I sighed. 'Okay. I'm with Mitchell, but I'm sure he won't mind.'

'Won't mind what?' asked Mitchell.

'Sue's got two flat tyres. She needs a lift,' I said. 'We'll be right there, Sue. We're not far away.'

'Just not a word about what Morrie just told us. I don't want any information leaks before I'm ready to go public.'

'Fine,' I said. Ungrateful bastard, after all the help Sue had given him. I sent Sue a text saying we were on our way.

Sue's station wagon was easy enough to locate.

'Hi,' she said as we pulled up, shooting a winning smile at Mitchell. I wondered if this was all a ruse so she could see him again. 'Thanks for coming and getting me. I hope I didn't interrupt anything important. It was probably just kids mucking around, but it's got me a little spooked.'

'What are you doing out here?' I asked.

'I got a lead from Joe, that parking inspector you intro-duced me to,' she said. 'He reckons there was a witness to Otto's accident—a dishwasher who was having a smoko in an alleyway at the time. But he was too scared to go to the police because he wasn't supposed to be working on his visa. I think he lives at these flats, but I've been door-knocking and I've had no joy. It'd probably help if I spoke Arabic. Why we learned French in school I have no idea. Com-pletely bloody useless language.'

'We'd better give you a lift then,' said Mitchell. 'I assume you don't have two spares.'

'I don't even have one at the moment,' said Sue, climbing in the back seat.

CHAPTER NINETEEN

Monday came and I found myself awake before dawn as usual. My nightmares were getting worse and worse, and with each passing day I was becoming more and more scared that I was never going to see Baz again.

The kitchen was quiet as I made a cup of tea, but I could hear the shower running so I assumed Mitchell was up. His laptop was on the counter and I could see that he'd been searching a newspaper archive. I navigated the mouse to the search field and typed 'Delilah Russell'—the name on the birth certificate that we'd found in Baz's safe. Nothing came up.

Then I went back to the search field and typed 'abandoned', 'baby', 'Melbourne', and set the date field to 1975–85. As the search icon flickered, I considered slamming the laptop shut and walking away, but it was hardly secret information. I could have gone to a library at any time in my life and done a similar search.

The search results loaded and I clicked on the top result, BABY FOUND OUTSIDE BETTING SHOP, but then found my hands were shaking so much I could barely scroll to the story.

> *Police are seeking the parents of a baby found on Saturday night outside a betting shop in Brick Lane in Melbourne's city centre. The baby girl is thought to be about two months old.*
>
> *'She's obviously been cared for,' said an officer. 'She was not malnourished or mistreated. We hope that the mother will come forward and claim the child.'*
>
> *In the meantime, the child has been taken into the care of the authorities.*

If this child was me, then Baz had been telling me the truth. I'd sometimes wondered whether he'd told me I was abandoned because my parents were serial killers—or worse—although I don't know what's worse than a serial killer. Port Adelaide supporters, maybe?

I went to make a cup of tea and was staring at the kettle when Head-butt the cat came by and banged his head violently into my leg. I looked down at him and he appeared to wag his tail.

'Are you sure you're not really a hound dog?' I asked as I gave in and put down some food. 'What if I said I ain't gonna feed you no more?'

The cat let me stroke him for a bit and then bashed his head into the sliding glass doors that led to the backyard. I opened the door and he disappeared without a backward glance.

* * *

When the clock ticked around to nine, I called in sick to work. I didn't want to risk being run down by a luxury German car, and I also feared that Selena might be lurking in the bushes outside council, waiting to run at me with a microphone and a camera as fast as her high heels would permit.

I didn't know exactly why Selena had taken such an instant dislike to me back in Year 4. Was it simple racism due to her assumption that I was Black like Baz? Or was it an innate bully sense that I was just the weakest lamb in the flock, with my stutter and lazy eye? Well, I wasn't that little lost lamb anymore and I wasn't going to be her victim again.

It was several minutes before anyone in the office answered the phone. Being a Monday followed by a public holiday Tuesday, a plague had evidently passed through most of council—and probably most of Melbourne. Finally Brucie picked up.

'On the sickie bandwagon, are you?' Brucie sounded more tired than usual.

'What are you doing in at work?' I asked.

'Apparently my status as gatekeeper to Gail isn't as secure as I'd previously thought. I don't want to give Eve any excuse to say I'm not meeting my job description.'

A thought struck me. 'Shit. The office car. Has Eve noticed it's missing?'

'Not yet, but don't worry, I can come and get it,' said Brucie. 'If Eve has noticed, I'll tell her it was getting serviced. Give me your address and I'll be there in ten.'

I wondered how far I could trust Brucie. He loved gossip and might want to name drop if he thought I was shacked up with a semi-famous journo—particularly if he felt the need to deflect heat from Eve.

'You can trust me.' He'd read my mind and it made me feel bad. I was probably headed for a sacking anyway, but until then I needed all the friends at council I could get.

When Brucie arrived, I could see there was something he wanted to tell me and braced myself for more bad news. 'This is strictly confidential,' he said as I hustled him into the hallway, 'but I know I can trust you, Brick. I've been doing a bit of work on the side. Viral marketing. Have you heard of it?'

I'd barely got my head around marketing, let alone viral marketing.

'It's the next big thing,' said Brucie. 'Newspapers and TV. Forget about it. They've only got a few years left in them. People don't realise it yet, but there's big bucks to be made from social media like Myspace and Facebook and I'm aiming to get on board. If I'm lucky, I'll be able to retire before I'm thirty.'

At this point, I was just hoping to live to thirty. 'So how can I help you? I don't know anything about all that stuff.'

'I just might need you to cover for me a bit, if business takes off. I still need my job. Major credit card debt. Party lifestyle.'

I remembered the memo I'd found in Eve's office. 'I'm happy to help you out if I can, Brucie, but I'm a worried I might get sacked soon. Gail really doesn't like me.'

'I knew you'd be cool. And don't worry. It's really, really hard to sack people from council. Take Gavin for example. He hasn't done a shred of work in twelve months.'

'Is Gavin the one who likes to wear blue shirts, or is that Grant?'

'Not sure,' said Brucie, shrugging. 'Anyway, got to run. Don't get too hungover while you're sick, luvvy.' He pocketed the car key and left again.

I'd barely closed the door when there was another knock. So much for keeping a low profile; suddenly our quiet cul-de-sac was like Bourke Street. I looked through the peephole to see Mavis DuBois. She was still dressed like a homeless person, and when I opened the door she gave a start like a scared stray.

'Sorry for skipping out on you the other night,' she said, looking at her feet. 'I've been a little freaked out lately.'

I felt like telling her to bugger off, but that wasn't charitable. What would Baz do?

'Do you want to stay with me and Bunny for a few nights?' I asked finally.

She looked up at me and nodded, her eyes filling with tears.

'Are you still driving the Kombi?' I took her arm. 'Come on, we'd better get it off the street in case it catches the wrong kind of attention.'

I opened the corrugated iron back gate while Mavis returned to the Kombi. Somehow we managed to wedge the van next to the clothesline. It helped that we didn't care about dings.

I closed the back gate again as Mavis retrieved numerous plastic bags from the van. They looked to be filled with clothes and bedding. Through the glass door at the back of the house I could see that there were various people up and about in the kitchen.

'Are you ready to face the masses?' I asked Mavis as I helped with her bags.

She produced two tablets from her pocket and swallowed them without water, then nodded. 'Valium.'

I resisted the urge to frisk her for more and do the same.

We entered the kitchen to find Mitchell, Bunny and Timmy in the midst of a fry-up. 'Do you want a bacon and egg ...' Bunny's voice trailed off as she saw Mavis following me in.

I sat Mavis down on a spare seat and stacked up her plastic bags by the back door.

Mitchell poured her a large coffee. 'Mavis, we've got a few questions about the Kombi you've been ... er ... living in. Where did you get it?'

Mavis looked furtive, or maybe it was just a lack of eye make-up. 'I found it in a back lane about a block away from the council building. It had one of those stickers on, you know, saying that council was going to tow it. I think it had been dumped. My dad used to collect old cars and fix them up. I used to hang out in his shed with him a lot to keep out of my mum's way. Kombis are really easy to hotwire.'

'Did Brick tell you that it may have been used to transport a dead body?'

'I think I need a shower,' said Mavis, setting down her coffee carefully. She left the room without further explanation.

'If you need to leave,' I called after her, 'please use the door and not the window, or the paint-sniffing kids from around the corner will climb in and rip off anything they can find.'

Mavis came back into the room carrying a fresh towel. 'I'm sorry about last time, I won't do it again.' Then she delved into one of her plastic bags and pulled out a photo. 'I took your photo, Brick, I'm sorry,' she said as she handed it back. It was the photo of me with Nora. 'I saw it in your room, and it scared me because— Who is this?' Her voice sounded mildly hysterical.

'It's me,' I answered in as soothing voice as I could muster. 'It's me as a kid.'

'No, I mean the woman. Is she your mum?'

It was such as innocent question, but it was like a punch in the stomach. Nora was the closest thing I'd ever had to a mother and the memories I'd recently uncovered had left me dealing with a feeling of deep sadness. 'No. It's not my mum. She's a woman who fostered me when I was little. I was a foster kid. Her name was Nora, but I can't tell you much else.' I tried to keep the emotion out of my voice. 'She liked high heels, jewellery and the Fitzroy Football Club.

She was kind to me ...' My voice trailed off and there was silence in the room. Everyone looked from me to Mavis.

'This is the same woman I saw in the photo of Errol— the photo that sent him crazy,' she said. 'I'm sure of it.'

I felt sick and dizzy, as if I was about to faint.

'What happened to Nora?' Mitchell asked.

'She died.' I could no longer control my voice and it cracked.

Mitchell put his hand on my arm. 'How did she die, Brick?'

I looked down at his hand. It had a pink scar running clear across the top. 'I don't know.'

He tightened his grasp. 'You don't look like you don't know.'

'It's complicated.' I closed my eyes so I didn't have to see his hand any longer. 'I've had nightmares my whole life, but lately I've started to realise that they might actually be memories.'

'What happens in the dreams?' Mitchell relaxed his grasp and his voice sounded gentle for once.

'A man is hurting Nora and he wants to find me and hurt me too.' I wrenched myself away, ran into the bathroom and vomited.

I washed my face and then lay down on the cool tiles of the bathroom floor. The foster care system wasn't perfect, I knew that. But it was awful to think I'd been exposed to such violence as a small child. Baz must have known Nora. Did he try and protect her? Is that why he felt he had to protect me too? Who was the man who'd hurt Nora? Was he the reason she died? How did she die? Another wave of nausea hit me.

There was a thrumming in my head. The memories of my life before Baz were starting to seep back into my everyday consciousness. The genie was out of the bottle—and there was no shoving it back in.

I wished Baz was with me. I felt unmoored without him, without the Phoenix. What if I lost both? They'd been the constant in my life as I remembered it—the touchstone— and I didn't know what my future would look like if they weren't there.

An hour later, after a powernap with the help of a couple of tablets from Bunny's bag of magic tricks, I felt almost human again. There was a soft knock on my bedroom door and Mavis slunk into the room.

'I'm sorry I upset you. I haven't been getting enough sleep lately and it's made me a bit paranoid. Here, I bought a frame for your photo.' She handed me a beautiful silver frame.

'Thank you. That's really lovely.' I forced myself out of bed, holding the frame to my chest. 'I'm going to make a sandwich. You can have a nap in my bed if you like.' In reality I couldn't think of anything worse than eating, but I wanted to do something normal.

Mitchell was still in the kitchen, tapping away at his laptop and drinking coffee. He looked up briefly. 'All good?'

'Yes.' I avoided eye contact. 'I'm going to make sandwiches.'

'Whatever gets you through. I could eat a sandwich.'

I inserted the photo of Nora and me in the silver frame, set it on the counter, and then began buttering bread like my life depended on it.

'So, the premier of Victoria is a pretty high-profile person,' Mitchell said as I inspected a tomato that looked like it was probably best consumed several days earlier. 'Has his face ever rung any bells for you? Or triggered any of these bad dreams you mentioned?'

'It's hard to say.' I sawed at the tomato. 'Obviously I've seen his picture in the newspaper and on TV ... but you know how it is, men in suits all look a bit similar.'

'You have trouble distinguishing men in suits?' Mitchell looked the most amused I'd ever seen him.

'They look the same!' I felt defensive for some reason. 'Am I the only one who tells them apart by their neckties?'

'I'm not wearing a necktie. Can you recognise me?'

'Do you even own a suit?'

Mitchell took one of my sandwiches. 'Getting back to business. While you were having your little lie down, I did some research. I don't want to give you another turn, but I looked up the newspapers from that time. To give you the brief version: Nora Strange, twenty-nine years old, was found dead in her home. Her estranged husband was arrested a few days later.'

I dug a jar of pickles out from the back of the fridge. Looking at the use-by date, they should have been eaten at least five years earlier.

'I rang an old journo mate of my father,' Mitch said. 'He did the police round for decades and knows more about

Melbourne crime than most criminals. It took a bit of prodding, but he finally remembered something about this woman, Nora. Her estranged husband was a former football player, that's why my mate remembers it. Played for Fitzroy. The husband had no alibi, had been drunk off his head at the time of her death. No trial, though. He hung himself in the lockup and the case was closed.' Mitchell watched me wrestle with the lid of the pickle jar. 'A couple of years later—while my dad's mate was covering a completely different case—it came out that this woman's husband was actually in the drunk tank for the entire night that she died. The paperwork was misfiled. The old fella tried to get some interest in the story, but the woman had no surviving relatives and the police closed ranks as usual. As a long-time police reporter, sometimes he had to choose his battles.'

'So your friend reckons that Nora's ex-husband didn't do it.' I gave the jar's lid a whack with a knife edge in a bid to loosen it up.

'Unless the cops were way off about the time of her death, which is another possibility of course. But judging by the blackmail attempt, I'd say Errol Grimes may have been romantically involved with Nora at some time. Is that possible?'

'If he was playing football and she was part of that scene, I guess it's possible they knew each other.'

'From the photo, she was a pretty woman. It's no secret he was a bit of a pants man before he got into politics. Since getting into politics he's been discreet—only dated the posh types like Mavis—probably so people don't think he's gay.

Is there anyone who would know if Grimes and Nora had had some kind of relationship?'

'Well, Baz maybe … but we can't ask him since he's still bloody missing.'

'Nora's husband's dead. No kids. Did she have any friends that you remember?'

'No idea. I was only about ten, I barely remember her.'

'Yet your memory now is near photographic. Am I right?'

'It's not photographic.' I shook the jar, wondering whether smashing it on the footpath outside was too extreme. 'I've just worked in a bar for too long.'

'We're getting nowhere with this speculation.' Mitchell took the jar off me and opened it with a quick twist. 'I'm sick of powerful men who can hide in the shadows. Politicians like Grimes and their big business buddies like Mullett. They surround themselves with minders and bully boys who control access. Where's the accountability? How can reporters do their job properly if they're not allowed to even question the power brokers? How can anyone be expected to keep them in check?'

'I know where you can find Mullett and Grimes.' Mavis had entered the kitchen without us noticing. She was wearing my tracksuit pants and one of my favourite jumpers. 'Flemington Racecourse. They've got horses running in the Melbourne Cup.'

I rolled my eyes. 'Of course they do.'

Mitchell, however, had a manic gleam in his eye, and I almost expected him to embrace Mavis. 'That's a great idea! The best idea I've heard all day!'

'What idea?' She took a step back from him, looking worried.

'The Cup. Mullett will be there! I'll confront him face to face. I'll finish my father's investigation once and for all.'

I nibbled a pickle. It still seemed edible. 'That's the dumbest idea I've ever heard. You can't just rock up to the Melbourne Cup and find people like Dave Mullett. He'll be in one of the VIP areas.'

'Getting into Uruzgan Province wasn't easy. People said it couldn't be done.'

'Didn't you get kidnapped?' I recalled the photo of Mitchell as a hostage. 'I'm not letting you go there. Your body will be found in a burnt-out car under the Bolte Bridge. I think your boss may have been right about you having PTSD.'

'That's the pot calling the kettle black.'

I decided to shut myself in the bathroom for a while.

I put on a Dinah Washington CD and then sat on the edge of the bath with a cold flannel on my face. I couldn't seem to stop images of Nora's face rising up in my mind. Maybe I just needed to confront the past head on—find out if Errol Grimes was the bogeyman from my nightmares, or just a run-of-the-mill arsehole with too much power and a nasty attitude towards women.

'Okay, let's do it,' I said when I returned to the kitchen. 'If you're determined to go on this fool's mission to the Cup, I'm coming with you. You want to talk to Mullett. I want to see Grimes in the flesh. And you need a minder or you'll get yourself killed.'

'I didn't know you cared.'

CHAPTER TWENTY

The bonus of Mitchell's Melbourne Cup idea was that it gave me a project to help keep my mind off things. I stayed up half the night rebirthing a dress I'd worn on stage a few years earlier when an extra back-up singer was required at short notice. It had a bit of a fifties feel to it and matching gloves—a handy way of covering my shredded nails.

Timmy loaned Mitchell a suit he'd recently worn to a family wedding. It didn't fit too badly—a little tight around the shoulders perhaps, but otherwise Mitchell looked disturbingly suave. He'd even run a comb through his hair.

I inspected myself in the mirror, but still felt my outfit was missing something. 'You don't have a hat or a fascinator, do you?'

'I barely even know what a fascinator is.' Bunny wasn't big on dressing up.

I made do with a large silk flower in a complementary shade of pink sewn to a hair clip. The colour reminded me of the dress I'd worn as a small girl. The one Nora had bought me. A memory appeared of us together at the shop. I'd never had anything so beautiful before in my life and I'd loved Nora from that moment.

I tied my hair back into a chignon, which I lacquered to within an inch of its wilful life. Then I put the hairspray in my handbag. I read somewhere that you could use hairspray for self-defence in lieu of mace. You just had to have the presence of mind to retrieve it from your bag, take off the lid and spray it directly into your assailant's eyes. It was that or stab them with a nail file.

I emerged from my bedroom, quite happy with my efforts.

'Brick. You look like a princess,' said Bunny.

'Spoken like a true imperialist.' I gave a vampish twirl.

'No, you like one of those old-time movie stars,' said Timmy.

'You mean from the 1980s?' I looked at Mitchell to see if he had any feedback.

He looked me up and down. 'You'll do. Let's go.'

We caught a taxi to Flemington to save us battling with public transport. The racing carnival is always a bit of a strange time in Melbourne. Some years I'd forget it was happening and then wonder why people on the street were dressed as if they were going to a wedding. A very large, very posh wedding.

Hours later, of course, it would be another story. Women would be sporting panda eyes and ruined hairdos, men would have crumpled jackets slung over their shoulders. Most would be weaving and twenty per cent would need to use their hat as an impromptu vomit bag. No one could lower the tone faster than an Australian.

It was just after two o'clock when we set off towards the gates and there were people everywhere. The only bonus of the crowds was that I felt sure that whoever had chased me the other day would have no hope of finding us among the tens of thousands of people. I hadn't been to the Cup in about eight years. I used to do some casual waitressing during the carnival but finally decided that no penalty rates were worth walking through that much vomit.

In the 150-odd years of the Melbourne Cup, it had grown to develop its own sociological system and the Flemington Racecourse is divided accordingly. The general admission area is the domain of the so-called lower classes, fondly known as bogans. In this area the men usually wear exactly the same outfit as their ten best mates. The more high-minded hoi polloi fork out more cash to enter the grandstand areas. They generally wear a suit or dress and a hat scrounged off a mate or bought from a chain store. But Australia's high society and semi-celebrity class plan their designer outfits in the same way people plan an Everest expedition. They have tickets to exclusive VIP marquees in an area known as the Birdcage and their tickets cost hundreds of dollars—or can't be bought at all but are distributed by the corporate entities that thrive on the worship of the Great God of Gambling.

'I've looked into it,' said Mitchell. 'Mullett will be in the Emirates tent.'

'So have you managed to swing us an invitation as well?'

It worried me that Mitchell did not reply.

He steered us towards our target like a safari guide beating a way through the jungle. Alcohol had been flowing freely since dawn and people were starting to revert to their animal state.

The word 'marquee' didn't really accurately describe the pleasure domes that were erected at Flemington for the rich and/or beautiful people. They were more like palaces. And like palaces, there were guards at the door. It was strictly invitation only.

'Follow my lead,' muttered Mitchell as he strode up to the bouncer outside the Emirates marquee. 'Hello, I've lost my invitation, but I'm Mitch Mitchell, you probably recognise me from TV. James Packer can vouch for me.'

The bouncer was as large and as impassive as an Easter Island statue. 'Invitation only.'

'No, really, I insist.' Mitchell was nothing if not persistent. 'Is there a manager we can talk to?'

'I am the manager.' Either the bouncer didn't watch much current affairs or he wasn't a fan of Mitchell's work. 'If you don't leave, I'll have you removed.'

We skulked off. '"You might recognise me from TV"? Is that the best you could come up with?'

'Have you got any better ideas?' Mitchell sounded cranky.

I remembered from my waitressing days that there was another entrance for the staff. 'Let's go around the back and see if there's a way in there.'

I led the way through the throng, but there was some heavy-looking security placed at the hospitality entrance as well.

'It's not looking good,' I said. 'We can't pass for waitstaff dressed like this.'

'Maybe we could cut our way in via one of other the marquees,' said Mitchell.

'You got a knife on you?'

'No.'

An idea popped into my head. 'Can I borrow your phone?'

'Sure.'

It was a new-fangled smartphone like Brucie's, but luckily I'd humoured Brucie when he'd wanted to show me every single aspect of this wonderful new technology. I opened Mitchell's contacts and sure enough, Selena was there. Before Mitchell could see what I was doing, I sent her a text. *I hear you're looking for Brick Brown. Get me into the Emirates tent and I'll give you exclusive vision rights.*

Where R U? The quick response made me think we had a chance.

Outside. Problem with bouncers.

Wait there.

Don't bring camera now or she'll run.

Five minutes later the boofhead at security got a call and decided to let us in. I couldn't help but be a bit impressed: Selena had connections and knew how to use them. But I still wasn't convinced that this mission was going to come up with any goods.

As we entered the marquee I grabbed a glass of champagne from a passing waiter. Dutch courage. Inside it was amazingly lavish, including a chandelier that looked like it had been acquired from a French aristocrat who was downsizing. Among the crowd I recognised various faces—TV weathermen, soap opera actors and footballers were stuffing down the hors d'oeuvres and free grog. Already some of the soapie starlets looked a bit wobbly on their stilettos. Not surprising since most of them didn't look old enough to drink.

'Is there some super VIP area that he might be in?' I asked. 'These guys all look pretty C-list.'

'Let's mingle and see what we can find out,' said Mitchell.

'You lead the way. I won't know anyone here. Except maybe a couple of guys in the band.'

'Fine.' Mitchell grabbed my hand and pulled me towards a throng of people hovering near a food table. They had to be journalists, judging by the speed with which they were ambushing any waiters who emerged with trays of food.

'Biggsy,' said Mitchell, grasping the hand of a short, thickset man and shaking vigorously. 'Long time no see.'

'Mitchell.' The man nearly coughed up a smoked mussel on his shiny-looking suit. 'I heard you were back in the country. Good to see you. You're looking well after the whole kidnap thing.'

'This is Brick,' Mitchell said, and my own hand was pulverised by a large sweaty mitt.

'Nice to meet you,' said Biggsy, his eyes hovering at my chest area. 'She's lovely, Mitchell. Well done.'

I decided to spill a drink on him as soon as practical, although I doubted it would make his suit look any worse.

'So, what movers and shakers have we got here this year?' asked Mitchell.

'It's the same group of wannabes and hangers-on as last year,' said the man, stuffing another hors d'oeuvre in his face.

'What about the serious money? Where are they hiding?'

'I think they're upstairs watching the races, boring old farts. It's much more fun down here. This champagne is sixty dollars a bottle!' He lurched after a waiter, who saw him coming and swerved in the opposite direction. I grabbed a fresh glass from another passing waiter. Who knew when I'd get another chance to taste real French champagne?

'Steady on.' Mitchell frowned. 'You may need your wits about you.'

I rolled my eyes, but no sooner had he spoken than he was proven true. Emerging from the crowd was Selena in a shimmery blue dress and some headwear that looked like a cross between a hat, a fascinator and a pandanus plant. It was hanging down over her eyes, obscuring most of her expression, but judging by the amount of teeth she was flashing, she was very happy to see us.

'Mitch, sweetie, and my old friend Brick! I didn't know you two knew each other! Is there something going on here?' She waggled her finger flirtatiously.

'Selena! Fancy seeing you here,' I said as insincerely as possible.

'I'm here every year, babe. Haven't you seen me on the news? I was runner-up in Fashions on the Field last year. The designers were all begging me to wear one of their dresses this year. What do you think, Mitch?' Selena gave a twirl as she smiled coquettishly at Mitchell.

'It's unusual.' Mitchell looked singularly unimpressed.

'You're looking so well, Mitch. I'm glad you're getting on with things.' Selena attempted to look sensitive and caring.

'Who are you here with?' Mitchell asked.

'Oh, my boyfriend's just over there.' She waved gaily at a man whose large stature was unsuited to his baby blue suit with dark blue trim, reminiscent of something I'd last seen in a John Hughes flick from the 1980s. Footballers were bigger fashion victims than their girlfriends these days. I would have hardly thought it possible.

Mitchell pointedly avoided looking interested in Selena's romantic choices. 'So can you get us into the VIP area?'

Selena smiled like a joyful Cheshire cat. 'Follow me.'

She set off through the crowd, swaying in her teetering heels yet still managing to text as she walked. No doubt she was summoning a camera crew so she could ambush me as quickly as possible.

Mitchell was striding behind Selena without a backward glance—totally focussed on his mission—and the crowd parted to let them through. They attracted glances from people who would no doubt be gossiping about their alleged reunion the second they had the opportunity. I was content to be attracting no attention at all.

We approached a door with more bouncers either side but this time, due to Selena's magic, they let us through with a mere nod. I scanned for exits and gave thanks I was wearing waitressing-appropriate heels. I was going to run for it at the first sight of a grumpy-looking man in a polo shirt, well before he could hoist his camera onto his shoulder.

This second room was even more luxuriously decorated than the first. A life-sized ice sculpture of a horse stood on the bar, melting quietly under the designer lighting. Garlands of exotic flowers were woven around columns, adding to the scent of power and money that rolled off these people who occupied a strata of society high, high above the nouveau riche, famous, drunk and giddy crowd we'd just left behind. This room was more sparsely populated with tastefully dressed people who wouldn't blink an eye at thousand-dollars-a-bottle champagne and caviar on a biscuit that definitely wasn't a Jatz.

'Here we are.' Selena made a sweeping gesture as we entered, in the manner of a gameshow hostess.

Mitchell leaned forward as if to whisper a special thanks in her ear and tipped his entire glass of champagne down her front. Although there was very little cloth to get ruined, Selena looked horrified. Like an enraged baby, she opened her mouth to scream, but no sound came out. Mitchell took my hand as he strode over to the bar to get a refill, leaving Selena to run straight for the ladies' room.

'She is really going to get you for that,' I said as I accepted a glass of the special room champagne. 'She's already out to get me.'

'Wear it as a badge of honour,' Mitchell replied as he scanned the room in a businesslike fashion.

'I reckon we've got about five minutes before she comes back with a camera crew. Do you see him anywhere?'

Mitchell didn't answer, but I could see by the way he squared his shoulders that he'd spotted his target. I looked over. In the flesh, Dave Mullett was not an overly big man, but he stood out even in this group of super VIPs. More than his startling white hair and impeccably tailored navy suit, he wore an aura of power. Ruthlessness and power. A large man, the same one who'd attended the planning meeting, was hovering nearby. He was wearing a black suit like before and designer sunglasses, although he'd changed his facial hair design from a goatee to sideburns.

The three glasses of champagne I'd drunk had given me a slight buzz, but the sight of Mullett and his bodyguard sobered me up at once. Again I looked down at my shoes. I could run if I needed to. Mentally I planned an escape route—one that wouldn't go past the toilets, in case it led me straight into Selena.

'Stay here, if you like,' said Mitchell. 'No point you getting mixed up in all this.'

'Hello? What page are you on? I'm mixed up already. Whoever took a pot shot at us in council must have seen us together because they tried to run me down on my bike.'

'Fine. Do whatever you want.' Mitchell obviously thought I was snubbing his gallantry. He strode off towards Mullett, leaving me to trot inelegantly behind him in an effort to keep up.

Unlike most of the hundred thousand people at Flemington on this day, Mullett was actually watching the horses, albeit via a giant plasma TV. I wondered how much he had riding on the result—probably more than I'd earn in my entire lifetime.

'Mr Mullet,' said Mitchell in what I now realised was his special 'news' voice. 'Mitch Mitchell. So glad to see you here.'

Dave Mullet was too powerful and too male to show any reaction beyond a slight narrowing of his eyes. 'How did you get in here?'

Mitchell ignored the question—probably a good tactic since I estimated we had less than a minute before we were going to be thrown out.

'Mr Mullett. I want to ask you about a building application your company recently made for a tower block on Brunswick Street.'

Mullett's face darkened slightly, but otherwise his expression remained impassive. 'I don't believe you were invited here, Mitch Mitchell. Or you, Miss Brown.'

I was chilled that Mullett knew my name. Until the bicycle incident, I'd convinced myself that I was an insignificant player in this whole debacle—one who didn't deserve to have her legs broken. They weren't the most shapely pins in the world, but I was still very fond of them.

Mitchell had also noticed Mullett's reaction and switched to a different line of questioning. 'I also want to ask about a woman called Betty Jones,' said Mitchell. 'I believe you may have adopted her twin sons. The Chinese consider twins lucky, you know. Do your sons happen to know where their mother is now? I'm interested in talking to her.'

Mullett's eyes looked dangerous—as if he could turn people to stone. 'I'm warning you, Mitchell.'

In a moment of clarity, I realised we were in real danger. It was quite possible that no one would remember we were here. They were all distracted by the horses, the alcohol, the 'scene'.

Mullett looked to his left as if to beckon someone to come and evict us as violently as possible, but his body-guard, for once, was not present. People were beginning to drift towards the windows. It's said ad nauseam that the Melbourne Cup is the race that stops the nation. I'd never been so thankful for Australia's obsession with major sporting events.

'We'll see ourselves out,' I said, grabbing Mitchell's arm. The race had begun—the caller's voice was piped through the entire complex. Three minutes and it would be over. We couldn't get out of Flemington in three minutes, so I dragged Mitchell towards the door Selena had taken after her dress disaster.

The ladies' room was decorated with even more vast swathes of flowers than the bar. I could see only one of the toilet stalls was occupied, but Selena wasn't alone.

'I called you here to help me fix my dress not to give you a head job, you moron.' Selena's voice had lost its plummy TV tones.

'Please, ba—'

The whine was cut off as I kicked the door open as vio-lently as I could manage in formal wear. The door caught

Selena's boyfriend on his temple and he was felled like a giant tree, pinning her to the cistern.

'What the fuck?' she gasped.

Mitchell was looking at me like I'd just lost my mind—which wasn't far from the truth.

'We're switching places,' I said. 'Help me.' Together, Mitchell and I pulled Selena out from under the incredible hulk, who was sleeping like a drunken baby.

I balled my hand into a fist. 'Give me your dress or I'll mess up your face.' Selena's dress was already unzipped, so it was easy enough to get her out of it. 'And give me your phone.'

She handed it over reluctantly.

'Grab his jacket and hat.' Luckily Selena's boyfriend had already taken off his jacket and left them on the tasteful couch in the corner of the rest room, because there was no way we'd be able to move him without the help of small crane.

I pushed Selena back in the cubicle. Her near nudity would hopefully keep her in there for a while.

'You've always been a fucking slut!' she yelled through the door. 'I'm going to get you for this!'

'Unzip me,' I said to Mitch. 'And put on his jacket.'

I wiggled out of my own dress and into Selena's. It was a bit like getting out of a neck-to-knee swimsuit and then into a string bikini, a confusing string bikini at that. 'How the fuck did she get her boobs into this thing?'

'Selena has tremendous willpower,' muttered Mitchell as he pulled on the footballer's hideous blue jacket. 'But really bad taste.'

I arranged my shawl over my chest—in the absence of Hollywood tape (or gaffer tape), it was the best I could do—and pinned Selena's fascinator on my head. 'Take his hat as well.' I picked up the blue top hat and shoved it on Mitchell's head. It also featured decoration that resembled a pandanus plant.

'Let's go. Once the big race is finished, all bets are off.'

I grabbed my dress, rolled it into a ball and shoved it under my arm. 'If we're lucky we'll be mistaken for two pot plants.'

We left the toilets as casually as possible and made a beeline for the VIP room exit. People were cheering and hugging as the horses crossed the finish line. We made it out and into the general area of the marquee without being spotted.

Although we'd spent less than ten minutes with the high rollers, the people in the Birdcage looked fifty per cent drunker. They were also fifty per cent more difficult to cut through. It was like a Tokyo train platform in rush hour. If Selena's dress hadn't already been covered in wine, it was now.

We were tantalisingly close to the exit when the goon squad turned up. Mitchell held up his hands, as if this somehow indicated that he was harmless, but the bouncers, led by Mullet's bodyguard, weren't in the mood to talk. Mitchell was soon in a headlock. I fared slightly better in that only my upper arms were being crushed by a hand the size of an LP record.

They began to move us—but not towards the exit. I realised they were heading for a more private area, intended for the super celebs to come and go by. Were we about to be shoved into the back of a black Mercedes and driven off to some industrial wasteland before receiving a quick bullet in the head? Surely they wouldn't. We'd been seen at the event by a number of people—journalists even—who could attest to our last movements. Or could they? They were all pretty drunk.

Pessimism began to overwhelm me. Was my life going to flash before my eyes when the end came? Was it going to be a life I could feel proud of? Or was I going to wish I'd had someone else's life? Would all my memories suddenly come rushing back? Would I see the man's face? The bogeyman of my dreams?

Then we were outside and Melbourne's weather had worked its mysterious charms. It had been sunny a mere half an hour ago, but now there was a crash of thunder and the next second there was a deluge. Melbourne's weather god was feeling really cheeky this year, waiting until just after the big race—when the crowd was at its pulsating zenith—to pull a 180-degree turn. Instant chaos ensued as people tried to prevent hundred-dollar hats from being ruined and the ground turned to mud under a thousand stiletto heels.

Mitchell took advantage of the drenching and the slippery gel in his hair. He twisted his head out of the headlock with a pop and grabbed my free arm. I was being pulled at like a Christmas cracker between Mitchell and a thug. My boobs broke for freedom before I did, popping out of Selena's ridiculous dress. The split second of distraction allowed me to wriggle out of one glove like an X-rated Rita Hayworth.

Without pausing to try and recover my modesty—I was well and truly beyond caring—Mitchell and I ran straight into the madding crowd.

At first the crowd was almost worse than being manhandled by bouncers. I was stabbed several times by wayward fascinators, but my shoes held up well and Mitchell and I managed to make it to the train station—along with a thousand other soggy, drunk and very cranky punters. Mitchell happily donated the baby blue jacket to me to restore my modesty and we threw what was probably a thousand dollars' worth of pandanus headwear in the nearest bin.

CHAPTER TWENTY-ONE

After forty-five minutes we managed to get on a train—neither of us felt up to the street-fighting required to catch a taxi. We stood with the rest of the throng like sheep waiting to be dipped until North Melbourne Station, where we were able to catch a taxi back to my place. It had been a long and fretful day. I didn't even know who had won the race that stops the nation and frankly, I didn't give a damn. I wanted a hot shower, dry clothes and a supportive bra. I stomped up the steps to the porch, fumbling for my keys, and it was several moments before I realised that the door was ajar.

Mitchell gestured for me to be quiet as he gently pushed the door. It swung open with a creak and we tiptoed into the hallway. The front bedrooms looked undisturbed, but as we neared the loungeroom I could see that the boxes of files we'd left there were gone. As was Mitchell's computer, which I'd convinced him we couldn't take to the Cup with us.

'My laptop!' said Mitchell.

'Shh, they might still be here.' I continued to the kitchen while Mitchell remained frozen like a tragic statue. Through the doorway, I could see that a coffee cup had been smashed on the floor and the pieces lay in a brown puddle. My heart lurched. Bunny must have been home—perhaps sitting at the breakfast bar having coffee. I could just see a pair of small feet emerging from behind the bench.

I rushed through the door to find Bunny lying on the floor. Her hands were bound behind her back and she'd been gagged with a tea towel.

'Bunny. Oh my God.' I crouched down next to her and she opened her eyes. She looked wild with fury and started making frantic noises through the gag.

'It's okay, I think they're gone.'

I pulled the tea towel down from her face and grabbed a bread knife to saw through the ties. It looked like they'd used a bit of our washing line. 'Who did this to you? Did you see them?' I could feel a sob starting in my throat.

With the gag off, Bunny started coughing and making disturbing choking noises. 'It was a man, a big man. He was wearing a balaclava. I didn't see his face. He hit me and then tied me up.'

Another awful thought assaulted me. 'Where's Timmy? Was he here too?'

'No, he went to one of his 48-hour-straight computer game tournaments, thank God. But Mavis was here. Where's Mavis?'

A quick search uncovered Mavis in the bathtub, also tied and gagged. She sobbed as we pulled her out and cut the cord binding her wrists.

By this stage Mitchell had regained his composure so I decided to lay into him, in lieu of the actual perpetrator being present. 'This is going too far! Bunny and Mavis could have been killed. What the hell have you got us mixed up in?' Then despite my best efforts to supress it, I began to cry as well.

'It's okay, Brick.' Bunny put her arms around me in an awkward manner, making me miss Baz and his bear hugs even more. 'I was tied up heaps of times that summer I worked in Zimbabwe. I'll have a chat to a shrink and I'll be fine.'

'We'd better call the police so you can make a report for your insurance,' said Mitchell. 'But I don't think there's much else they can do.'

'This sucks,' said Bunny, summing up the situation succinctly. 'And what happened to your dress, Brick? You left the house looking like a million bucks and you've come back looking like a two-buck hooker.'

* * *

Bunny and Mitchell dutifully went through the motions of making a police report although they both agreed to leave out some details for the time being in case it pushed Mavis over the edge. I took the opportunity to have a long, hot bath while I tried to pull myself back together, both physically and emotionally. In all the excitement, we hadn't managed to lay eyes on Errol Grimes at the Melbourne

Cup—if he was even there. I couldn't help but feel relieved. In my mind's eye I recalled the photo from the newspaper taken when Grimes had been targeted by the anti-highway protesters. He'd looked dangerous.

I emerged from the bathroom to find Bunny and Mavis sitting at the breakfast bar, each with a large glass of wine. Through the glass of the back door I could see Mitchell in the yard. He was smoking and talking on his phone.

'What a day it's turned out to be,' said Bunny. 'Help yourself to some wine.'

'I don't mind if I do,' I said, opening the fridge.

I was just pouring myself a mug when Mitchell came back in. 'Before you get liquored up, Brick, we have to work out what we're going to do next.'

'I think you'll find this is a bottle of wine.' I took a big sip. 'And I thought there was no "we". Suddenly there's a "we"?'

Mitchell nearly knocked over the wine bottle as he slammed his phone down on the table. Both Bunny and I grabbed for it the way a mother lunges for her endangered child.

'I'm not letting Mullett get away with this! It's intimidation! Not to mention all the documents they've stolen that belong to Sister Margaret.'

'But what can we do?' I asked. 'We can't just rock up to his mansion in Toorak or wherever and knock on the door! And I'm sure he'd have a security system that's beyond anything I can take on—even if I am pretty good with a bobby pin.' I grabbed another mug and poured Mitchell some vino. 'Besides, there's a very real chance that he'll have us killed if we create too much fuss. We need to rest and regroup. We're out of leads.'

'I suggest we get pissed,' said Bunny. 'It's still Cup Day after all.'

Bunny's ability to emotionally compartmentalise went a bit too far sometimes and I feared that one day she would develop a split personality—but she did have a good point about Cup Day. Mitchell gave in and accepted a mug of wine. He was a journalist after all.

Mavis finished her drink and then looked so wobbly we considered putting her back in the bathtub for her own safety. 'I took a couple of valium,' she mumbled. 'I might just need a lie down.'

'How many valium?' Bunny asked. 'Because I'm planning to get too drunk to drive you to Emergency if you need your stomach pumped.'

'Nah, I'll be fine—just need a li'l sleep.'

'I'll put her in my room,' said Bunny. 'In the recovery position.'

Bunny returned from tending to Mavis and we broke open another bottle of wine, which went down very easily. Mitchell was back outside on his phone. I told Bunny about our encounter with Mullett at the Cup and our subsequent run-in with Selena. We turned on the TV to watch the news. The ABC in particular loved to focus on all the drunk punters and with the rainstorm, there was some extra funny footage—but thankfully none of me. We'd just opened a third bottle of wine when there was a knock at the front door.

My stomach lurched. 'Are you expecting anyone?' I whispered.

'No, are you?'

We tiptoed down the çorridor to the front door and Bunny peered through the peephole.

'I think it's Mavis's mother,' she said in a theatrical whisper that was probably heard next door.

'How do you know?'

'I recognise her from the social papers. My mother reads that shit.'

'Mavis must have called her.'

Bunny took a deep breath in an obvious effort to look less drunk before she opened the door to reveal a woman who epitomised Toorak matron: facelift, tasteful make-up and manicure, expensive trouser suit and more pearls than a small island nation. I could see where Mavis got her beautiful hair. Winsome DuBois's bob was an artful ash blonde colour and fell with the grace of a hundred-dollar blow wave.

Her face was curiously smooth and without expression, so I couldn't tell if she was surprised to be confronted by two very drunk women. 'I'm looking for my daughter Mavis.' Even her voice was Toorak.

'Yes, of course, do come in,' said Bunny, suddenly sounding like she was about to offer tea and scones.

The older woman took a hesitant step into the hallway, clearly afraid to touch anything lest she catch hepatitis. Luckily Bunny's bedroom door was not far from the front door, sparing her from venturing too far inside our den of iniquity.

'Mavis, your mother is here,' I called as I entered Bunny's bedroom.

Mavis appeared to be asleep, clutching her phone to her cheek as if it were a security blanket.

'Mavis.' I shook her gently. 'Your mother's come to get you.'

Her eyes shot open. 'My mother! What the fuck is she doing here? Why would you call her?'

'Calm down. I didn't call your mother. How would I know her number? You must have called her.'

'Why in the name of fuck would I call the old bitch?'

'Maybe you wanted to tell her "she done raised you wrong", I don't know.' I took a deep breath and attempted to recover my patience. 'But she's here and she wants to take you home. I think it's a good idea.'

'What the fuck would you know?'

I gave up trying to be nice and left the room as Winsome entered.

'Good Lord, Mavis, you look dreadful,' I heard her say as I headed back to the kitchen. 'What have you done to your hair? You look like a lesbian.'

I poured myself a glass of cool water while I tried to lower my blood pressure back to something in the normal range.

Bunny appeared in the kitchen a few minutes later.

'Mavis has gone home with her mother,' she said. 'And Lady Winsome asked us to be discreet about her daughter's "little breakdown".'

'So do you want to ring *Woman's Day* or shall I?'

Three hours later we'd drunk all Bunny's good stuff and were onto a nasty little cask wine that was left over from a Christmas party—possibly a 1980s Christmas party, judging by the outfit of the woman on the cardboard box.

Mitchell had given up talking on his phone, and he and Bunny were trading war stories in what had rapidly become a game of one-upmanship. Mitchell was winning on the horrific traffic accident stories, but Bunny had the upper hand with regard to tropical diseases.

'I had malaria and cholera at the same time.' Bunny was slurring. 'You should have seen the shit that was coming out of me—looked like custard. It was unbelievable. And the pain was excruciating—like I was shitting out my intestines.'

'That's nothing,' said Mitchell. 'I was in a motorcycle crash in Cambodia and I broke my ankle. The skin was hanging off all over the place because I'd been wearing flip-flops. The bloody doctors wanted to cut my foot off. I had to refuse all painkillers while they set the bone and stitched the skin back on. I was afraid if I took any drugs, I'd wake up an amputee. The pain was unbelievable.'

'And this little incident,' slurred Bunny. 'It was nothing compared to this one time, in the Sudan, my entire medical convoy was taken hostage by militants. We were held in a goddamn cave for two nights, guarded by twelve-year-old soldiers hyped on speed. It was unbelievable. Hey, weren't you kidnapped, too? I think I read about it in the paper. How many days were you held?'

'Forty days and forty nights. Bloody biblical, hey?' He gave a bitter laugh that seemed to be edging towards hysteria the longer it went on. 'It was … it was …'

For once, Mitchell seemed to run out of words. He covered his eyes with one hand and for a second I thought he was going to break down and cry, but he removed his hand and his eyes were dry.

'It was all because of a dumb little shit who thought all you needed to be a journalist was a laptop and a fucking smartphone,' he continued. 'And bloody social media. This bloody social media shit nearly got us killed. The idiot posted photos of his hotel. Told everyone where he was going and with who. May as well put up a sign saying "kidnap me".'

'Have you ever been up in a hot air balloon, Mitchell?' I asked in a bid to change the subject.

He took a deep breath and recovered himself. 'Sure, once or twice.'

'What's it like?'

'Peaceful.' From his tone, I gathered that he didn't think this was a good thing.

'I was in one that nearly crashed,' said Bunny, returning the conversation to its previous bent. 'It was in Kenya. I didn't even really want to go up in the bloody thing. But I was with a group of people who wanted to see the wildebeest migration or some shit like that.'

Bunny was starting to look seriously drunk. She was holding her eyelids open by raising her eyebrows and tipping her head back. It was amazing how such a small person could put away so much alcohol, but there had to be a limit and she was nearing hers. We were just about to find out what happened during her balloon ride when she slumped suddenly into the beanbag and began to snore loudly.

'Okay, you're the winner, Mitchell.'

'What do you mean?'

'You've drunk a fifty-kilogram woman under the table. You've proved your manhood.'

'I'm sensing a lot of hostility towards men, Brick. Why is that?' he asked, moving down the couch towards me.

'Too many saxophone players,' I said, moving away. 'Not to mention the drummers. But it's okay. I'm celibate now and so far it's working out for me.'

'Celibate?' Mitchell said loudly, as if addressing an audience. 'Celibate? Why would a woman like you decide to be celibate?'

'A woman like me?' I asked, my eyes narrowing. 'What's that supposed to mean?'

'You being celibate—it's like having a Lamborghini and then just leaving it in the garage.'

'You're comparing me to a fast car? Mr award-winning journalist, representative of the oppressed and downtrodden. You're no better than Selena. You probably think I shagged the mayor as well.'

'What? How did we go from me giving you a compliment to you shagging Dickie Ruffhead? Is that what people are saying about you?'

'How did you go from shagging Selena to giving me a so-called compliment?' I countered.

'Ahh.' Mitchell smiled in an annoyingly smug fashion. 'I get it.'

'Get what?'

'You think I'm comparing the two of you. Well, don't worry. There may be a passing resemblance, but there's no comparison. Anyway, I was off my head on pills and booze when I hooked up with her. I'm not even sure if we even had sex.'

It was more than I needed or wanted to know. 'I think it's time for you to hit the hay, Mitchell.'

'I'm just saying,' he said, as he staggered off, 'the offer's there.'

I left Bunny on the beanbag—although I did roll her into the safety position first and put a glass of water next to her—and then headed for bed myself, after stacking every chair in the house against the front and back doors.

I could already hear Mitchell snoring through the door of Bunny's room. Typical. Proposition a girl and then pass out in someone else's bed before she has a chance to reconsider.

CHAPTER TWENTY-TWO

I collapsed on my bed, but it seemed I'd only just closed my eyes when the telephone shrilled. I wondered if I was dreaming, and then I scrabbled for it, trying to answer before it could wake Bunny or Mitchell.

'Brick?' said a voice as I answered. In the background was a hubbub of shouting and sirens; not the kind of thing you want to hear when you answer the phone in the middle of the night. A heavy breather would be preferable. 'Brick, it's Gene. You'd better come down here. The Phoenix is on fire.'

Naturally, my first thought was of Baz and then Flora. 'Is anyone inside?'

'I'm not sure,' he said. 'The fire brigade's just got here. You'd better come down.'

'I'll be right there,' I said, dropping the phone. For a second I was frozen, not knowing which urgent action to undertake first. Then I grabbed the nearest clothes and ran to wake Mitchell. It seemed he liked to sleep naked.

'Mitchell, wake up.' I shook him by the shoulder, but he barely stirred. I considered throwing a glass of water on him but settled for a violent face pinch. 'Muggerdich!'

'Mum?' said Mitchell, opening one eye.

'The Phoenix is on fire. Come on. I've got to get down there.'

I didn't have to say it twice. Mitchell went from a groggy, half-asleep mess to wide awake and seemingly completely sober, pulling on his clothes.

'I'll drive,' he said as we cleared away the chairs I'd stacked in front of the door. 'Wait.' He suddenly stopped. 'This could be a trap. Who called you?'

'It was Gene. I could hear the sirens in the background.'

We resumed moving the chairs I'd stacked.

'Hold on.' It was my turn to hesitate. 'I don't want to leave Bunny here. What if one of those thugs comes back?'

'Fine, I'll grab her,' said Mitchell. 'We'll have to hot-wire the Kombi. It won't matter if she vomits in that.'

'Bunny hasn't vomited since 1995.'

Bunny was still on the beanbag where I'd left her. She didn't stir as Mitchell put her over his shoulder and transferred her to the van.

The hair-raising drive to the pub was the longest five minutes of my life—I could see why Mitchell had been in so many car accidents. I clutched at Bunny, who had roused momentarily at one hairpin turn, but was now once again blissfully unconscious. It was probably a good thing that I was still drunk. I could kid myself that it was the alcohol that was making me feel like throwing up, instead of the fear that I was about to find out that Uncle Baz's charred body had been discovered in the smoking remains of his own club.

When we arrived, the scene was strangely orderly. Two fire trucks were parked in the street and firefighters were hosing with a minimum of fuss, the blue and red lights sparkling off the wet concrete. A small group of civilians watched from the sidelines. I couldn't tell if they were residents from nearby buildings or just passers-by who'd stopped to see what was going on.

The acrid smell of smoke burned my throat as I jumped out of the car ran towards the club. I scanned the crowd for Gene and found him not far from the fire trucks. He looked more death-like than usual, clutching Bojangles the cat, who looked a bit singed, but otherwise as grumpy as ever.

'Brick.' Gene's voice was croaky. He clutched at me with one hand and my heart sank into my ugg boots. It's some indication of my deranged state of mind that I'd actually left the house while wearing them; usually I wouldn't even answer the door with them on. Gene's dire expression seemed to be confirming my worst fears.

'I must have fallen asleep in the shop. I'm still packing up. I'd had a few cones and I got woken up by the sirens,' said Gene. 'There was smoke everywhere, man.'

'Who called the fire brigade? Was it you?' asked Mitchell.

'No. I don't know who called them, man,' said Gene. 'I just hope the smoke doesn't hurt my vinyl.'

'Fuck your vinyl, Gene.' I shook him forcefully. 'What about Baz? Is there any chance he was in there?'

Gene looked hurt that I might not care as much about his records as about my uncle. 'No, man. I don't think so. One of the fire dudes said they caught it pretty early. They sent some guys in there and they haven't found anyone.'

'Oh, thank God,' I said. 'Baz is insured for fire. It was the one insurance I insisted we had to keep.'

A fire officer approached and I identified myself as a relative of the owner. He told us more or less what Gene had just said—only with less 'man's. Unfortunately he couldn't—or wouldn't—say what had started the fire. It was hard to see how much damage had been done from the outside: the brickwork was blackened, but otherwise it looked the same. The firefighters said I wasn't allowed to go inside.

Mitchell disappeared off to do his newshound thing, leaving me with Gene. Flora pulled up in her old Mini. She was wearing a patterned dressing gown and slippers.

'I jumped right in the car when Gene rang,' she said. She grabbed me in a rough embrace. 'Have they found anything? Have they found Baz?'

'No, they haven't found anyone,' I said. 'And they say there hasn't been too much damage inside. Do you think it could have been arson?'

'It's the fat cats. They bought my place, and now they're out for the whole block. They're prepared to smoke everyone out if necessary. If my nonno was still alive, he'd stop this, I'll tell ya. But the old days are gone ... they're gone.'

For once I had to agree with him.

'I'm not going to stand for it,' said Gene. 'Like the time the FBI crashed my computer and stole all my maps of Atlantis. I stood up to them and I can take on these guys, too.'

Once again Gene had gone off-piste, so to speak. 'Don't worry, Gene,' I said, giving him a reassuring pat. 'We can take you home if you like.'

Flora extracted Bojangles from Gene's arms and headed off to interrogate the firefighters. Mitchell returned. He was like a man reborn, zinging with the adrenaline of the war zone.

'What have you found out?' I asked.

He put his arm around me. 'Let's get out of here and I'll fill you in.'

'We'd better take Gene with us.'

Gene was now staring at the blackened building and sodden sidewalk as if he was about to enter a catatonic state.

'Come on, Gene,' I said, gently.

He was just starting to take a few baby steps towards me when I was blinded by a floodlight full in my face.

'Miss Brown. Is it true you were having relations with a respected married man, a pillar of the community and basically your boss?'

I blinked, scrabbling to comprehend what was happening. My brain just didn't seem able to catch up with my eyes. It was Selena. It was four in the morning and she was wearing a full face of make-up and a grey power suit— sensible considering the amount of ash in the air. She was holding a handicam with a bright light attached to it.

'Is this your new lover?' She spoke loudly in her weird singsong news voice as she directed the camera and light towards Gene. 'Aren't you afraid of dying in her bed? Like the mayor did?'

Gene was looking at Selena as though he was having an acid flashback. But before the situation could get any more mortifying, Mitchell snapped into action.

'Back off, Selena, or I'll have a word with your managing editor about your creative use of expense accounts that time in Geneva. And then I'll get on to the Broadcasting Commission.'

Selena—always the professional—didn't miss a beat. 'Or is it you she's sleeping with, Mitchell? You really get around, don't you, Miss Brown? How many other men are there?'

At that moment, a familiar-looking van pulled up behind us with a screech. I was simultaneously overjoyed and horrified to see Bunny behind the wheel. 'Get in,' she slurred.

I pushed Gene through the sliding door and jumped in after him while Mitchell got in the passenger seat. Bunny burned rubber, nearly hitting Selena in the process. Maybe she'd been taking tips from third world taxi drivers or maybe it was because she was still at least five times over the legal limit.

'Pull over,' said Mitchell when we were safely clear of the chaos. 'You shouldn't be driving.'

'Fine,' said Bunny. 'But what's going on? Last thing I remember I was at home on the beanbag and then I woke up in the van. I couldn't find the keys, but Kombis are pretty easy to break into and hotwire. I learned in Somalia. Who was that woman with the floodlight and camera crew?'

'That was Mitchell's ex-girlfriend.' I'd decided to channel my mortification into anger. 'Lovely girl. I don't know why you two broke up—oh, I remember. She dumped you for a footy player whose IQ was lower than the number on his jumper.'

Mitchell didn't say anything, but I could see he was bothered by his clenched jaw.

'Could it be a worse time for her to ambush me? I'm wearing ugg boots, for Christ's sake. I should have let her get me on camera on Cup Day. At least I looked nice then.'

'Stop moaning,' said Mitchell. 'Nobody takes Selena seriously. I thought you were more worried about your uncle.'

'Don't tell me to worry about Baz.' My voice was nearing a scream. The horror of not knowing whether Baz was alive or dead, seeing his beloved club put out of action and being erroneously shamed for sleeping with a 68-year-old sleazebag while wearing pyjama bottoms, a shapeless, poo-brown jumper and ugg boots, it was all too much. I punched Mitchell in the arm as hard as I could and burst into tears. He looked equal parts horrified at the sight of a crying woman and outraged at being attacked while driving.

'You've made her cry now,' said Bunny protectively. 'You really are her type.'

'Her type?'

'Yeah. A total dickhead.'

CHAPTER TWENTY-THREE

My hysteria had subsided somewhat by the time we got home. Gene, meanwhile, had slipped into a catatonic state. We brought him inside and put him on the couch so Bunny could keep him under observation. While still in her Dr Bunny mode, she gave me a sedative and I sank into blissful oblivion.

When I opened my eyes again, I could almost believe the previous night's events were a hallucination brought on by bad cask wine, but there was no mistaking the reek of smoke in my hair.

Worse was when I remembered the encounter with Selena. I hid under my doona and groaned softly to myself to see if it would make me feel less mortified. It didn't. I would have stayed under the doona indefinitely, but I was desperate for water.

I shuffled towards the kitchen, dreading what I might find—the days were getting progressively more and more demoralising. Only Bunny was in the kitchen. She was slumped at the breakfast bar nursing a cup of tea, looking a little worse for wear but still way better than I felt. The world was not a just place.

'Morning.' I looked at the clock. 'Or afternoon, rather.'

'I feel like ten kinds of shit,' said Bunny. 'Including camel shit. I'm never drinking again.'

I silently seconded the motion while I washed down a couple of headache tablets with a litre of cold water.

'I called in sick for you at work,' said Bunny. 'I said you had food poisoning.' She rubbed forehead. 'Sorry if that's a bit uncreative, but it's all I could think of—my brain's coming out my ears.'

'Shit.' My mobile phone was on the breakfast bar. I had missed eleven calls and a text from Brucie (*WTF girlfriend?*). 'Selena must have told someone at council her disgusting theory about me and the mayor. I'm going to have to resign so I never have to face any of them again. I suppose it doesn't matter whether I keep the council job or not anymore, since I don't even know if Baz is still alive.' I heard my voice rising towards hysteria again, but I didn't seem to be able to control it.

'I'm sure Baz is fine.' Bunny dragged herself off the stool at the breakfast bar and held my shoulders firmly. 'He's got more lives than those mangy cats you've let into my house. And I've been keeping an eye on the news. Selena hasn't gone public with the story yet. She might drop it.'

'Yeah, right. You don't know what she's like. In Year 5 she tried to set my hair on fire.'

'I think you've got more to worry about than Selena if what Mavis says is true.'

'What do you mean?'

'If the premier of Victoria had anything to do with your foster mother's death, he is not going to want that to become public knowledge.' Bunny looked me in the eyes. She had on the this-is-serious expression I imagine she used on patients who weren't following their treatment plans. 'I know you don't like to talk about your past, but you were a traumatised child when Baz took you in. It seems to me that Nora's death might have had something to do with that trauma.'

'Traumatised?'

'Baz told me that you hardly talked for the first two years you lived with him.'

I picked up a dishrag and began wiping the counter. 'Baz said that about me?'

'It was after I'd had a particularly gruelling time in the Sudan. Seeing hordes of dying and damaged children day after day … it's not great for a person's mental health.'

'You talked to Baz?'

'Why not? He owns a bar. Bartenders are known to be good listeners.'

'He never mentioned it, that's all.'

'Baz can be discreet. And I'm sure he only told me about what you were like as a kid because he knows how much I care about you. He worries about you, you know. He worries that you're not reaching your full potential, that you feel obliged to stay working for him at the Phoenix.'

It was turning out to be a week of discovery—about Baz as well as about myself. 'I love the Phoenix. I've never felt that Baz was holding me back.'

I rinsed the dishrag under the tap and pulled a thread that was coming unravelled from its edge. 'I've remembered some things: things from before I lived with Baz. They started as dreams, or I thought they were dreams, but now I'm remembering more and more.'

'It's not uncommon for children to repress traumatic memories until they're ready to deal with them.'

I couldn't stop unravelling the thread from the dish rag. It meant I didn't have to see any look of pity on Bunny's face. 'What if I'm not ready, though? What if I can't take the truth?'

'You're not a child any longer, Brick, you're a grownup. Baz gave you a pretty stable life—unconventional but stable. It was probably more stable than what I had with my parents' trainwreck divorce. We all have our traumas. That's just life.'

I put down the dishrag and squeezed Bunny's hand. 'Speaking of people avoiding their personal trauma, where's Mitchell?'

'He's out in the caravan using one of Timmy's computers. He's been there for a while.'

'Did you tell Timmy about getting tied up?'

'No.' Bunny frowned. 'No sense worrying him.' She was overly protective of her brother, but it was kind of sweet.

'Fair enough.' I sighed heavily, then continued with my hangover abatement process of another cup of tea and some Vegemite toast. Eventually I felt strong enough to go and see what Mitchell was up to.

I staggered through the disturbingly sunny backyard and into Timmy's caravan, only to discover the two men were sitting on Timmy's threadbare bed playing a video game, looking like they didn't have a care in the world.

'Brick! Finally,' said Mitchell without looking up from the screen. 'I thought you were going to sleep all day.'

'I wasn't asleep.' I closed the caravan's door to keep the sunlight out. 'I was unconscious. There's a difference.' The difference was that I felt in no way refreshed or reinvigorated.

Mitchell put down his game console. 'Whatever. I've got some interesting information for you.'

He was looking way too chirpy. I wanted to puke on him, and the van's usual smell of fake cheese pasta was making projectile vomiting a real possibility. I rode out the wave of nausea. 'What have you found out?'

'We think we've found out who set fire to Baz's club,' said Timmy, who'd been bursting to get in the conversation.

I began to feel dizzy. Mitchell grabbed my arm, opened the caravan door and steered me outside. 'Why don't we go back in the house and have a cup of tea? You're looking a bit green.'

I gulped some fresh air as we headed back to the house. Mitchell put on the kettle for more tea and we all sat around the kitchen bench. He opened Timmy's laptop and typed for a moment without speaking. For some reason, the gesture made me think of the Gail's PR department meetings—but in a fond way. I never thought I'd long to return to those days of unmitigated boredom, but if I still had a job, I vowed I would never complain about a meeting again.

'Timmy managed to hack into some CCTV from the 7-Eleven near the Phoenix.' Mitchell brought up a photo on the laptop, and we crowded in.

'Someone called the fire brigade at 2am. But look at 1.35am—this car drove past the 7-Eleven. Recognise it?'

'It looks very much like the Mercedes. The same one you nearly ended up in.'

'I reckon Mullett had his goons set the fire. Maybe he was trying to smoke your uncle out, literally.'

There was a ping and an email notification popped up on the screen. Its subject line caught my eye: *For Brick Brown.*

Mitchell looked over his shoulder at me. 'Are you expecting anything? Did you give out my email address?'

'No.' My nausea returned, but I couldn't help but watch as Mitchell opened it.

'It looks like more security footage.'

The picture was grainier than the 7-Eleven footage and shot from a high angle. It showed a small room lined with shelves. There was no audio.

'I think it's the stationery cupboard at work,' I said.

A man walked into the footage.

'That's Dickie Ruffhead,' I said. 'I recognise the hair. You don't see a bouffant combover like that much anymore. What's he doing?'

'He doesn't look interested in the stationery,' said Bunny. 'I'd say he's waiting for someone.'

I held my breath.

'So far it's about as exciting as watching reality TV,' said Bunny.

'Someone's coming in,' Mitchell said as the door to the stationery cupboard opened.

A woman entered the room and Dickie grasped her in a passionate clinch.

'Okay, too much reality now,' said Bunny.

Mitchell leaned in to scrutinise the screen. 'That doesn't look like you, Brick.'

'Of course it's not bloody me!'

'It pays to be sceptical in my line of work,' said Mitchell. 'Do you recognise her?'

It was hard to say with Dickie Ruffhead all over her— and I mean *all over*. 'I can't see her properly, if he'd only move her around a bit.'

As if on cue, Ruffhead turned the woman around, bent her over some boxes of photocopy paper, hitched up her skirt and started undoing his pants. If this wasn't revolting enough, I could now see clearly who the woman was. It was Gail. My uptight, pain-in-the-arse boss was having a quickie with the mayor in the stationery cupboard.

'Okay, seen enough now,' I said, running for the safety of the bathroom. 'I may want to have sex again myself one day and I don't need images like that in my head.'

'I think I'll stick with being a lesbian,' said Bunny.

'Okay, the deed's over,' Mitchell called. 'Didn't last long. She's leaving the cupboard. He's fixing himself up …

Oh, that's interesting. He's taking out a little box. It looks like he's taking a pill. He's fixing up his hair and he's out the door.'

'Well, now we know what he was doing without his pants in the archive room. Maybe he got wise to fact that there was CCTV in the stationery cupboard and decided the archive was more private. I hope they never did it in the photocopier room.' I'd spent a lot of time using that photocopier.

'He obviously had a pre-existing heart condition and was taking medication,' commented Bunny.

'Bugger,' said Mitchell. 'He probably did die of a heart attack then. That's no help to us. I was hoping he might have been murdered.'

'Well, it does at least prove that I wasn't having an affair with Ruffhead,' I said, annoyed that Mitchell had such a one-track mind.

Mitchell raised an eyebrow. 'Well, it doesn't completely prove it, but I think this footage will be enough to get Selena off your case.'

'Who sent it to you?'

'It's a Yahoo account, and I suspect pjsc97sdk5 is not their real name. It must be from someone who doesn't like your boss.'

'That could be a number of the people I work with. But how would they have gotten this footage?'

'The same way Timmy got the 7-Eleven footage. People often choose really stupid passwords for things. It's a hacker's paradise out there.'

I couldn't imagine that any of my colleagues were smart enough to hack, unless it was Brucie—and he'd be unlikely to send me anything anonymously. He loved taking credit.

Mitchell interrupted my thinking. 'I really hate to do Selena any favours, but I think we have to email her this footage. As long as you don't mind your boss being in the hot seat instead of you.'

'At times like this we have to be self-sacrificing. No wonder Gail didn't come to the mayor's memorial service. It all makes sense now.'

'Okay,' said Mitchell, hitting the computer keys with a flourish. 'It's done! Your honour is saved!'

'Hooray!' said Bunny, patting me on the back.

'Hooray!' I echoed, with less enthusiasm.

'Now, I've got some information to give you guys,' said Bunny, looking smug. 'I've also been making a few calls. I remembered what you said about Mullett's adopted children. When I was doing my internship, Mullett came into the hospital for a bone marrow transplant. It was a big deal and no one was allowed near him except the top specialists. It was a big secret who the donor was—but a friend of mine assisted on the surgery. I just rang him. I had to promise him a very expensive bottle of alcohol, but he told me that the donor was one of Mullett's sons and it was a particularly good match—the kind that's usually only possible between blood relatives.'

'What are you saying?' asked Mitchell.

'I'm saying that Mullett must be related to his adopted children. In fact, I'd say that they're probably his actual biological children.'

'It's like the Hollywood stars in the 1930s,' I said. 'Some of them adopted their own illegitimate children to keep their reputations untarnished.'

'Mullett probably did it for the same reasons,' said Mitchell. 'Strict Catholic wife and father-in-law to whom he owed his business. They wouldn't take kindly to some illegitimate children turning up, particularly when he and his wife had been unable to produce any offspring.'

'So he adopted them,' I said. 'But what happened to their mother?'

It was like a dozen pieces of the puzzle suddenly slotted together in my head.

'Oh my God. Baz went to see Sister Margaret for information about Betty, and then he started searching the Phoenix cellar with a sonogram machine! Didn't you say Mullett used to hang out at the Phoenix? Maybe Baz thought she was buried in the cellar for some reason.'

'It's my fault.'

I spun around. I'd completely forgotten about Gene, who was still there on the couch, albeit slightly obscured by cats. 'I told Baz how my family used to store bodies in a tunnel that ran between the Phoenix cellar and the cellar next door.'

'What are you talking about, Gene?' I asked. 'What do you mean your family used to store bodies in a cellar?'

'You know me as Gene, but I changed my name in the 1970s to sound like Gene Simmons from Kiss. My real name's Gino. My family owns the building where I have my shop—or they did own it until Uncle Nino went senile and sold it to Mullett.

'When I told Baz about it, he remembered that, back in the late 1960s, around the same time Betty Jones went missing, Dave Mullett had done some building work for the old fella, Pascoe, who owned the Phoenix. He thought that maybe Mullett had stashed her body in the cellar there.'

'I think we need to check this tunnel story out ASAP,' said Mitchell. 'Before Mullett can get a demolition order.'

'Baz and me, we couldn't find the tunnel though,' said Gene. 'I even got my hands on a ground scanner, but we couldn't find anything. Maybe my uncles were bullshitting. If we could get our hands on some actual blueprint-type plans it might help. But I looked through Uncle Nino's papers and couldn't find anything.'

'I have the blueprints for the Phoenix,' I said, suddenly remembering. 'They're under my desk at work. I nicked them out of the archive department. But then Mitchell got zapped and I forgot in the excitement.'

I rang Brucie and asked if he could bring the box over before Eve had a chance to clear out my desk. He arrived within minutes of me hanging up the phone.

'What's going on, Brick? I've heard these awful rumours about you!' he said, as I felt my head begin to throb again. 'Of course, I know they're not true. Unless he drugged you. Disgusting old man—did he drug you?'

'No,' I said, ushering Brucie inside and closing the door behind him. 'Wash your mind out for even thinking it!' I grabbed the laptop and showed Brucie the footage. 'Someone sent this to Mitchell. Was it you?'

'Oh my God, no! Why would I do that? That is the most repulsive thing I have ever seen,' said Brucie, visibly shaken. 'Poor Gail.'

'Poor Gail?' I was stunned at his reaction. 'Poor *Gail*?'

'She's obviously more desperate and lonely than any of us had imagined,' said Brucie. 'I feel kind of sorry for her. She really hates her job.'

'Why doesn't she quit then?'

'She's afraid to. Although if Evil Eve gets any weirder, I think that could be the thing to push her.'

'Well, this footage is going to get out. Maybe that'll spur her on.'

'Oh God. What if Selena does one of her doorstep ambushes and then puts it on national TV? Gail will kill herself! I have to warn her.'

I was still amazed at Brucie's compassion for our boss. 'Do what you like, Brucie.'

He gave my shoulder a squeeze. 'I'm sorry I even thought for a second you'd let that troll into your vagina. But as that footage shows, heterosexual women are completely beyond understanding when it comes to sexual partners.'

With that, Brucie presented me with the box, safely retrieved from my workstation, and left again, saying that he didn't think Gail should be alone when news broke of her tryst with the mayor.

'Underneath that bitchy exterior lies a heart of gold,' I told Bunny as I lugged the box back to the lounge room and we all grabbed a handful of papers to peruse.

Immediately something strange caught my eye.

'Hey, this is weird. It says here that Baz inherited the club from a Mrs Pascoe. He always tells people that he bought it.'

'Why would she leave it to him?' Bunny asked. 'Was she a relative?'

'I don't think so.'

Mitchell took the papers from Bunny. 'Daphne Pascoe. She'd co-owned the club with her husband Ron Pascoe and was the sole owner after her husband died. Maybe she and Baz had something going on.'

'Wait. Did you say Daphne?' I went to snatch the paper, but Mitchell held it out of reach. 'Does it have her maiden name in there anywhere?'

'Previously known as Daphne Russell.'

I recognised the name from the birth certificate for Delilah Russell in Baz's safe. Had Baz fathered a child to this woman, Daphne Russell? Was that why she left him the club? I took the club's title deeds from Mitchell and hid them in the pantry, behind the flour tins. I'd worry about that later.

'Okay, here's the cellar schematic,' said Bunny. 'You can take this and compare it to the real cellar.'

'The power might be turned off after the fire, so we'll need some torches,' Mitchell said.

'I've got some gear you can borrow,' said Gene. 'I've got all kinds of gear that I've been storing for … some people. I can't say too much about who.'

'We don't want to know.' Mitch and I spoke in unison.

Gene and Mitchell disappeared and thirty minutes later, Mitchell returned in a windowless white van.

'It's a loaner from Gene,' he said. 'But I didn't bring him with me. He was looking a bit ragged.'

'Good move,' I said. 'I feel worried enough about Baz without worrying about Gene too.'

'Do you want me to come with you?' asked Bunny.

'No,' said Mitchell. 'I think you'd better stay behind. We'll drop you somewhere safe.'

Much to my surprise, she didn't argue. 'Timmy's got a shift at the Black Possum,' she said. 'I'll go there with him and we'll stay there after he closes up for the night. But if you don't contact us by 2am, I'm calling the police. I mean it.' She looked at me. 'I'd tell you to come with me to the Black Possum, but I know I'd be wasting my breath.'

I hugged her. 'Thanks for understanding. And if worst comes to worst—take care of the cats.'

'I don't think it will come to that,' said Mitchell. 'But we might find something unexpected. Are you sure you wouldn't rather stay with Bunny?'

I knew what he was alluding to. We might find Baz's body. I was touched by his last-minute sensitivity.

'I'd like nothing more than to stay with Bunny. But I'm coming. I owe it to Baz.'

'Okay then,' he said, squeezing my hand.

We set off like soldiers heading out of the trenches— soldiers who knew they were pushing their luck.

CHAPTER TWENTY-FOUR

Mitchell and I got into Gene's van and set off for Baz's club. Neither of us spoke for at least five minutes, then I reached out to touch his hand. 'Thanks for helping me look for Baz.'

A light rain made the roads gleam like black silk. The street outside the Phoenix had returned to normality after the previous night's excitement. The only reminder was some orange tape across the doors. I yanked it off and unlocked the side door. Mitchell shone a torch through the doorway. The interior smelled smoky even though the firemen said they'd caught the fire early.

'How do you get to the cellar?' asked Mitchell.

'Behind the bar.'

I shone my torch on the trapdoor and Mitchell lifted it to reveal the breakneck stairs leading into the cavern below.

'Let's do it.' Mitchell threw down the bag of tools then led the way. I followed at a distance. The iron stairs always wobbled so much that I didn't like to put them under too much strain.

The cellar was almost as big as the bar above it—about ten metres by ten metres. Along one side were kegs, lowered through the metal trapdoor that opened out onto the footpath, as well as tall canisters of gas, necessary to propel the beer up the pipes. I looked at Mitchell, attempting to gauge how he was doing in the windowless environment. He was in his war-zone mode and barely looked shaky at all. 'Where do you reckon we should start?'

'I guess we look for any signs of digging.'

I paced the walls of the cellar, scouring the floor with my torch. Mitchell had a coping mechanism, but I was definitely feeling claustrophobia and dread descending. Being in the cellar was like being smothered.

'Nothing over here.' The beam of my torch showed up spider webs, but nothing else remarkable.

'Nothing here either.' Mitchell stopped. 'If you were going to bury a body here you'd need a biggish hole. I'd go for that big flagstone over there.' He pointed to a metre-wide flagstone in the middle of the floor. 'Let's try that one.'

Mitchell set to work with a crowbar and a pick while I shone the torch. It didn't look as though the flagstone had been moved in decades—if ever.

'Set down the torch and come and lean on this crowbar.'

It took both of our full weights before I felt the stone move slightly. We rested and then renewed our attack. Like a tooth, once loosened it just needed to be jiggled to come free. At last the huge stone came up. We laid it aside to reveal the dirt beneath.

Breathing heavily, Mitchell knelt down and felt the dirt with his fingers. 'I wouldn't think anyone would bother digging too far down if they were just going to drop that huge block on the body.' He grabbed the pick and starting swinging. The dirt was hard packed. 'I don't reckon this has been disturbed since the hotel was built. There's nothing here.'

I shone my torch upwards. People don't often look up. I spied a weird depression in the upper section of one of the walls behind the metal staircase. Like the hot air balloons in the morning, some things you didn't notice until you saw them out of the corner of your eye.

'Check that out,' I said to Mitchell. 'It looks like there used to be an alcove there and it's been covered over. Give me a look at the blueprint.'

Mitchell ran his finger over the area. 'You're right. Judging by the blueprint, that wall is about a meter closer than it should be. This wall must have been built later. This might be the entrance to a tunnel.'

He stood on the stairs and, despite the awkward angle, managed to swing the sledgehammer at the wall. It crumbled surprisingly easily.

'Whoever put this up did a lousy job,' he wheezed as dust filled the air. 'It's coming apart like Lego.' He shone his torch through the hole. 'I can see some old drums in there—really old, Brick. There's no way Baz is in here, but do you want to squeeze through and take a closer look for me?'

'Why me?'

'I don't think I can go in there, Brick. To be honest, I'm hanging by a thread.' His war-zone mask dropped and I saw real fear in his eyes.

If Mitchell was admitting weakness, then his claustrophobia must be worse than mine. I gestured for him to come back down the stairs so I could go up. I slung my bag across my body, put my torch in my mouth and then went feet first through the hole, using the metal bars on the side of the stairs to lower myself in.

The air on the other side of the wall was stale but dry and so still that it changed the acoustics. It felt like being in a sound studio that deadened every echo. I shone my torch around the cavity. It contained half-a-dozen metal drums, each about a metre high. I was just about to take a closer look when I heard footsteps ringing out on the cellar stairs. I looked back through the hole in the wall, expecting to see Mitchell's scuffed boots on the stairs, but the shoes I saw were shiny and expensive looking. Then they were joined by another set of black boots—very large black boots. I had a bad feeling that the two men coming down the stairs were Dave Mullett and his giant bodyguard.

I extinguished my torch in case the light attracted their attention and scrabbled through my bag for my phone. I tried to dial Bunny but being underground had killed my reception. I held my breath. Mitchell was trapped in the cellar like a rat in a cage, as was I. Even worse—I could see that there was now not one set of giant boots on the stairs, but two. Mitchell was well and truly outnumbered.

'Mr Mullett.' Mitchell was using his TV voice, and I could hear him clearly. 'Fancy seeing you here. And you've brought your two identical bodyguards with you.'

My suspicions regarding the owners of the large boots were confirmed.

'Are they your bodyguards, though? Or are they your twin sons? You're all wearing gloves so I can't quite see if one of them has a scarred arm from a house fire. It's a warm evening, I'd hardly think it calls for gloves. What brings you here to this cellar in Brunswick Street in the middle of the night wearing gloves?'

'Mitch Mitchell.' Mullett's voice was also distinctly audible. 'You are one huge pain in the arse. I didn't want to get rid of you, I know all your hack mates will kick up a big stink, but you're not giving me much of a choice.'

The stairs' metal joints creaked, no doubt straining under the weight of three men, two of whom were very, very large.

'Have you been digging your own grave for me?' Mullett must have noticed the dislodged flagstone on the floor. 'Thanks for the effort, but this might not be the best place for your body. The government's planning a new freeway tunnel and if I have anything to do with it, it's going to come out right here. This whole block is going to be wiped out. I'll have to put you somewhere else.'

I climbed up onto one of the metal drums, praying it would hold my weight, and tried my phone again, holding it as high up as possible. But there was still no reception. I needed to do something and quickly. One of the men was so close, if I had a knife I could have slashed his Achilles tendon. I used the light of my mobile to scour my handbag for anything I could use as a weapon. The only thing that caught my eye was the can of hairspray. I must have thrown it in my handbag after the Cup expedition. I grabbed the can and scrabbled through my handbag again, this time more frantically. Like any good bartender, I usually carried a cigarette lighter and sure enough, I found one down the bottom of the bag. I prayed it still worked.

I looked through the hole in the wall again and positioned the can, took a deep breath, then flicked the lighter while I depressed the spray button. A fiery plume of hairspray went directly through the hole—and onto the legs of the man still standing on the rickety stairs.

The sudden flare burned into my vision, then I saw a trouser leg catch fire. The reaction was immediate. The man looked like he was dancing a jig as the flames took hold, but there was no mistaking the panic in his scream. The bodyguards were definitely the twins from the orphanage, still with the trauma caused by the fire that had injured one so badly. The legs disappeared out of my field of vision and there was a sound that could only be that of a large body propelling down the metal stairs at speed before a sickening crunch as it impacted with other bodies. The screaming continued, and Mitchell yelled: 'Watch out! The gas canisters are going to explode!'

I didn't really think the canisters would explode, but from the frantic sounds of bodies scrabbling up the metal stairs, I'd say the other men did believe it. Then a surprisingly large amount of acrid smoke started spewing through the hole in the wall and into the cavity. I felt my throat starting to close. Maybe the canisters were going to blow after all.

I scrambled off the drum and got as low to the ground as possible. It was now totally dark—no light or noise at all coming from the cellar next door. I curled up in a ball, burying my face against my knees and wrapping my arms around my head. I could only hope that Mitchell's war-zone training would get him out of the cellar in one piece. I didn't know how I was going to get out. Tears and snot streamed down my face. I felt helpless, trapped and terrified. And maybe that's what triggered it.

Suddenly I found I did remember and it wasn't a dream. I was in Nora's house. It was dark and I was sitting scrunched up with my arms wrapped around my knees, dripping tears and snot onto the hem of my nightdress. I was desperate not to make a sound. I had been in bed earlier when I'd heard voices: Nora and a man were arguing. The voices were getting louder and louder and the man sounded angry. 'Get out,' I heard Nora say, more than once.

I crept out of bed. My bedroom door was ajar and I could see down the hallway of her small terrace house to the front door. Nora was standing there with the door open as if to let someone leave the house. She was wearing a blue dress with red flowers and I could see from her face that she was scared. It made me scared too.

A man walked down the hallway. I saw him from behind. He was very tall, almost giant-like, with a golden blond mane of hair. He walked down the hallway towards Nora, but instead of exiting through the front door, he hit her across the face and then slammed the door shut.

The force of the blow sent Nora tumbling to the floor. The man grabbed her by her beautiful dark hair and dragged her back towards the lounge room. I saw his face clearly.

I was terrified, yet I wanted to help Nora. I crept down the corridor to the lounge room after them. Through the doorway I saw that Nora had collapsed on the floor. Blood was streaming from her nose. She saw me and her face grew frantic.

'Run,' she whispered. 'Run and hide.'

I heard a noise from the kitchen and I crouched down to make myself small and crawled under the couch. The carpet tickled my nose but I didn't dare move.

I heard awful noises. Nora began whimpering, begging and pleading for him to stop. But he didn't stop and soon the sounds became too much for me to bear. I rolled out the other side of the couch and crawled towards a small nook deep under a table behind some curtains. It had been my special hiding place before, where I played with my dolls. Nora was screaming now, but the sound was quickly muffled by something. I curled up in a ball in my special hiding place. I heard what he did to her. And then, finally, Nora went silent.

The next few minutes felt like hours. Time blurred. I realised that a part of me had been frozen that day—caught as if in amber. Since that day, a part of me had been left in that dark, scared place. A terrified little girl, listening to the footsteps of the bogeyman as he tried to find me.

When I heard someone at the door and the splintering of wood, I was still too afraid to move. I hadn't moved in hours, days. I didn't know how long. There was a man's voice.

'Nora? It's Baz. You alright?'

The footsteps passed and then I heard a strange cough, as if someone was trying not to be sick. 'Sweet Jesus.' The man's voice was now a whisper.

My heart was racing. I was frightened of leaving my little space, but I was also frightened of being alone again. I could hear Baz running through the house, opening doors, shouting, 'Little girl. You here? You here? Please. Please. Please. Please, God!'

I crawled out of my hiding spot, weak from dehydration and terror. Baz was kneeling on the floor next to Nora. I saw he was crying. I had never seen a man cry before.

Crouched in the tunnel underneath the Phoenix, I knew for certain that the man I'd seen on that long-ago night was Errol Grimes, and he was the one who killed Nora. He killed Nora and he took away my chance to have a mother. Then he'd locked me in the house and left me there. Too afraid to move, to go to the toilet. Hungry, thirsty, petrified. Her body lying there all that time. I'd been left with the terror and the blank spaces in my memory.

I was brought back to the present by approaching sirens. Everything I knew about myself needed rethinking, rebuilding. I felt like I was only just beginning to understand who

I was—and now it was likely my life was going to end before I'd worked out the full puzzle. It was like getting halfway through a book and then finding the last few chapters were blank.

Yet I felt strangely calm.

I opened my eyes and saw that the smoke was dissipating.

CHAPTER TWENTY-FIVE

When I crawled out of the hole in the cellar wall, then up the stairs to go outside, the night air was the sweetest I'd ever tasted. I collapsed on the concrete and coughed my lungs up, snot and tears running down my face.

Someone wiped my face with a wet cloth. 'Tip your face up, I'll pour some water over your eyes,' said a familiar voice.

'Joe? What are you doing here?' The hi-vis blur began to solidify and Joe the parking inspector's beautiful long-lashed eyes came into focus.

'Sorry about the tear gas. Gene told me what you and Mitch Mitchell were planning and I thought we'd better come down here in case something went wrong. When I saw those goons going in, I had to think fast. I wasn't sure the police would get here in time.'

Tear gas? What was a parking inspector doing with tear gas? I continued to blink my streaming eyes, my focus blurring again.

I could make out three men lying face down and trussed on the concrete. One of the prone men was screaming and babbling. It was an awful sound. There were two familiar men standing over them, having made some kind of citizen's arrest. It was Gene … and Baz.

'Baz!' I staggered to my feet and ran towards him as best I was able.

'Brick.' For a minute he just held me while I coughed mucus onto his jumper. 'Bub, I'm so sorry you got caught up in this big mess. I tried to warn you to keep out of it.'

'Where have you been all this time?' The feeling of relief was passing quickly and I was moving on to anger. 'I've been going out of my mind.'

'I was hiding at Gene's house—didn't he tell you? I came here with Gene and Joe. They said you might be in trouble.'

I decided I'd need to stay in the angry phase a bit longer. 'No, he didn't tell me you were at his house! I've been going out of my mind with worry and you've been hanging out at Gene's drinking beer—and smoking too, I bet!'

'He said he'd let you know I was safe. I would have called you, but Gene said the council was bugging everyone's phones.'

'Baz, how could you listen to Gene? You know he's completely paranoid.'

Baz looked so sad, I couldn't stay angry.

Baz took me to sit on a nearby bench and I was relieved to see Mitchell sitting there, pouring a bottle of water over his face. His eyes looked red raw and as painful as mine.

'There you are, Brick. I was about to send someone down into the cellar to find you. And this must be Baz.' He shook my uncle's hand. 'I was beginning to wonder if Brick had made you up.'

'You're so full of it, Mitchell.'

'Gene told me you were on Mullett's case,' said Baz. 'I was hoping you'd keep Brick safe.'

'Brick can look after herself,' said Mitchell. 'But I think we'd better get out of here unless we want to get arrested.'

We piled into Gene's van and watched as the ambulances and police arrived. Mullett and his sons were loaded in two ambulances and Mitchell rang for a taxi, saying he would follow them to the hospital. 'I just wish my father could have seen this.'

Joe dropped Baz and me back to Bunny's place, and I rang Bunny at the cafe to tell her we were safe. Then I drank about my body weight in ice water while I held a wet flannel over my sore eyes. Baz made a pot of tea.

'What I don't understand is why you went looking for Betty Jones,' I said as Baz poured the tea. 'Did you know that Mullett had adopted her twin sons?'

'Ah, Betty … Betty Jones. That was her stage name. Her real name was Kasinsky. She was a girl that used to hang around the Phoenix back when Pascoe still owned it. She did a bit of singing, that's how I knew her. I always liked her, though not as a girlfriend. We were just friends. But I knew

she'd been involved with Mullett because he had some of
his mates beat me up one time. They told me I should stick
to girls my own colour.' Baz wiped his face, as if wiping
away the bitter memory.

'After the beating I didn't see her for a couple of years
until she came to me one day, asking for help. She'd had
twin boys by Mullett, but he wanted to take them away
from her. She was staying at the convent and she asked if I
could help her and her kids get out of town. I bought her
a bus ticket to Adelaide and arranged for her to stay with
one of my aunties who was living there. But when the time
came, Betty didn't show up for the bus. She'd left her boys
at the convent and disappeared. I thought she'd done a run-
ner. There wasn't much else I could do. It wasn't long after
that that I went to the US.

'I felt bad about it. I should have tried harder to find her.
Years went by and I only thought of her again when Gene
told me that Mullett was buying up properties on Brunswick
Street. Gene found out his Uncle Nino had sold the building where he had his shop. Mullett probably tricked poor
old Nino. He'd gone a bit senile. Nino sent me an envelope
of cash through the mail about the same time, so I reckon
he felt bad about the sale.

'Gene had heard stories of an old tunnel joining the two
cellars between that building and the Phoenix. Apparently
his uncles had stored a couple of bodies there, back in their
mafia heyday. Mullett was a brickie once upon a time, and
I remembered that he'd done some work at the Phoenix,
including in the cellar. It occurred to me that Mullett might

have killed Betty and buried her body there. Gene thought if we found something suspicious it would bring attention to Mullett and how much real estate he was buying on Brunswick Street. He's not a popular man in that part of town. Too many lefties living there now.

'Gene had the bright idea of getting a ground scanner machine to take a look around. But we couldn't even get the bloody thing to work. He said he got it from a spy from ASIO who was investigating Mullett.'

'Gene knows someone who works for ASIO?'

'Yeah, you wouldn't believe it. It's Joe! You know, the chubby guy that likes to dress up like Mama Cass from the Mamas and the Papas. Takes all types, hey?'

'Joe's not with ASIO. He's a parking inspector who seems to be tied up with that crazy mob of anti-freeway activists.'

'Well, that kind of makes more sense, now that you say it.'

I drank some more tea. Baz made it so strong you could stand a spoon up in it.

'I'm glad to be out of Gene's place,' said Baz. 'It's pretty freaky.'

'Poor, crazy Gene.'

'He swore to me that he'd given you a secret message that you'd understand—letting you know that I was safe.'

'A secret message?' Then I remembered all the lost pets—a cat called Barry and a dog called Brownie. 'Gene is just too paranoid sometimes,' I said. 'Did you see that tunnel he has going out from under his shed? And all that weird equipment in there?'

Baz nodded. 'Like I said, pretty freaky.'

CHAPTER TWENTY-SIX

I let Baz take my bed, figuring that sixty-two was too old to sleep on our couch and still hope to walk in the morning. Then I turned out the lights in the lounge room and attempted to bed down myself, although I left a lamp on. I wasn't ready for complete darkness.

Sleep was not coming. I gave up and was just making myself a cup of Milo when Mitchell tapped on the glass of the back door.

'I came in the back gate. Can I come in?'

I crawled out of my cocoon of blankets and unlocked the door.

'It'll be all over the news tomorrow morning.' Mitchell sounded tired but buzzed. 'Police have taken the barrels away for forensic examination. It's too early to know if Betty Jones is in one of them, but my gut is telling me that she is, poor woman. Either way, Mullett is toast. He's in the hospital under police guard. I heard from a source that his sons both completely lost the plot and started airing all kinds of dirty laundry.' He produced a bottle of sparkling wine from his satchel. 'Want to join me in a celebratory drink?'

'Sure.' I put the Milo tin away and took out two halfway decent glasses from Bunny's mismatched collection.

'Where's everyone else?' Mitchell popped the cork and poured.

'Baz is snoring up a storm in my room, Timmy's in his caravan and Bunny's asleep in her room, she took a Serepax.' I took a long sip of the bubbles. It wasn't quite on par with the Melbourne Cup champagne, but it wasn't Two-Buck Chuck either. 'Bunny gave me a couple of Serepax too, but they haven't worked. I'm too wired.'

We settled on the couch. The bubbles in my glass glinted in the dim light.

'Adrenaline,' said Mitch. 'It can take a while to wear off even if you're dying of tiredness. That's what used to really wipe me out in war zones.'

'I think there may be another reason,' I said. 'While I was in the cellar, when I thought I was going to die … it triggered something.'

'Do you want to tell me about it?' Mitchell's voice was gentle and his eyes looked black in the low light.

'I *did* see his face, after all. The man who killed Nora.' I pulled a blanket around me, then continued before I could lose my nerve. 'It was Errol Grimes. I saw him clearly and there's no mistaking it. I don't know what I should do about it.'

There was a long silence between us, then Mitchell put his arm around me.

'I'm going to be honest with you, Brick. I'm not talking as a journalist now. You've got Baz back safe. Mullett's going to be in deep legal strife for a very long time. You won't have to worry about anything being built next door to the Phoenix—not in the next couple of years, anyway. As long as they don't build a cross-town tunnel through there.'

'But if you were in my shoes, you wouldn't let Grimes get away with murder, would you?'

'I'm not you, Brick. Errol Grimes is Victoria's most powerful politician. He has friends in high places and historical charges are a minefield. You'd be putting yourself up to the worst kind of scrutiny—Baz, too. I've seen that kind of thing destroy people. Good people. People who wanted to do the right thing.'

I leaned against his chest. He smelled of smoke and sweat, but it was good to have someone there to cry on since I didn't seem to be able to hold the tears in any longer.

Mitchell let me cry, providing me with refills and human warmth. He held me until the sedatives kicked in and I fell asleep.

* * *

When I woke there was sunlight coming in the windows. I was tucked under a blanket on the couch. My mouth felt dry and there was no sign of Mitchell. I went to the fridge for some water and found a note from Baz under a magnet. Flora had taken him to check on the Phoenix and start the paperwork for the insurance claim—if they were allowed to make a claim.

I sat at the breakfast bar, sipping water and attempting to pull myself together enough to make a pot of tea. I turned on my phone but before I could dial Baz, it rang. According to caller ID it was Brucie.

'Brucie, I'm not coming into work,' I said as I answered. My voice came out as a croak. Then I remembered there was a council meeting scheduled. 'Someone else will have to go to the council meeting tonight.'

'Shut up, Brick,' Brucie cut me off. 'I think Selena McManus has just been taken away in an ambulance.'

The grogginess left me immediately.

'I was having a smoke out of the third-floor toilet windows and I saw it all. Only at first I thought it was you who was hit. I thought I saw you walking down the road and I was going to yell something out the window—you know, "nice tits" or something, because I know how much you girls love that—when a car came barrelling across the road straight up onto the footpath! I thought you'd been cleaned up!

'I called the ambulance, obviously, then I ran outside. There was a crowd of people around, but I bashed my way past them. I still thought it was you for a moment, she was wearing black jeans and boots and an old green jacket like that one you insist on wearing. She had almost no make-up on and must have put a red rinse through her hair. She looked so different that I didn't recognise her at first. I think she was trying to look like you.'

Mitchell chose that moment to return to the lounge room. It looked like he'd just had a shower.

'What's the matter, sleeping beauty? A pea under your mattress?'

'Brucie says Selena was just hit by a car outside council. He reckons she was dressed like me at the time.'

Mitchell dropped his smartarse expression. 'Shit. I bet she was trying to sneak into the council chambers to get an exclusive with your boss about her sexcapades with mayor. You must have given her the idea when you switched clothes with her on Cup Day.'

'This is my fault? Someone was trying to get me?' I went back to my burrow on the couch still clutching my phone.

'What do you think?'

I was tempted to pull a blanket over my head. 'I don't know what to think anymore.'

'Tell Brucie to keep quiet about it being Selena and not you.'

Brucie agreed immediately to keep it under his hat. 'I know you're mixed up in something bad, Brick. Just call me if you need anything and stay safe. I'll cover for you here.'

Mitchell sat next to me on the couch, his face serious. 'Let's think this through. My father was killed in a hit and run: no driver found. Old mate Otto was skittled in the street: no driver found. And now Selena gets run down outside your place of work.'

'Do you think Mullet's put out a hit on me?'

'He's still in hospital. His sons, too. They have burns, broken bones ... and at least one of them is in the middle of a major psychotic episode. And why would Mullett put a hit on you? No, I've been thinking it over. I can understand Mullett might want to kill me. But why didn't his sons just come here and grab me, if they were so keen? Why did they risk returning to the Phoenix?'

My mind was refusing to function, but luckily Mitchell's question was rhetorical. He kept on thinking out loud. 'I reckon Mullett didn't *know* I was staying at this house which means he *wasn't* behind the raid here on Melbourne Cup Day. Maybe I wasn't even the target of that raid. Maybe *you* were.'

He paused and I was suddenly aware of how quiet it was in the neighbourhood. It was as if we were in the middle of nowhere.

'I hate to tell you, Brick,' Mitchell continued, 'but I think someone must know about what you witnessed as a child.'

'How? I only just remembered it myself. And you're the only person I've told. I didn't even tell Baz yet.'

'Well, Mavis told us that someone was using Nora's death to blackmail Grimes. Maybe Grimes decided to find Nora's foster daughter and neutralise the threat—you. He doesn't want people to know he killed a former girlfriend and got away with it. It would ruin his career—or I hope it would. These days, honestly, nothing would surprise me.'

'But how would Grimes know that I was Nora's foster child? It was fifteen years ago. I look totally different, my name is different. There's no legal paper trail, thanks to Baz.'

'Your first name isn't different.'

'Still, it's a stretch ...'

We sat in silence and I heard a plane flying high overhead.

I suddenly felt very angry. 'Mavis must have told him about me. She knows that Nora was my foster mother. She knows about Grimes and Nora.'

'Why would she do that?' asked Mitchell.

'Because she's fucking nuts, that's why.'

Bunny entered the kitchen looking ridiculously well rested and headed straight for the kettle. 'Morning, folks. What trouble and hijinks have you cooked up for today?'

'Bad news,' I said. 'We think someone other than Mullett may have been behind the break-in that ended with you tied up in the kitchen. Which would mean that we should really get out of here ASAP, in case they come here again.'

Bunny put down the kettle without filling it. 'What? But if it wasn't Mullett, who was it?'

'We're starting to think Errol Grimes might have been behind it,' said Mitchell.

'Are you fucking kidding me?' Bunny looked at Mitchell. 'You must be really talented at pissing people off.'

'What can you tell us about the guy who tied you up?' I asked.

Bunny abandoned her efforts to make tea and sat down. 'He was big and wearing black. Balaclava. Gloves.'

'What about his voice?'

'He didn't talk. Just whacked me, and when I came round I'd been tied up and gagged. Actually, one thing I remember now: he took some photos with his phone, particularly of something that was on the kitchen bench.'

We looked at the bench. There was a knife block with no knives in it, a vase with no flowers in it, and the silver-framed photo of me and Nora, exactly where I'd left it on the day Mavis gave it to me.

'Do you think he could have recognised Nora from this photo? Like Mavis recognised her?' I asked.

There was another knock at the back door and there she was, as if conjured by the devil. I opened the door, grabbed Mavis roughly by the arm and pulled her inside. Her hair had now been completely cut off, but in an expensive way that was quite stylish. Otherwise she looked grey and haggard.

'What have you done, Mavis? Did you tell Grimes about me? Why would you do that?'

Mavis crumpled onto a stool and put her head on the breakfast bar. 'I didn't tell him anything. I haven't seen or spoken to him since the day he hit me.'

'Are you sure?' I asked. 'Because Selena McManus was just hit by a car outside the council building. And we think it may have been an attack intended for me. What do you remember about the man who tied you up on Melbourne Cup Day? Could it have been Grimes? Because we didn't see him at the Melbourne Cup. Maybe he came here.'

'No. I'm sure it wasn't Errol. I know how he walks. What he smells like. I'd know if it was him.'

'But do you think the man could have been working for Grimes?' asked Mitchell. 'Did he say anything to you?'

'No. He didn't talk at all. I don't even want to think about it.' Mavis pressed the heels of her palms against her eyes.

I sat down next to her and put my hand on her forearm. 'We really need you to think, Mavis. I know it's a scary memory and you don't want to think about it. But this is really important.'

She opened her eyes again. 'I'd been in the bathroom having a shower,' she said. 'I was about to get dressed when I heard a loud crash out here, so I threw on my clothes and I came out. There was a man in black, wearing a balaclava. When he saw me, he hesitated—I think I surprised him. Then he grabbed me, tied my hands and shoved me in the bath. He smelled disgusting, a mixture of body odour and cheap cologne.'

'BO and cologne. I know who that reminds me of.'

'Timmy?' asked Bunny.

I frowned. 'Well, yes, but also Hugo Clark.'

'Yes,' said Mavis, although she didn't sound convinced. 'A bit like Hugo Clark. But a lot of people like cheap deodorant.'

I turned away from Mavis. 'Mitchell, could Hugo have been the person who attacked you in the archives department?'

'I didn't see anyone and it was pretty stinky in that room, but Hugo Clark would have after-hours access to the council building.'

I sighed. 'Why are you here then, Mavis? If you're not here to kill me on behalf of your psycho ex.'

'I want to go public.' Mavis' face was grim. 'About Grimes and what he did to me. Will you help me, Mitchell?'

'This day is getting out of hand very early.' Mitchell exhaled loudly. 'First things first, we should get out of here. It might not be safe.'

'Where can we go?' I asked. 'Baz's flat's still out of action from the fire.'

'Ring Baz and tell him to stay with Flora,' said Mitchell. 'Then wake up Timmy and tell him to grab his laptop. I know a place that's definitely safe.'

'What about the cats?' I looked around, wondering whether Bunny had a large box anywhere.

'I'm sure they'll be fine,' said Bunny and Mitchell in unison.

We all squeezed into a taxi and Mitchell gave the address. When we arrived, Gene did not look best pleased to see me, Mitchell, Bunny, Timmy and Mavis on his doorstep.

'What the fuck, man?'

'Gene. It's an emergency,' said Mitchell. 'Mullett and his boys are out of action, but we think there's someone else involved in this whole bloody mess. Someone just tried to take out Brick with a car.'

'Shit, Brick, are you okay?'

I was glad to get some sympathy—even if it was from Gene. 'They got the wrong person. But we're worried they'll try again.'

Gene let us into his house and we were soon huddled on the couch in his lounge room. I accepted his offer of a beer so as not to offend.

'We need to think logically about this,' I said. 'What do you know about Hugo, Mavis?'

'Not much. I usually tried to stay as far away from him as possible. He gave me the creeps. Sometimes I'd catch him watching me and, seriously, it was like the hair on my neck would stand up.'

'We know that someone played hardball to make Mavis give up the development committee chairman position,' said Mitchell. 'A position that Hugo then slipped into. Maybe Hugo was behind the scare campaign.'

'I can imagine him doing something like that,' said Mavis with a shudder. 'Like I said, he's creepy.'

I took a tiny sip of my beer, but it was so disgusting that my stomach nearly rebelled. 'You looked into his background, Mitchell. Is there anything that connects Hugo with Errol Grimes? Did Hugo play football? Was he into horse racing?'

'No. The thing that drew my attention to Hugo in the first place is all the blanks. It's like he didn't exist until about ten years ago.' Like me, Mitchell was looking wary about drinking any of Gene's homebrew. 'We know Selena is the third hit and run that may be connected, so maybe this has something to do with Grimes as well as Mullett. We know they've scratched each other's backs in the past. It's highly possible my father also uncovered some information the premier doesn't want to come to light. Your friend Sue was onto a lead regarding a possible witness to Otto's accident. Do you think she had any luck in finding them?'

I grabbed my phone and dialled Sue. It barely rang before she picked up.

'Brick? Are you okay? I heard on the radio that they're trying to identify a young woman who was run down by a car outside the council building. From the description, I was worried it was you!'

I'm glad there was another person who was concerned for my welfare. 'It wasn't me, Sue, it was Selena.'

'Thank goodness for that!'

'Listen, Sue, this is very important. That night we picked you up, you'd been looking for a witness to Otto's hit and run. Did you ever find them?'

There was a moment's silence and I knew Sue had indeed found the witness.

'This is not a time to worry about a scoop,' I said. 'It's a matter of life and death.'

'There's not a lot to tell—I'm still working on it. But the witness saw a man get out of a car carrying Otto. He was unconscious, if it's any small mercy—I can hardly bear to think about it. The man lay Otto down on the road, and before the witness could really believe what he was seeing, he drove right over him and then off down the street!'

'Did the witness give you any description of the man?'

'He could only say that the driver was big and that his face was mostly covered by a beanie. But he did say that the man had a big, bushy beard.'

'A beard. Like Hugo Clark.'

'Yes,' said Sue. 'Like Hugo Clark. I'm still a long way from having anything I can run with, if I can run with it at all. But in any case, my newspaper's an inconsequential piss fest. It would never publish something this big. Do you think Mitch would help me pitch the story to one of the big news agencies?'

'Mitchell is here with me,' I said. 'We're in Coburg. Can you come over?'

'I'll be there in thirty minutes.'

I gave Sue the address and she must have broken a land speed record for a station wagon because she arrived in less than twenty.

'We may not know much about Hugo Clark,' said Mitchell. 'But there's plenty on the record about Errol Grimes. He's been in the public eye since he was a star football recruit as a teenager.'

'I have a login for a newspaper database,' said Sue. 'I could do a category search on Grimes.'

We set her up on Timmy's laptop.

'What should I try? How about "Errol Grimes" and "police"?' Sue typed. 'No, that's just brought up heaps of stories about him and the Minister for Police.'

'Let's check for family,' I said. 'If Grimes has someone committing murder for him, he must trust them completely.'

'According to his bio, he has no brothers, only a sister, much older than him.'

'What about a nephew or cousin?' Mitchell asked.

'Here's something: Football star's nephew linked to suspicious death.'

'What does it say?' I asked.

'To summarise: In 1997 Grimes's seventeen-year-old nephew Jayden Grimes was arrested, accused of the rape and murder of a sixteen-year-old girl. Overdose of a date-rape drug.'

'Interesting,' said Mitchell.

'But there's more. It seems Jayden Grimes went missing while on bail. His clothes were found at a beach past Frankston, a presumed suicide. He literally did a Harold Holt.'

'Do you think he was picked up by a submarine? Like Holt.' No surprises it was Gene who piped up here. 'I told you how I saw him in Goa one time?'

We all ignored Gene.

'They didn't find a body,' said Sue. 'I guess it's possible he faked his own death.'

'Is there a photo of this nephew?' I asked.

'Yes, but it's your typical court shot, hand up to obscure his face.'

'I'm googling him on my phone now,' said Timmy. 'But there's not a lot—it was the days before social media.'

We crowded around to look at the photo of a skinny teenager with badly dyed blond hair and acne.

'He looks nothing like Hugo,' said Sue.

'But what does Hugo really look like? He has a beard that covers half his face. He's years older and forty kilos heavier than the kid in that photo. Do that to anyone and they'll look completely different.'

'Are there any more photos?' Mitchell asked. 'We need to look at things like ear shape, tattoos or hands. They're the things that don't change when you put on weight. And we need a photo of Hugo to compare it with.'

'We've only his official council headshot,' said Sue.

'Is there seriously no other photo of him on the web?' asked Mitchell as we held Timmy's phone with the picture of Jayden Grimes next to the laptop with the picture of Hugo.

'Their ears aren't dissimilar,' Sue said. 'But they're pretty standard ears.'

'And their hands?' asked Mitchell.

'That's interesting,' I said. 'In this shot where Jayden has his right hand up to shield his face, it looks like he's missing a fingertip.'

Timmy zoomed in and sure enough, the tip of his index finger was missing from the first joint.

'And Hugo?' asked Mitchell. 'His hand's not in the photo. Can you remember, Brick? Have you ever noticed his hands?'

I shook my head. 'I can't say I have. Mavis, have you noticed?'

She pulled a face. 'I generally tried not to look at him too closely.'

'Are there any other photos of him online?' I asked.

'Not a lot,' said Sue. 'And none with his hands visible.'

'I just remembered,' I said. 'I took some photos of him at the memorial service for Dickie Ruffhead. He wasn't happy about it, though. He came by my office later and asked to see them. He wanted me to delete the ones he didn't like.'

'Did you delete them?' asked Mitchell.

'No. They'll still be on my desktop at work. I'll ring Brucie and get him to email them.'

A few fraught minutes later, the photos arrived with a pointed note about the amount of unlabelled crap on my desktop. I held my breath as Timmy clicked through them.

'There, look!' In one photo I'd managed to catch Hugo Clark shoving a sausage roll in his mouth while simultaneously juggling a napkin and a glass of orange juice.

Timmy zoomed in. The photo clearly showed Hugo's right hand and its lack of the top segment of his index finger.

'I don't fucking believe it!' said Mavis.

'That clinches it,' said Mitchell. 'As far as I'm concerned, Hugo Clark really is Grimes's nephew.'

'But if he went to the effort of faking his death and getting a totally new identity, why would he stay in Melbourne?' Sue asked. 'Wouldn't you start again in a different town, a different country even?'

'Family ties can be strong,' I said.

'And why would he go into local politics?' Sue was still staring at the computer screen, her mouth agape.

'Same reason his cousin went into state politics,' said Mitchell. 'The same reason anyone goes into politics: power, influence, prestige. No offence, Mavis.'

'I don't know why I did anything anymore.' Mavis had drunk an entire glass of Gene's beer and was looking worse for it. 'My whole life I've been told what I should be doing. I guess I was trying to be like my grandfather, the big hero. He was a complete arsehole to my grandmother, though. No one ever mentions that.'

I offered her the tissue box. She took one and blew her nose loudly.

'I still want to go public.' Mavis wiped her face with her hand. Her nails were bitten to the quick. 'I want to tell my story ... about Grimes and what he did to me. I want the Victorian public to know that he's a woman-bashing arsehole who tried to ruin my career.'

'Are you sure?' Mitchell looked worried as Mavis accepted a second glass of Gene's beer. 'I don't need to tell you that this may not work out how you expect.'

'I know.' Mavis eyes were red-rimmed but steady. 'But someone needs to stop him or he's just going to keep on going, taking everything he wants, any time he wants.'

I took Mavis's hand. 'I'm sick of it, too,' I said. 'Sick of being afraid to look at the past or the future. Now he knows who I am, I'll never be safe. And what if he does something to Baz? Makes him disappear for real? Going public isn't going to do it, though. It'll just be "he said, she said" and legal stuff, and police and courts. It could take years—and I don't want to be looking over my shoulder the whole time. We need to get him and get him fast. We need to outsmart him. He's an ex-footballer. It shouldn't be that hard!'

Mitchell raised an eyebrow. 'Should I tell Baz you said that?'

'I'm thinking of Baz. The law doesn't always protect the right people. Often it only protects the people with the power. And Grimes isn't just relying on the law either. He's been having people murdered! We need to fight fire with fire. I've got a crazy idea to get Grimes … and Hugo.' I closed my eyes and took a big gulp of the awful beer. 'But I'm going to need help.'

'A crazy idea? I'll help you.' Naturally Gene was the first to come on board.

'I'll help you, too,' said Mavis.

'And me,' said Sue, Bunny and Timmy.

'That's a whole lotta crazy,' said Mitchell. 'I guess I'm in, too.'

'Okay,' I said. 'Thanks to Mavis, we know about Grimes's bolthole in Fairfield. And we can assume that Hugo told Grimes that Mavis and I know each other. I suggest that Mavis rings Grimes, tells him Hugo ran over the wrong woman and offers to bring him the right one, in exchange for being left alone. Do you think he'll buy that?'

'Mavis has been acting pretty off the charts lately,' said Mitchell. 'No offence, Mavis. And Grimes is probably feeling the pressure too, with Mullett under arrest. Grimes may not be thinking in the most rational manner right this moment.'

'We just have to work out how to put a wire on Mavis so we can get him confessing on tape,' I said.

'That probably won't hold up in court,' said Sue.

'It doesn't need to hold up in court,' I said. 'It just needs to ruin his career. But we'll need to get Hugo out of the picture first—separate Grimes from his usual back-up. That's where my crazy idea comes in.'

'You mean getting Mavis to ring him wasn't the crazy idea?' asked Mitchell.

I ignored that comment. 'But we've got to act fast. Hugo's due at a council meeting this evening, and he may not know about his Selena mix-up.'

'I'll ring my police source,' said Sue, 'and see what they know.'

A minute later Sue reported back: 'The police are calling for witnesses to the hit-and-run. They don't know the woman's identity. If she had a handbag or phone with her, someone's nicked it in the chaos. What kind of a world are we living in?'

'It's a shit world, Sue,' said Mitchell. 'But now is not the time to dwell on it. Is Selena still alive?'

'She's alive but she's in an induced coma. Hard to kill, like a cockroach.'

I couldn't help but feel sick. For all the lousy things Selena had done to me in primary school, it was hard to stomach that she'd been hurt in my place. It was also hard to imagine Selena in a coma—she was one of the most alive people I'd ever met.

Mitchell was less affected by the news. 'We need a back-up plan. What if Grimes doesn't take the bait?'

I refilled my glass and took another swig. 'Then I'll ring the murdering bastard myself and tell him to come and get me. But let's try it the other way first.'

We didn't have a lot of time to get organised, so it was lucky we were at Gene's house. It turned out he was storing some very interesting stuff in his front room, including tasers. Bunny and Timmy disappeared in Gene's van for an hour and came back with some more specialised requirements.

'This is a hospital-grade emetic,' said Bunny gleefully as she stood in Gene's kitchen doctoring a packet of Monte Carlo biscuits. 'Hugo Clark will be voiding from both ends in no time. When it hits, I'll be waiting in the toilets to jab him with a hypodermic of ketamine. Don't ask me where I got the ketamine.'

We didn't.

Timmy rigged up a system of wireless microphones and earpieces to connect me, Mavis and Mitchell, borrowing the equipment from a gaming buddy, who also lent him an extra van. 'The microphones will be open the whole time. You don't have to worry about turning them off and on. I'll record everything from the van. It's just like a spy movie!'

We decided that Mavis and I would take Gene's van, but first we'd all travel to the council building together for the sting on Hugo. Mavis said she was afraid to be left alone and I was afraid she'd change her mind about the whole thing and call her mother to come get her again.

I rang Brucie and he agreed to fill in for me at the council meeting and make sure the special Monte Carlo biscuits went to Hugo. Brucie offered to put a web cam on his laptop and then Skype to Timmy's laptop so we could see the council meeting. 'The councillors won't realise,' he said. 'They're all completely clueless about technology.'

We parked outside the council building. Bunny and Mitchell went in wearing hi-vis disguises from the gear Gene was storing for the Anti-Freeway Alliance. I stayed in the van with Mavis and Timmy and we watched the council meeting get underway from the laptop.

Even via a sketchy Skype connection, I could see Hugo Clark was looking as cool as a cucumber, mere hours after running a woman down in the street. Brucie came into shot and put the plate of Monte Carlo biscuits down in front of Hugo. He ate one immediately and then another and another. Five minutes later, with the meeting yet to get underway, he left the room with alacrity.

'He's just left the meeting room in a hurry,' I said into my microphone so Mitchell could warn Bunny to get ready. 'He should be on his way to the toilets now.'

Through my earpiece I heard the bang of a door being slammed open and then the sound of someone heaving their guts up.

'The eagle has landed,' said Mitchell's voice quietly. 'Or should I say walrus?'

A few minutes later Bunny and Mitchell returned to the van.

'He'll be out for at least four hours,' said Bunny. 'We put him in the recovery position, so he probably won't choke on his own vomit, and Brucie's locked the toilet door so no one can walk in and find him.'

CHAPTER TWENTY-SEVEN

We decided it would be best if Mavis sent Grimes a text message, hinting that she knew about Hugo running down 'Brick' and asking him to call her. He rang Mavis less than ten minutes later. We tried to give her some space but since we were all crammed in the back of a van, I couldn't help overhearing.

'I don't want to say much on the phone,' Mavis mumbled into the receiver. 'Meet me at your house in Fairfield and we can talk there.'

When she finished the phone call, Mavis looked as if she might vomit at any moment.

'He said he'd meet me there in half an hour. Is that enough time?'

Timmy gave us the thumbs up. 'I've set it up so I can record. The microphones should pick up a person talking within a couple of metres.'

'We need Grimes on tape saying something incriminating,' said Mitchell. 'Once we've got something in the bag, we're coming to get you.'

'What if he has a gun?' I asked.

'This is Australia,' said Mitchell. 'I don't think he'll have a gun. But if he does have one, let me know.'

I touched the gaffer tape that was holding the mike to my chest. The way it pinched made me feel suffocated. I looked at Mitchell. 'This is insane, isn't it?'

'Yes.' Mitchell took both my hands with his own, his face serious. 'I've seen some pretty insane things in my life, so I can tell you definitively that this is insane.'

I looked at his hands holding mine. 'Does it have any chance of working?'

He shrugged. 'I'd say it's about fifty-fifty, so if you don't want to do this, you have another option. You can leave Melbourne—leave the country even. I don't think Grimes will bother trying to hunt you down.'

It was true. If I left town, Grimes would probably figure I'd been scared into silence, the way he'd scared Mavis into a mental breakdown.

'But if I leave Melbourne, I'd have to leave Baz and the Phoenix,' I said. 'Maybe I'd never be able to see him and Aunty Dot again. Or Bunny or Flora … and all the other nutjobs who hang out at the Phoenix. What kind of a life would that be?'

'I think you should ring Baz and tell him what you're doing,' said Mitchell as he let go of my hands and went back to checking the equipment with Timmy.

I took out my phone, but I decided I wouldn't ring Baz—I knew he'd try to stop me. Instead I found a pen and a scrap of paper in my bag and wrote him a note. Just in case.

What do you say in your last words? 'Such is life'? 'I'm popping to the shops and I may be some time'? In the end I just wrote: *I love you, Baz. Thanks for everything.* Then I folded the note in four and addressed it to Baz.

Outside it was grey and drizzly. I hoped this wasn't the last time I'd see Melbourne's skies. They weren't looking their best. I stowed the note for Baz in Gene's glovebox, and then closed the passenger side door and returned to the back doors of Gene's van, feeling like a gunslinger with a taser taped to my thigh. Mitchell was waiting there for me. He bound my hands in front of me with a cable tie that had been cut and then stuck back together with gaffer tape.

'You should be able to break out of these,' he said. 'Not exactly like Houdini, but the best we can do at short notice.'

I twisted my wrists. The ties were too tight for my liking.

'Houdini came to Melbourne once, you know,' said Mitchell. 'He jumped into the Yarra, chained and bound, and lived to tell the tale.'

I was glad of his effort to lighten the tension. 'Thanks for that weird piece of trivia. Any other words of wisdom?'

Mitchell touched my cheek, looking serious for a second. 'John Batman wanted to name Melbourne Batmania.'

I smiled at him. 'What a lost marketing opportunity.'

There was a pause, and for a second I thought Mitchell was going to kiss me. But then Gene appeared and the moment was gone.

'One thing with the tasers,' said Gene. 'Make sure you're not touching the person you're tasing or you'll feel the shock as well. And it's not fun.' He winked at me. 'I found that out the hard way.'

The plan was for Mavis to drive to Fairfield with me in the back of Gene's van. Mitch, Timmy, and Bunny would follow in the second van, borrowed from Timmy's gamer buddy.

'If Grimes lets Mavis through the gate at his Fairfield house then we'll know he's taken the bait,' said Mitchell.

Mavis was quiet on the way to Fairfield. Rush hour was ending but she drove slowly, so as not to shake me up too much in the back.

'You can change your mind at any time,' I said to her through the headset. 'I can drive myself to see Grimes.'

'No. I'm going through with this.' The headset's speaker made her voice sound extra shrill. 'I'm sick of being Little Miss Perfect, it gets you fucking nowhere in life. After this I just wanna move to London—work in some crap PR job for a while. I'd even work in a pub if I had to.'

I was happy to travel in silence for a while after that, until finally the van came to a halt.

'We're at the gate.' Mavis still sounded stressed.

'Deep breath,' I said. 'You can do it.'

I heard the buzz. Mavis had pressed the intercom button, and a few seconds later I heard a man's voice, slightly distorted by the intercom speaker.

'Mavis?'

'Yes, it's me.' Mavis's voice sounded steadier than I'd expected.

'I'll let you in,' said the male voice.

'No, you come out here to me.'

'No way, Mavis.'

There was a pause, and then I heard Mavis press the intercom button again. 'You listen to me, Errol. Hugo got the wrong woman. Brick Brown is alive and well, and I've got her in the back of this van. Tied up. I'll give her to you if you promise that you and your people will never bother me again. But you have to come out here and get her. I'm not going in there.'

'Are you fucking serious?' Even with the static I could hear he was not happy.

'Yes, I'm fucking serious. I'll send you a fucking photo right now.'

I heard the click of the van's driver's side door, and a few seconds later the back doors swung open. Mavis took a photo of me with her smartphone and then slammed the door shut again.

She was making me feel very nervous. I wondered whether I should break the cable ties now in case I needed to make a run for it. But before I could take action, the van doors opened again and Grimes himself was standing there. He was wearing trousers and a shirt as if he'd just removed his jacket and tie.

'So you're Nora's brat then, all grown up.' He sounded hostile and spoke without looking at my face. 'What do you reckon you know?'

I took my time to assess him. He was older and his clothes and haircut were more expensive, but his voice hadn't changed and it left me with no doubt. Errol Grimes was the bogeyman of my night terrors.

I looked at his hands. They were large and well-shaped—strong hands. They didn't look like the hands of a monster. And yet they were.

'I know you killed Nora on February 6, 1992.' My voice sounded strangely calm despite my inner turmoil. 'You came to her house on Station Street. She was wearing a blue dress with red flowers. You bashed her and raped her, and then you smothered her. And you left me locked in the house with her dead body.'

I kept my eyes locked on his face, but his expression remained unchanged, as if I was reading out a shopping list.

'It was nearly two days before anyone found me,' I said.

Finally he met my eyes and I saw a flicker of emotion. It was annoyance, possibly anger.

'I knew Nora had a kid living with her—a kid named Brick,' he said. 'But I gotta say that at the time I thought you were slow. I never even heard you talk.

'Then someone told me there was a girl called Brick who had a photo of Nora and who'd suddenly become best mates with Mavis and that up-himself reporter Mitch Mitchell. I thought it might be best to get you out of the picture.'

'So you had Hugo Clark run me down? Only he ran down the wrong woman.'

'If you want something done right, sometimes you have to do it yourself.' Grimes produced a gun that must have been tucked in the back of his waistband.

'Is that a gun?' I said loudly in an effort to alert Mitch to the new danger.

Grimes didn't bother to answer me before he slammed the van doors shut. This was not going smoothly at all.

'You!' I heard him say to Mavis. 'Get in and drive. Or I swear I'll shoot you in the fucking face right here.'

'Shit. I hope you guys are close,' I spoke into my microphone. 'This is not working out as planned.'

The van's engine started up and I was tossed into the side as it went into reverse before abruptly accelerating again.

'Mitchell,' I said again. 'Grimes is in the front of the van with Mavis. He's making her drive and he's got a gun. He's got a gun!'

There was no response from Mitchell. All I could hear in my earpiece was Mavis breathing heavily and Grimes barking directions.

'Can you hear me, Mitchell? Is this fucking thing working at all?' I hissed.

'No, it's okay. I can hear you.' Mitchell's voice finally hummed in my ear. 'It's just … the van we're in, it's broken down. We're trying to jump-start it.'

'What?'

'Don't panic. We'll get it going or we'll get a taxi. We'll be right behind you.'

'This is a fucking disaster.' I was mostly speaking to myself.

'Where are we going?' Mavis's voice was clear.

It suddenly occurred to me that I'd been really stupid. Why had I put my life in Mavis's hands? I didn't really know her. I didn't even like her. It now seemed entirely possible that she was still in Grimes's thrall, and she was helping him drive me to a shallow bush grave.

'No, turn right, you dumb bitch.' Grimes was not sounding happy. It gave me a glimmer of hope.

'There's less traffic by the river,' said Mavis. 'I can cut through Yarra Bend Park.'

'What are you fucking talking about?' Grimes sounded close to the edge.

The sounds of traffic died away. Mavis was taking us somewhere secluded. I broke the ties holding my wrists together, thinking it could be time for me to risk jumping from a moving van. But then I heard another vehicle approaching at speed, its motor straining. I relaxed a sliver, and it was lucky I did, because the next second there was an ear-splitting crunch and I was flung violently into the side of the van.

Mitchell must have deliberately crashed into us. Or maybe it wasn't deliberate—he was a pretty crap driver. When the van came to a standstill, I saw the back door had come open slightly. I kicked it until it sprang open and I tumbled out and onto the ground outside.

I looked up, stunned, and it took a moment for my brain to catch up with what I was seeing. We were on a gravel service road not far from the river, having narrowly missed running into a river gum. But it wasn't Mitch who'd collided with us. It was the old Kombi—and trapped in the driver's seat was Hugo.

It had all gone spectacularly wrong. I'd found Baz but now I was going to be the one who ended up dead in a ditch.

'Brick, are you there? What just happened?'

In the chaos I'd forgotten about the earpiece and microphone.

'Hugo's here. He just crashed into us in the fucking Kombi! He must have lost control on the gravel.'

'Are you okay?'

'I think so.'

'Where's Hugo?'

'Still in the Kombi. I think he's stuck.'

'And Grimes?'

The passenger side door of Gene's van was open. Grimes was not there, and Mavis was slumped, possibly unconscious.

'I can't see him anywhere, and Mavis looks hurt.'

'Run and hide, Brick. We've called the police and we'll be there soon. Run and hide!'

Run and hide. There were trees and shrubs around. The sun was setting and in the dusk there were places to hide. It was the sensible thing to do. That's what Nora had told me too when I was a little girl.

But I was a grown woman now, and I was done with running and hiding. I touched my thigh. The gaffer tape had done its job well—the taser was still in place. I wrenched it off my leg and switched it on. I felt something warm and sticky near my ear and realised I was bleeding.

I had the advantage while Hugo was still pinned by the Kombi's dashboard. He saw me coming and started to struggle, but the steering wheel had been pushed into his bulk by the impact of the crash.

'You're dead, bitch!' The motor gave a sick cough as he tried to start up the van and I took this to mean he didn't have any other weapons handy. I stepped up to the Kombi window and shoved the taser into the rolls of his neck without hesitation, releasing a long burst of current.

The effect was instantaneous. Hugo made a weird gurgling noise and his chins shook like a bowl of jelly. I gave him another burst and his eyes rolled up into his head as he lapsed into unconsciousness.

'Mitchell, are you close yet? We're on an old track near the river. I may have killed Hugo and I still don't know where Grimes is.'

'We're almost there.' Mitchell's voice in my ear sounded frantic, but I could feel my pulse slowing down. Everything was going in slow motion. I limped to the back of the van to check on Mavis. Strangely, the doors were now closed. I almost knew what I'd see but I pulled the passenger side door open anyway.

There was Grimes, crouched over Mavis's body. It looked like he was strangling her. I hoped this meant he'd lost his gun in the crash.

'Hey!' I shouted, as I primed my taser. 'Arsehole!'

Grimes's head snapped around and he lunged at me like a cornered cat. I went to slam the door on him but I wasn't anywhere near quick enough. He knocked me down and pinned me to the ground, his hands now around my neck. My taser went flying.

All I could see now was his face, red and twisted. He hardly looked human. I flailed my arms, my palms grazing gravel. Then my fingertips brushed the taser again. Frantically I reached for it and then I brought it in contact with his leg and pressed the button.

Nothing happened. I pressed the button again, but nothing. I must have used up all the charge on Hugo.

My mind was still operating as if divorced from my body, although a lack of oxygen meant that my vision was starting to fade out. I didn't want the last thing I saw to be Grimes's face. I closed my eyes.

Then there was a sickening crunch. Grimes relaxed his grip and collapsed on me. I took a huge gulp of air, then pushed him with all my might. I freed myself and rolled away.

As my vision returned I saw Mavis. She was gasping for breath and holding a large rock in a menacing fashion. I rolled further out of Grimes's range, in case Mavis took another swing. My heartbeat almost drowned out the sound of approaching sirens.

'The police are coming, Mavis. It's okay.'

But Mavis wasn't stopping. She took out her taser this time and shoved it into Grimes's side and shocked him until her taser ran out of charge. By now Grimes was shaking like he was having a seizure. Mavis threw down her taser and started kicking him again and again and again, until I grabbed her and made her stop.

The pink and red colours of the sunset glinted off the muddy waters of the Yarra River as a pair of ducks floated past serenely.

CHAPTER TWENTY-EIGHT

Mitchell and the rest of the crew arrived as the police sirens were getting louder. It was quickly decided that Timmy, Bunny and I should slip away, so we hiked through the park—Timmy lugging the recording equipment—and caught a tram home. Mitchell sent a text later to tell us that Mavis had been arrested for assault, and Grimes and Hugo had been taken to hospital, but charges were pending against them also. Mitchell thought he'd be at police HQ for most of the night, answering questions.

Needless to say, Baz was wild when he found out what we'd done.

'You could have been killed! You could have disappeared like Betty and never been heard of again! How could you worry me like that? And Aunty Dot? Do you want to kill that old lady? Do you want to kill *me*?'

Baz calmed down after about an hour, and we settled on the couch with a pot of tea. As the adrenaline wore off, I felt more tired than I'd ever been before in my life. I was wrapped in my couch cocoon, my eyes almost closed, when Baz brought his chair close to me.

'Before you fall asleep, bub, there's something else I've got to tell you.'

It was so dark I couldn't see his face, but I knew him so well I could picture his expression.

'When I went to see that old lady in Moonee Ponds,' he said, 'the one who used to be a nun, I found something out about you.'

'We went there too and I saw a folder with my name on it. But there wasn't anything in it.'

'That's because I took it,' said Baz. 'I was going to give it to you, but then with the way things went, I didn't get around to it.'

I hardly dared breathe for a moment. 'Where is it?'

'I posted it to Dot for safekeeping. I didn't want you to find it accidentally. I don't know if it's arrived there yet. Post is terrible slow to Darwin.'

I was glad Baz had waited to tell me this in person. 'What did it say?'

'It was a police report about how you were found in the lane, but there was also a photo in the file. It was a photo of someone holding a baby. I'm not sure if the baby is you, but I guess it could be. Maybe you could find out about your real mum and dad. If that's something you'd like to do.'

'Thanks, Baz.' Something about the dark made the words flow more easily. 'I've got something to tell you too. I've remembered about Nora.'

'I knew it would happen one day, bub. Poor Nora. She was a good girl really. She just married the wrong guy—and then she got mixed up with Grimes. She loved kids, though, that's why she fostered you. She used to come by the club sometimes, do a bit of singing, and she brought you with her once or twice. I could see you liked the music. You'd sit there with your big eyes, quiet as a mouse.

'When I found you alive after all that time alone in that house, I couldn't let you go back into foster care.'

I felt my eyes well with tears. 'How did you do it? How did you adopt me?'

'Your social worker helped me. Her name was Beryl. I called her as soon as I found you and she told the police we'd gone round to Nora's house together. I'm not as paranoid as Gene—I hope—but as a Blackfella, you've got to watch yourself round the coppers. Beryl died of lung cancer not long after. I reckon she already knew she was sick.' Baz stopped to clear this throat.

'She suggested I get a birth certificate for a baby girl who'd died, so I found one. I even found one with my last name: Beloved Baby Brown—poor little thing, lived just a couple of days. Beryl told the department you'd run away. To be frank, it wasn't that hard. There was nobody else that wanted to take you.'

It was good to have my suspicions about the adoption confirmed, but there was something more pressing I wanted to know. 'Baz, I've got to ask you about Mrs Pascoe, the woman who owned the Phoenix before you.'

'I thought this might come out with all the council complaints and renovation business. I promised I wouldn't tell, but ... most of the people who would be hurt are dead now.' Baz drew in a breath. 'Mrs Pascoe was my aunty.'

'Aunty? As in a blood aunty?'

'Yes. She was Dot's second youngest sister. But she was passing herself off as white. Not even her husband knew she was Aboriginal. She was scared, maybe shame. There's always been racism in Australia—we've still got a long way to go there.' Baz sighed. 'I never told Dot that I'd met Daphne; there would have been no stopping her coming to Melbourne and trying to see her, and I didn't want Dot to go through that kind of rejection. Not after everything she went through in her life.

'Daphne had a daughter from before she married Pascoe. I don't think Pascoe liked the girl much—or she didn't like him. One day she ran away and no one knew where she went. I hope she found a better life. She was a bit wild, but who am I to talk, hey? Anyway, long story short, my aunty left me the Phoenix. But I always thought that if Delilah came back she should at least have a share of it.'

His long fingers ran over his face. 'I know it might not seem fair, bub, I know how much you've put into the Phoenix over the years—it's yours as much as it's mine. But if there's any way we can find Delilah or find out what happened to her or if she's got kids that are still living ... I feel like I have to offer them at least a stake of the Phoenix.

And if I want to leave a part to you, I think we should do the paperwork for real. I'll adopt you properly. How do you feel about that?'

'I don't need a piece of paper to tell me you're my father,' I said. 'But a piece of paper would still be nice. And if we find Delilah, we'll cross that bridge when we come to it. It's not like you're going to die tomorrow.'

'I dunno. Aunty Dot might kill me when she finds out about all this.'

I hugged him. 'Aunty Dot will be happy her sister left you the Phoenix. If that's not looking after family, I don't know what is. And if anyone can find Delilah, it's Dot. Cheaper than a private detective.'

'You can't go past family,' said Baz, mimicking Aunty Dot and her favourite saying.

'Thank you for giving me a family, Baz.'

* * *

I'd had the foresight to unplug all the phones before Baz went to bed, so we managed to sleep until midday before Bunny woke us up to hear about what had happened. I told her what I could. Already it sounded like one of Gene's paranoid ramblings, even to my ears.

An hour or two later Flora came round to yell at me for worrying her and Baz, then she stayed for dinner. Bunny cooked a roast, with potatoes and everything. Timmy even helped. We watched all the TV news broadcasts and taped them as well. Baz said Aunty Dot would want to see them.

Every bulletin was dominated by the premier's massive fall from grace, as broken by Mitchell. There was footage of Grimes as he was hustled between the court's back door and a police van. His back was stiff and proud. 'I'll beat this,' was the message his eyes conveyed as the wagon door was slammed. The police dropped the charges against Mavis.

Selena's sordid exposé of Gail Fawcett's 'deadly' affair with the late mayor had second billing in the bulletin. She'd written it from her hospital bed and even did a piece to camera, make-up caked over the bruises on her face. It was a performance sure to win her a Logie at the very least. More likely we'd see her anchoring a breakfast show before the year was out.

After we'd watched the news, I felt secure enough to let Baz go home with Flora. Maybe he'd talk her into making an honest man of him.

The media frenzy continued in the newspapers the next day, with the added bonus of Sue's exclusive on how Hugo Clark had been charged not only for Otto's hit and run, but for killing Mitch's dad and injuring Selena. Hugo remained in hospital with serious internal injuries from the car crash.

'I still don't know how he got out that tiny bathroom window,' said Bunny. 'The man must be part octopus. And after all that ketamine as well! They should use him for medical research.'

'But how did he know we'd gone to Fairfield?' I asked.

'Grimes must have contacted him somehow—after Mavis sent that text.'

The only thing that was still a mystery—for me, at least—was who had moved the mayor's body. I rang Brucie to see if I still had a job and he gave me the last piece of the puzzle.

'You're not going to believe it,' he said breathlessly. 'Eve's been fired for putting illegal spy cameras around the building. Gavin shopped her to the CEO, and I think it was Gavin who leaked that video of Gail as well. Eve left the building screaming that she never should have helped Gail move the mayor's body. Apparently the old goat died in this very building, having a cheeky nooner with Gail. That's what was behind the smell everyone was complaining about. And Gail was just going to leave Dickie there, stinking up the place, until Eve came back from long-service leave and helped her move it in the middle of the night. How weird and disgusting is that?'

I was still puzzling over this strange turn of events when I received a text message from Mitchell: *Meet me for a balloon ride tomorrow morning at 5am. Princes Park.*

My first thought was: how lovely and romantic. My second thought was: I'm still not sure about the safety of balloons. And having been nearly killed several times already this week, I'd really prefer something more pedestrian.

All the same, the next day I got up at the insane hour of 4.30am and rode my bike to Princes Park. The world seemed to have returned to normality. I no longer had to worry about people trying to run me over—other than your usual aggro motorists. I could even legitimately take a week off work, citing stress. I thought I'd probably be wise to keep the council job a bit longer, with the Phoenix out of action. The fire damage wasn't bad, but it had spurred along Baz's plan to redo the wiring and some other renovations. The regulars were planning a fundraiser.

The only worry I had was my feelings for Mitch Mitchell. Although I now had to admit that he wasn't a complete dickhead, he did behave like one a lot of the time. Meanwhile, I was just starting to find out where I belonged in the world. Did I really have room for a relationship right now? Was I just repeating my usual mistake, but with a good-looking journalist instead of a good-looking saxophone player?

I pushed the thought into the back of my mind and pedalled harder. The cool air was bracing but held the promise of the coming summer.

I arrived at the take-off point to see a giant pink balloon waving above me, reminding me strangely of Hugo.

'Brick?' The balloon handler was a wiry man in his sixties.

I looked around, but there was no sign of Mitchell.

'You just missed Mr Mitchell,' said the man. 'He stopped by on his way to the airport. He has to catch a plane to Iraq, but he wants you to take the ride anyway. It's all paid for.'

Yes, Mitchell was a dickhead, all right. But a slightly better class of dickhead. I thought I might as well take the ride. After the week I'd had, I was beginning to think I was indestructible.

The gas hissed as the balloon took off smoothly.

'He also asked that I give you this,' said the man, handing me an envelope.

There was a message scrawled on the outside: *John, Paul, George and Baz*. I opened it to find some shiny new photo prints and the negatives that we'd removed from Baz's safe. Baz had been telling the truth the whole time. He *had* met the Beatles while they were in Australia and from the looks of it, they even had a jam session. Trust Baz to put them in the safe and forget about them. I laughed out loud.

The balloon continued its rise and I looked down at the suburbs of Melbourne. From up high you'd never believe the joys and the heartaches that lay beneath roofs—nor the secrets buried in the gardens. Who knows? Maybe I was looking down on my mother's house, or my father's.

I took a deep breath and let go of all the anguish I'd been harbouring. I felt it float off into the atmosphere and join with the clouds flying high, high above. Mitchell was right about the balloon ride. It was peaceful. And I loved it.

ACKNOWLEDGEMENTS

Firstly I'd like to acknowledge that although *Brunswick Street Blues* is set in Melbourne, many of the venues are invented: including the Phoenix Hotel, the council building where Brick works, the orphanage and most of the cafes. I hope Melbourne readers won't be too offended.

Next I want to thank everyone who's helped me on my long journey of writing this novel—and subsequent journey of actually getting it published and out into the world.

A huge thank you to the Australian Society of Authors and Harlequin for offering the ASA/HQ Commercial Fiction Prize. Winning this prize in its inaugural year made my dream of being published come true.

Thanks to the Harlequin and HarperCollins team, especially Rachael Donovan, Julia Knapman and Laurie Ormond. Thank you to editor Kylie Mason for making me chase up all the loose ends, as well as Melanie Saward for her cultural advice. Thanks to Debra Billson for the awesome cover design.

Thanks to the NT Writers' Centre and the NT Writers' Festival. Creative arts support organisations, writing workshops and festivals are so important to aspiring novelists and the literary ecosystem in general.

Thanks to my dear friend Marilyn Hanson for reading numerous early drafts, and for being my Melbourne brains trust when my memory wasn't so good.

Thank you to the CAL Scribe Fiction Prize for shortlisting an early manuscript, and to HarperCollins for selecting me for their Varuna program in 2011. Huge thanks to the Varuna House and its community for being so awesome, and especially to Carol Major for her early encouragement and invaluable creative writing advice.

Other people I'd like to thank for their expert advice include: Louise Thurtell, Christopher Wakling, Stephanie Smith and an anonymous manuscript assessor who made some very useful points for improvement.

Thanks to the fellow writers I met during a Curtis Brown course. I'm sad it was online rather than in London. Maybe next time!

At the very end of my journey writing this novel, I finally found some writing group buddies. I wish I'd found you all earlier as it might have speeded up the process! But I really appreciated the friendship and words of advice as I tackled the final hurdles.

Thanks to the established writers who were kind enough to read early copies: Sarah Barrie, Angela Savage, Jock Serong and Toni Jordan.

Thanks to my friends and family, especially my mum and dad who let me move home for a few months to write the first draft all those years ago—and to my daughter Zoe who makes me smile every single day.

talk about it

Let's talk about books.

Join the conversation:

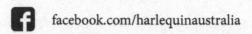 facebook.com/harlequinaustralia

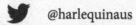 @harlequinaus

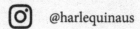 @harlequinaus

harpercollins.com.au/hq

If you love reading and want to know about our
authors and titles, then let's talk about it.